Book One

Large Print

Colter Bay Series

H. Amore

Veneta, Oregon

H Amore 2014

Cross-Trained

Copyright © 2014 by H. Amore. All rights reserved.

Published and distributed by Stonebridge Publications, P.O. Box 163, Veneta, Oregon 97487.

StonebridgePublications.com.

This book is a work of fiction. Any similarity to actual persons or events is entirely coincidental.

No part of this book may be copied in any form unless written permission is received from the publisher.

ISBN 13: 978-1-940473-20-8 large print edition.

ISBN 13: 978-1-940473-29-1 standard print edition.

ISBN 13: 978-1-940473-21-5 ebook.

Cover Photos: (rainbow): © Gina & Niko Plaitakis | Dreamstime.com
(Hand carabiner): © Rcaucino | Dreamstime.com

Cover design by Rob Trahan

Acknowledgment

Thank you to all of you who supported me during the entire process of writing this book. Your input is invaluable and without you, this story would have remained a dream in my heart.

Chapter 1

Caleb Cohen raked his calloused fingers through his strawberry-blond hair and glanced up at the sun. It was well past morning. He drew in a deep breath, coughed and spit out the taste of fumes from the downed plane. Wiping his mouth with the side of his sleeve, he bowed his head. The call had come in before he had arrived at the station. His boss, Joe, told him to head straight for the launch pad and to bring his gear. There had been a crash in South Bend—no survivors—and a fire stretched as far east as one dared look.

The fire didn't surprise him. October was Mother Nature's month for casting away the old, the dead and the weak.

Single-engine plane crashes seemed to be en vogue this year. He tried to distract himself with information, but the broken and charred remains of Gregg Dareme lay amongst the debris of the plane. Oh God, please. Caleb gasped, swallowing his words before they could be spoken.

"She wasn't on the plane," Brileigh, the team leader, said as he broke away from the group.

Caleb dropped his gear and sifted through the ashes. Nausea overwhelmed Caleb as the fumes attacked and seared his skin. He had combed these mountains for wreckage and survivors since he was sixteen. Now as an intern forest ranger at age twenty-two, the body of his girlfriend's father stared up at him, and Carrie was nowhere to be found.

"She wasn't on the plane." Brileigh knelt down beside Caleb and placed a strong hand on his shoulder.

"I drove them to the hangar myself." Caleb uncurled the blackened flesh of what remained of Gregg Dareme's fingers.

"She's not listed on his flight plan," Brileigh answered. "Are you sure she actually got on the plane?"

Caleb retrieved a small tube of honeysuckle lip gloss from Gregg's grip and placed the evidence in Brileigh's hand. He grabbed his radio and dispersed the search teams.

He ran his tongue over his grated lips, tasting the lingering remains of her kiss. The scent of honeysuckle and vanilla accosted him as he pressed further into the vast forest that swallowed the Dareme plane.

He pushed the sight of Gregg's body from his mind and searched the trails within the perimeter as he listened to the feedback from the teams. The weather wouldn't be in their favor much longer. October had always been the most unpredictable month in these parts—never a good time to be flying anywhere out of Wyoming. The wise people would be settling in, preparing for the arrival of the first breath of winter. Instead, Gregg had chosen to fly to Oregon. Caleb had tried to convince him otherwise, but Gregg's sense of purpose overwhelmed his sense of reason.

Until last year, Gregg had served as a pilot and missionary in Africa. Only the recent death of his wife Helen had brought him back to Colter Bay and to a daughter he barely knew. Gregg returned determined to see Carrie through graduation, but left no uncertainty that once she completed high school, he would return to Africa.

With Carrie entering her senior year, Gregg had planned the trip to Oregon to build support from sister churches to further his ministry in Africa. Gregg had told Caleb that he planned to take Carrie with him, in hopes that she would embrace the vision and purpose God had laid down.

"Are you sure she was even on that plane?" asked his partner Reyn as he grabbed Caleb's shoulder, turning him around before he could venture down another trail.

Caleb wiped the salty sweat from his upper lip and rolled the grit over his teeth with his tongue as he squinted up toward the sun. Gray cirrus clouds loomed in the west, offering an ominous warning. A heavy snow right now would prove to be vexing, but thunder snow could be fatal. His body shivered as the temperature dropped a few more degrees and the wind tousled his hair. He rubbed the back of his neck, looking toward the sky. *Lord, where is she?*

"Did you try texting her?" Reyn asked, as he followed him toward the open cliff.

Caleb held his tongue. Reyn was not his favorite person, but they had been partnered since Padraic left for anesthetist training. There would be no second-guessing if Padraic was with him. Most of the team members were familiar with the paths leading from Jackson Hole to Colter Bay, but it was his former partner, Padraic, who retained the skills and determination to unveil the secrets between and off trail. More than once Padraic had earned his stripes in the hollows of these hills.

Padraic's personality struck a chord in almost everyone, waging flagrant warnings of uncertainty. His reaction time and skills were unattainable by anyone else on the team, but he'd just as soon leave you lost as look for you, if the mood struck him.

He'd never leave Carrie. *Lord, I need him here.* Caleb shook his head at the thought, drawing in a deep breath. *No, I don't want him on my team. Lord, please, I just want to find Carrie without involving him. Please, Lord, let me do this.* Caleb gnawed on the reality that his stubbornness might cost him valuable time. Deep-rooted jealously surfaced at the thought of Padraic being Carrie's rescuer. Lord, don't do that to me.

"The only one who believes she was on that plane is you," Reyn said, as he pushed in front of Caleb, stopping their progression. "We need to bring it in."

"She's expecting us to find her," Caleb stated between clenched teeth.

"Ain't nobody walked away from that crash. Maybe she was incinerated."

Caleb felt his fingers curl as the blood heated his skin. He grabbed the front of Reyn's jacket and threw him to the ground.

Reyn quickly regained his footing and knocked Caleb down. "I am not your Cherokee patsy! You lay your hands on me, I'll give it right back to you!"

"He's Sioux." Caleb picked himself up and brushed the dirt and snow off his coat.

"Where is Chief Sitting Bull anyway? Didn't you at least call him?" asked Reyn, as he grabbed his canteen. He took a long drink before acknowledging Caleb's silence. "Well?"

"He's taking his boards today."

Caleb chewed the inside of his mouth, turning away from the obscenities Reyn threw at him as they headed back toward the crash site.

"You're putting the whole team in danger because your stupid girlfriend may or may not have gotten on a plane! And you didn't even call your village idiot!" Reyn changed to a patronizing tone. "If you really believed she was on that plane then why haven't you called the feather nit? He'd have found his girlfriend by now."

"She's not his girlfriend." Caleb rubbed his temples as

the group re-emerged at the crash site.

"Don't you and that timber nigger share everything?" Reyn spit on the ground and stomped his boot into the snow.

Caleb walked away. Padraic was taking his boards today, but that wouldn't have stopped him from turning around. The sun literally rose and set around Carrie in Padraic's world. She had chased them both from the time she was old enough to walk, but by the age of five, she proclaimed to everyone that she would be Caleb's bride. To this day that had not changed, regardless of how much more Padraic had to offer.

Caleb followed everyone to the launch pad and returned to the ranger station as ordered.

"There's no answer from her cell," Brileigh stated.

"It was on the plane with her," replied Caleb.

"Call Tonto." Reyn folded his arms across his chest, taking a deliberate stance in front of Caleb.

"We shouldn't have abandoned the search," Caleb said, rubbing his temples.

"Give me the phone. I'll call the feather nit." Reyn snatched the phone and shoved Caleb aside. "Gregg himself would have called the Injun before now, if he believed Carrie was really out there, and you know how much love is between them." Reyn turned away from Caleb's attempt to get the phone, as Padraic came on the line. "About time you answered, you good-for-nothing! Dareme's plane crashed this morning. Your best friend can't think worth nothing, and the girlfriend is missing." Reyn threw the phone at Caleb. "He's all yours, Opie."

"What's going on?" Padraic's voice echoed concern and hostility.

"Gregg's plane crashed over South Bend this morning. He's dead," Caleb heard himself answer. "There's no trace of

Carrie, but I know she was on that plane. They want to call off the search."

"We aren't calling off the search. Give me the coordinates. Where were they headed?" An engine started in the background.

"You can't help me! You're in the city! I need to get back up there. She's expecting me to find her!" Caleb unleashed his breath, unwilling to accept the calmness around him.

"I'm not in the city. Tell me what you know." Padraic kept his tone steady and committed.

"I know she was on that plane, and she's not at the site or within a ten-mile radius. Gregg is dead."

"My concern isn't for the dead." Padraic's radio was silenced, and there was a loud rustling as his truck door slammed. "If the crash was imminent, Gregg would have dropped her sooner. My guess is she's closer to home. I'm almost to Columbine now. Get an air team toward Ben's Lair."

"Padraic—"

"I've got my gear. Quit wasting time and back me up."

Caleb closed his phone and looked at Brileigh and Reyn. "He's right, Ben's Lair. Gregg would have put her out at the first sign of trouble. We need an air team for a medevac." Caleb felt his strength renewed as he grabbed his gear and headed for his truck.

He's going to find her. Why can't I be the hero just once? Why does it always have to be him? He's cocky; he's arrogant; he never follows the rules. A swarm of thoughts filled his mind. *Padraic will save the day and prove everyone else incompetent, especially me.*

He turned his truck toward the highway and stepped on the gas. *I should be grateful. I should be thankful. Instead, I'm jealous. Lord, take it from me. I don't want to be this way. I need to think clearly. I need help, Lord—Yours and his. Help me accept both.*

Chapter 2

To tether in would be a waste of time, an asset which was too valuable and already in short supply. Padraic barely noticed the eighty-pound pack on his back as he scaled the walls of Columbine and Wilderness Falls. The frigid mountain air condensed as he exhaled, unloaded his safety gear and looked up toward Ben's Lair. Dusk had settled, and a coat of icy rain licked the rocks, making them more treacherous than usual.

"Thanks a lot Lord," he mumbled, as he hefted himself up, dragging his fingers across the gritty surface in search of a stronghold.

Search blades from the medevac helicopters could be heard overhead, which served only to push his limits further. She simply wouldn't be at the top waiting for him. Things were never that easy. According to the radio traffic, no one had found her. *She's above Ben's Lair*, he thought. He cast his eyes toward the jagged peaks. *She needs a climber. There's no other way to descend.* The clanging of his clips echoed as the darkness engulfed him.

"Lord," he began, then shook his head and thought to himself, *No time for adequate prayer at this point, and besides Caleb's probably already at Your feet. You'll take the time to listen to him.*

Padraic launched himself forward and forbade himself the momentary jealousy. He redirected his thoughts to the only thing that truly mattered: Carrie Dareme.

"Marco!" His voice ricocheted off the distant rock faces.

"Padraic!" Her shriek forced him to turn left.

"Marco!" He pulled a ChemLight from the side pocket of his pack and snapped it, watching the chemicals mix to provide a fluorescent glow.

"Polo!" Her answer brought relief and sent him forward.

"Marco!" He yelled lower, in hopes of reducing the resounding echo.

"Polo!" Her voice saluted above him.

"Marco?" He lifted his ChemLight into the air and surveyed the trees.

"Polo." The weariness in her reply captured his attention.

He worked his way to the edge of the cliff and followed the sound of rustling nylon. In front of him lay awkwardly placed vines. With caution, he reached out his hands and grasped the ligaments. They were, he'd hoped, the ropes to her parachute.

"Where are you?" Padraic struggled in the darkness.

"I had to climb. Going down wasn't an option." Her crackling cough renewed his strength. He needed to get her out of there.

"Oh my Lord!" he said, as he snapped another ChemLight and stepped back, realizing the three- to four-hundred-foot drop to the havoc below.

"You better be praying!" Her attempt to sound shocked toward his language tickled his ears.

"I am now." He eased around the edge, trying to catch a glimpse of her outline. "I still don't see you." He tied a piece of nylon cord to a ChemLight and threw it toward the top of the parachute.

"Don't try that climb in the dark. I'm anchored in. I can wait." It was a feeble attempt to stop him.

"I'll get you down." he tossed another ChemLight in her direction and waited to hear the snap.

A green glow illuminated the outline of her face. "Please don't get killed."

"It's not my intention."

He wrestled through the equipment in his pack and secured a taut line to a sturdy pine. Then, he leapt over the drop-off and spread himself onto the rock face. Every finger dug into the surface, and the first layers of his skin tore from his chin and cheek. "Mercy, Almighty!" He said, as he lifted his face, spit out a mouthful of gravel and started his ascent toward her position. He hoisted himself over the crest of the ridge line and wiped the blood and dirt from his eyes.

"I'm here." She waved the green ChemLight but remained in position.

"Kimimela." The tension and anxiety escaped his body as he reached for her.

"Will you always call me that?" she asked, releasing a partial breath. She feigned a laugh with a slight grin, which he knew was the only thing keeping her from tears.

"Until my last breath." His thumbs wiped her dirty face. A gentle kiss of relief fell from his lips to caress her forehead. "Are you hurt?"

"I think my ankles are broken. I can't bear any weight on them at all. It only hurts if I try to move. Otherwise, I'm just kind of numb." She started to remove her sneakers, but he placed his hand over hers.

"No, leave them on for now. Let's get to safer ground." He pounded a stake into the rock. He tested the line, ensuring it could hold his weight. "Harness up. You remember how?"

She shook her head slightly, offering a passive grin. "I'm sorry."

"It's okay." He lifted her chin, returning the same coy smile. "I'll tie you up, but let's not discuss it with Caleb; otherwise, we both might get grounded."

"Where is he?" She lost her chiding tone as he tied her into a tight rope harness.

"Safety first." He secured a grappling hook to the loop and tested the tension on the line again. "It's like one of the gliders we used to have at camp. I'm going to get you over there. Just stay still and don't try to help me, okay?"

"Over the edge? You're pushing me over the edge?" Her voice rose, as he lifted her and tested the harness.

Padraic shoved her with as much strength as he could muster. She threw her hands out as she hit the tree and swung loosely but safely on the other side of the drop-off.

"Now what?" A loud gasp escaped her lungs as she swayed back and forth, suspended nearly ten feet off the ground.

"I'll be right over to get you down."

He debated jumping, but the lack of light caused him more reluctance than fortitude. Instead, he chose to slide over the edge and retrace his steps from whence he came. The misty coat of water that painted the rocks had turned to ice, serving as a reminder that time was not in his favor.

"Padraic!" Her shriek sent him over the divide, his body sliding toward the havoc below.

Spreading his body full eagle over the surface, he dug in and forced himself to ascend. "Carrie?"

An eerie green glow swung back and forth, rocked by the chilly wind. The outline of her unraveled harness illuminated in the fluorescent glare stole the mercies of his soul. Her disjointed position told him the rescue may have caused more harm than good. He pushed himself forward and eased her to the ground. He released her from the harness and knelt beside her. Her breathing was shallow at best, her pulse uneven and faster than he'd wanted.

Shock is getting worse. Now hypothermia, maybe internal injuries. Why'd I move her?

The wind whipped through the parachute as an icy sheet of rain assaulted his face and provided him with the answer. Curses rang under his breath as he tore into his gear. Using the internal frame of his pack, he made a back brace. He wrapped her in the shock blanket and hoisted the contraption on his back. *If Caleb was here…no.* He drew in his breath and forced himself down the trail. *I can't be bothered with the hundred safer ways we could have done this.*

Thurmond's Mound was only half a click from the canyon; there he'd find the trail hut. It wasn't much but it would get them out of the weather—a small edifice, but a refuge nonetheless. Sleet came over them in sheets as he reached the hut. Grabbing the lantern off the door, he lit it before releasing Carrie from the frame.

He removed her sopping wet clothes, eased her onto a cot and wrapped her frigid body in the wool blanket. "Just be still. I'm going to start a fire. Make some tea."

She hadn't opened her eyes, but the awakening would come soon. The change in her vital signs made that evident. He placed the lantern by her bedside and turned his attention to the small potbellied stove. Whoever had been here last had refilled the wood box and left an abundance of kindling, both of which had remained dry. A flint lighter lay on top of the stove, along with an old metal pot and a tea kettle. The fire was easy to start, and as for the tea, he'd always carried a version of it in his first-aid bag. Both were ready in minutes.

"I want my mom." Her lips trembled as she opened her eyes.

"Kimimela," he said soothingly. He wet her lips with the warm liquid, bidding her to drink.

It was a name that she would wear for life. Translated from Sioux, it meant "butterfly." He spoke little English when his mother left him on the Talons' doorstep fifteen years ago, but now it was a struggle to remember his native tongue.

Barely old enough for preschool, Carrie had wandered away from the schoolyard dressed in a sequined blue butterfly costume ready for a Halloween party.

"My dad? Is he—" she took the cup from him and sipped the tea.

"I haven't been to the crash site." Padraic grabbed the radio and tried to adjust the signal.

"Has Caleb?" The color now returned to her cheeks. She passed him her empty cup and secured the blanket around her. "You took my clothes?"

"Wet clothes and hypothermia, not a good combination." He offered her more tea.

"Caleb's going to be mad," she teased, tucking one of her blond ringlets behind her ear.

"How's that different from any other day of the week?" He checked the weather, then went back to the radio. "We should be picking up a signal. The weather is letting up." He brought the walkie-talkie to her bedside. "Try not to move too much." He stopped her from attempting to sit up. "I don't know the extent of your injuries, but moving around may make things worse."

"I don't hurt. What is in that tea?" She grabbed his arm before he could move away.

"That tea is why you're not hurting too badly right now.

We need to get you to a hospital. You need surgery." He squeezed her fingers then turned his attention to the radio. "Call Caleb, tell him your location. He will come and get you."

"Wait! You're leaving me here?" Panic gripped her, and she nearly came off the cot.

"You know better than that." He eased her back down and placed his hand against her cheek. "If the team finds me here, I'll be stuck doing paperwork all weekend with Caleb. I can't do that. I have a date tomorrow."

"You have a date?" She used what little strength she had to prop herself on one elbow and pull him to her.

"I do." He met her smile. "So be a good girl and keep Caleb off my back." He handed her the radio.

"Who is she? Is she pretty? Where is she from? Where'd you meet her?"

"Kimimela." He smiled and leaned in to kiss her forehead. "She will never be you."

"Please tell me. She's very pretty, isn't she?" Carrie sat up, perched on both elbows.

"Anapaytoo," he answered and dialed the frequency necessary for rescue efforts.

"She *is* special if you're speaking Sioux. What does that mean? Anapaytoo?" She blocked his attempt to give her the radio. "Tell me, Anapaytoo?"

"Radiant." He took her hands and placed the radio within her grasp, then caught her chin and lifted it with his fingers. "I need you to keep Caleb busy for me. I'll come find you later, okay?"

"Promise? And you'll tell me all about her? I want to know everything. Promise me that you'll come back and tell me."

"I think you're more excited than I am." He shook his head and knew he wasn't going to be let go without a promise. "Okay, but right now, you need to radio for a medevac. We need to get you to Mercy Hospital as soon as possible."

Carrie looked at the radio, then back toward him. "He's going to ask about you."

"I have a date." They shared a smile as he turned the radio on.

"What do I say?"

"Radio 1697 to base camp. Carrie Dareme requesting medevac transport at echo 3462." She took the radio, repeating his message verbatim.

Within seconds, a dispatcher responded and stated that a rescue team was being dispatched to her location. Padraic shook his head. A team could provide her with little more than what she had now. She needed transport to Mercy. She would need medical attention before the weather turned on them again.

"Request immediate medevac. Tell them that you are in stage three critical condition with multiple internal injuries." Carrie spoke the words he gave her.

"Tell Padraic to take the radio." Caleb's voice interrupted the dispatcher's transmission and caused momentary radio silence from both Padraic and Carrie.

Padraic shook his head. "Request the medevac again. Give him the location at echo 3462, and tell him that I'm not here."

Carrie did as instructed.

"Medevac has been dispatched to your location. Is he coming back?" Caleb asked.

Carrie lifted her eyes. Padraic gave her a slight wave and opened the door. "No," she reported. "He has a date."

Chapter 3

It took over an hour for the medevac helicopter to land on the roof of Mercy Hospital. Caleb waited in the emergency room and watched as they unloaded and brought the stretcher toward him. As far as he could tell, Carrie was asleep. An IV of heated saline ran to her left arm and she lay secured to a backboard. Mud, twigs and blood caked her honey-blond hair; multiple lacerations and contusions peppered her body. The paramedic pushed him aside and handed the nurse several vials of blood while firing off vital signs.

"Get the OR team STAT," was the last thing he heard as they pushed Carrie through the double doors.

"Caleb." A firm hand turned him around. Joseph Talons stood before him.

Joseph, Padraic's adopted grandfather, a rugged Irish outdoorsman, always had made it a point to look after Caleb, along with Padraic. Today more so than most days, Caleb felt he definitely needed looking after.

"I didn't really get to see her. I don't know what's going on." Caleb followed Joseph to the waiting area and threw himself in a chair.

"I'll wait with you." Joseph sat beside him. "Should we notify someone?"

Gregg was dead. The finality of Carrie's situation settled around him.

Caleb drew in his breath. He tried to focus, but his thoughts were a fury of activity. The scenes blurred together, adding confusion and frustration to his fear. He allowed his mind to stray away from the ER.

It wasn't so long ago that Caleb finished high school, enrolled at the city college and deemed himself free of the green-eyed pest who never allotted him any peace.

He had returned to Colter Bay a little more than a year ago, accepting a forestry internship that promised a ranger position in the National Parks System. He'd seen Carrie from a distance. Time had matured her into an attractive young woman, though still too young for him to entertain. He had kept his thoughts and feelings to himself.

The first Sunday he returned to church, she slid into the empty seat beside him. Taking his hand, she wrapped herself in his embrace and leaned close to his ear.

"I've missed you." Her breath felt warm against his skin.

He kept his arm around her, feeling a wholeness he hadn't realized was missing. He never asked her out; they just became the couple that she'd always said they'd be. He'd take her to school, church, and to the city to catch a ball game or just hang out with Padraic for a few hours. The more time he spent with her, the more certain he was that she would someday be his wife.

Helen Dareme, Carrie's mother, welcomed his presence immediately, setting a place for him at the dinner table. She needed a man in the house—someone to shovel the snow, mow the lawn, take out the trash, but most importantly to have a strong influence over her daughter. Carrie had grown into a stunning young lady, and there was no shortage of teenage boys trying to lead her astray. The one attribute Carrie had undoubtedly inherited from her parents was her level of commitment. Helen need not worry; Carrie would never have eyes for anyone else.

"You are my daughter's greatest blessing," Helen said as she sat beside him on the couch in her living room a few nights before her death. "I think she's been in love with you almost since birth." She glanced toward the closed door of her daughter's bedroom. Carrie had been asleep for several hours.

Caleb was just settling on the couch, tired from a day's work and from shuttling Helen and Carrie to an entourage of appointments. Helen's hands were gray and cold, indicating that her condition was worsening. Blood cancer was a battle she wouldn't win, and all of them were dealing with that realization. She took his hands in hers and placed them on her opened Bible on top a packet of papers. "She tells me the two of you will be married someday, and I believe it will be true. Age of marital consent in Wyoming is nineteen and that is a long time to wait."

"I won't lie. It gets harder every day." He wrapped the afghan around Helen's shoulders.

"We have no extended family, no one to look after Carrie once I'm gone. I'm not even certain her father will come home. Carrie wouldn't welcome him into her life even if he did. She still harbors bitterness in her heart for his choice to serve in Africa. That decision, coupled with how badly he treated Padraic, may cause her to never forgive him. I want my daughter to be happy. Not everyone would agree with my decision, but I believe it's the right one.

"You may never receive Gregg's consent; his ideals are far different from the lives we live each day. All I ask is that you allow Gregg to make his decision first. If he chooses not to come home, Carrie will need you. These papers are my blessing for you to marry Carrie, when you believe she is ready. I trust you. I've sent a copy to Africa, along with a letter to her father. The original will remain in my Bible, on my nightstand. These papers are legal and binding. I've already signed them and had them notarized. Gregg's signature is not necessary; I have general power of attorney over him."

Caleb suddenly sat up. *I need to stay focused on what is happening now,* he thought as he wiped his face with his hands and pushed back his hair before casting his eyes toward Joseph.

"Gregg's body was found with the plane. She has no one else." The words hit with an impact of finality.

Joseph nodded his head and remained silent. Caleb tried to steady his nerves, but there wasn't a position that could ease the restlessness building inside him. So much had happened since Helen's death, and now Gregg was gone, too.

She hasn't even recovered from the loss of her mother. How is she going to deal with this? His thoughts deviated from the present, and back to Helen's passing.

Carrie had called him at work the day Helen succumbed to cancer, and he took her to the hospital. She signed for her mother's body to be released to the funeral home. A Red Cross message was sent to her father, but no response was received. Why Gregg had not returned during the months prior to Helen's death was not something Caleb was privy to. The relationship between Carrie's parents had been vague to him at best. He didn't ask, and she seldom talked about it. Carrie never had a good word to say about her father. There would be no restitution for the man who chose to serve God in Africa over his family at home.

"I don't want to go home." Carrie tried to keep her voice steady. "Can I stay with you until my dad comes?" It was the evening of Helen's death, and no arrangements had been made for Carrie.

"No." Caleb had been firm with his answer. "I'll take you to the Talons'. Sarah's expecting us." The Talons hadn't said as much, but they were the closest thing he had to parents. They would know what to do.

As night fell, Carrie asked him to take her home, but wouldn't let him leave her on the doorstep. "Please, I just don't want to be alone."

"You should have stayed with the Talons." He unlocked the door and turned on the light. The emptiness overwhelmed them both.

"Padraic will be arriving tonight. Between his grandmother and him, that's too much company right now." She stayed on the threshold.

The mention of Padraic's name changed his whole attitude toward the situation. No, she couldn't stay with Padraic. "I'll stay, but I need you not to tempt me."

"I won't." She wrapped her arms around him, reaching for a kiss.

"I mean it." He pulled his face away from hers and released himself from her arms. "Go to your room and lock the door." She stood looking at him blankly. "I'll leave if you don't."

She had done as he'd asked. Over the next few days, they walked through the funeral together, and then the burial and the dinner. When it was over she sat still, with a lost, vacant look in her eyes. She barely spoke to anyone. He had to remind her to eat, to get up in the morning—sometimes even to breathe. The only glimpses of the old Carrie were late at night, when she'd tip-toe into her mother's bedroom and curl herself up on the foot of Helen's bed. He couldn't ignore the muffled sobs. He'd carry her out to the couch and hold her until morning.

It was on one such morning that Gregg unlocked the front door and woke them both up.

Gregg demanded that Caleb leave immediately. Outside, Caleb stood and listened to the conversation taking place in the house.

"He shouldn't be here. This whole relationship is—"

"Is what? Inappropriate? I'll tell you what's inappropriate: you coming back after the fact! Mom died two weeks ago. Where have you been? Anything that was going to happen between me and Caleb has already happened! Your presence isn't going to change any of my decisions. It wasn't you who held mom's hand when she took her last breath! It wasn't you who buried her. You have no right!"

"I have every right. I am your father."

"Caleb." A voice pulled him back into the present. "Do you want to talk about it?" Joseph sat down in front of him.

Caleb jumped to his feet and looked around the waiting room. He reeled around and settled his gaze on Joseph Talons. "I think I need some coffee."

"Me, too." Joseph slapped his knees, stood and led the way to a courtesy counter at the back of the waiting room.

Caleb poured two cups and handed one to Joseph. The aroma filled his nostrils in an attempt to awaken his senses, but the fogginess prevailed. He tipped the cup forward and closed his eyes as the steam singed his forehead.

The truth of the matter was that Gregg hadn't come home right away. Caleb had already asked Carrie to be his bride. She wasn't thinking like a little girl anymore. He had to force her to wait. She was all too willing to give him what they'd always been told to save for marriage. It wouldn't have been long before his resolve had abated. If Gregg hadn't walked in when he did, Carrie wouldn't have been innocent much longer.

They had re-established ground rules, in lieu of Gregg's return. Caleb limited their time alone together because he knew neither of them could be trusted.

A month after Gregg's return, Carrie stood on the threshold of Caleb's apartment, tears streaming down her cheeks.

"Please let me in." He stepped aside as she threw her book bag in the corner and placed herself in his arms. "I'm sorry. I know I'm not supposed to come here, but I needed you."

"Why are you crying on your birthday?" He lifted her chin, wiping the tears with his thumbs.

"Mom said she'd take me driving today. She said today we'd turn in my permit for my license. We'd go to the city to the Spaghetti Factory, meet you and Padraic, go to a game. She said..."

"I'm sorry." He knew about the plans. Helen had told him before she passed away. He had mentioned them several times to Gregg, but the message, like so many others, must not have sunk in. "Did you talk to your dad?"

"My birth is not something he celebrates." Her demeanor became suddenly rigid.

"He's lamenting the loss of your mother, just as much as you are." He followed her to the couch and pulled her onto his lap.

"He doesn't care about us. He never did—just those Africa people." She grabbed the afghan and covered her legs.

"He was called to be a missionary. Sometimes God's calling leads to great sacrifice."

"I don't enjoy being on the chopping block."

"You think Isaac did?" He settled her as she reviewed the Bible story in her mind.

"That's different. That was the Old Testament times. It has nothing to do with how I feel right now."

"You're wrong." He tightened his embrace as she tried to get away from him. "This is the second time your father has been asked to give up his life's passion in order to fulfill God's purpose. He has been faithful both times. That's something to be admired, not scoffed at. When he left you and your mom, do you think the African people embraced him? They welcomed him about as much as you did when he walked through the door last month."

"I don't care. Besides, Jesus said that you should meet the needs of your family first."

"Has Gregg ever left you in need of anything? It's the wanting in you that hasn't been met, and I don't think he can do that."

"Then who will?"

"I will." He offered her a tender kiss, crossing one of the established boundaries. "Let's give Padraic a call, and then I'll take you over to the DMV."

Caleb cringed at the indelible memory. It was the beginning of a series of choices that brought them to where they were. *It's not all my fault.* He finished the coffee and tossed the paper cup into a nearby trash receptacle. Joseph sat unmoving, like a sturdy pine in the midst of a harrowing storm. *Why can't I be that calm?*

"Are you still with me, Caleb?" Joseph leaned forward, placing a strong hand on Caleb's knee.

"I'm just trying to put it all together. None of it makes

any sense. They were just starting to get to know each other. It hasn't even been a year. Why would God do something like this?" He shook his head at his utterance. "I'm sorry, Granddad. I didn't mean to say that out loud."

"Why not? It's what we're all thinking, isn't it?" Joseph scratched his rust-colored beard. "Have you talked to Him about it?"

"I can't get my thoughts straight enough to be coherent to the people around me. How do I approach God? And with what? I couldn't even focus enough to find her. I had to call Padraic. I mean, this is what I do—I find people, I save them. But, I can't save my own girlfriend. I couldn't even find her, much less save her. It was enough when she lost Helen. Now what? What am I going to do? What do I say?"

Joseph's silence was expected if not welcomed. Caleb fought against the lump rising in the back of his throat.

There was so much that Gregg would never understand about his daughter. Those first few months after his return were the worst Caleb had ever endured in that household. As much as Helen welcomed him into their home, Gregg publicly condemned him, accused him of molesting Carrie. Twice, Gregg had him arrested, and had subjected Carrie to embarrassing and invasive physical exams.

Caleb sighed, recalling the many attempts he had made to reason with him. It was only in the recent months that Gregg would entertain his company, and only because without him, there would be no control of Carrie. When senior prom season approached, Gregg suggested he escort Carrie. To this day he still wondered if it was some sort of pernicious test from Gregg or God. Or maybe even both.

She had stood before him in her mother's emerald sequined gown. A string of baby pearls lined her neck as her hair cascaded in perfect waves down her back.

"You are beautiful." He tried to smile as she led him to the dance floor.

"You're really uncomfortable, aren't you?" she whispered, laying her head on his shoulder as they swayed slowly to the music.

"It's your prom. I didn't want you to miss it." He pulled away from her intended kiss. "No, too many people talking about us already."

"If you kiss me, it will give them something to talk about." She lifted her head, giving him a playful grin.

"Be a good girl," he stated in a low, barely audible whisper.

"It's still early. Let's go home, change and catch a movie." She toyed with his boutonnière.

"That's not what people will think we're doing." He drew in his breath as the music stopped.

"I don't care what other people think. I know you're uncomfortable, and so am I. I'm all prommed out. I really want to get into my comfy jeans and eat some theater popcorn." She took his hand and led him toward the door.

"Do you even know what's playing?"

"I don't really care." She handed him her coat.

It was a short drive back to her house, but when they arrived they found it dark and locked up tight.

"I don't have my keys." She stood on the threshold looking at him. "Gregg never said he was going out, so I didn't think I needed them. Mom would have never gone out. She'd be right here waiting." Panic had nearly brought her to tears as she stepped away from the door.

"Carrie, stop." He lifted her face toward his. "It's okay."

"No, it's not! All my clothes are in there! Why does he

have to be—?"

"It's okay." He wrapped his arms around her. "Walmart is open. We'll buy you some jeans, and you can change at my place."

"I hate him."

"No you don't." He led her off the porch and opened the door to his truck and helped her in. "He's just not your mom, and he never will be. The sooner you accept him for who he is, the sooner both of you will heal."

"I don't want to heal. I want my mom back," she informed him as he climbed in and started the engine.

"We need to accept the things we cannot change." He lifted her chin, placing a warm kiss against her pouty lips.

"I love you." Her eyes sparkled as he lifted her hand to his lips.

"I love you, too."

After they bought her clothes, Caleb drove her to his apartment. He walked her to the door and handed her his keys and the bag. "I'll wait for you in the truck."

"Aren't you going to change, too?"

"Actually, I'm going to stay out here and try to reach your dad on his cell. Find out where he is." He offered her one last kiss then opened the door and turned on the lights.

"Do you mind if I use your shower? I'd like to ditch this glitter and makeup."

"Towels are in the closet in the bathroom." He opened his cell phone and walked back to his truck.

Caleb sighed and bit into the side of his cheek.

Passed that test only to move onto the next. Lord, I'm tired. I don't want to be flooded with memories right now. I don't want to think about this. I just want Carrie to be okay.

I just want...

Joseph grabbed Caleb's shoulder and brought him to his feet as the doctor approached them. Caleb tried to regain his thought process as the physician introduced himself and discussed what was happening.

"She was given something—some tea or salve—during the rescue. Do you know what it was?" The doctor handed him a clipboard and a pen.

"I don't." Caleb shook his head.

"Yes you do." Joseph slapped his upper back. "That concoction you boys carry everywhere. I'll get it for you." Joseph started toward the physician, then grabbed Caleb's phone off his belt. "Go see how she's doing."

"Just a minute," the doctor said as he stepped toward Caleb. "We have a few questions that the medevac team couldn't answer. They reported that it was the ground team that stabilized her and provided most of her care."

"That's what we do." Caleb kept his eyes to the floor.

"Well, I certainly have a newfound appreciation for the level of skill your team has. Without the immediate care she received, she wouldn't be with us now. I'd really like to see a copy of that report." Dr. Anchorage offered a weak smile as Caleb tried to look at him.

"You and me both," Caleb mumbled under his breath.

There was no way Padraic was going to file anything. He left her at the hut, never sent a transmission and failed even to come to the hospital.

It doesn't matter; he'll call and they'll tell Padraic whatever he wants to know. He's always picking up shifts in the ICU for extra cash, and now he's going to be doing anesthesia for the entire hospital. He can get information on anyone he wants. Why does everything just fall into place for him? It isn't fair. He's got...

"Caleb." Joseph shook him. "You're wandering again."

"I'm okay. May I see her?" He stumbled over his words and handed the clipboard to Joseph.

"She's in room seven on the ICU." The doctor pointed toward the double doors.

Caleb glanced back briefly and saw Granddad and the doctor still speaking to each other. A wave of Granddad's hand told him he was free to go. Whatever it was that the doctor wanted, Granddad would try to supply. It's just as well, Caleb told himself.

The nurses buzzed Caleb in. He looked back as the door closed and the lock snapped behind him. He'd come to this floor a lot, but mostly just to find Padraic. This was Padraic's playground: trauma, codes, IVs—all the things that made Caleb's stomach churn, but completely fascinated and entertained his counterpart.

Hospitals are one step away from prison, or at least that's what his parents had told him. In their case, being meth addicts, there was probably a lot of truth to that belief. He let out his breath, unaware he was even holding it until he reached the nurse's station.

"Hi, Caleb, she's over here." A nurse stood on the threshold of one of the glass cubicles and waved him over. "Padraic called about an hour ago, said you'd be here. Surgery went well. She's starting to wake up."

He redirected his path toward the nurse who was speaking to him. *I should know her name, but I don't*. He swallowed his breath as he approached Carrie. She lay flat on the bed, tubes and wires sticking out from all directions. Bile rose in the back of his throat, and his head began to swim.

"Breathe." The nurse's hand was firmly on the center of

his back. "It looks bad, but given all she's been through, she's actually doing quite well." The nurse guided him to a chair beside the bed and directed him to sit down. "Talk to her. Let her know you're here."

The nurse placed a hand on his shoulder and reached for Carrie's free hand. "Open your eyes, Carrie."

Carrie's eyelids squeezed together tightly then fluttered open.

"You've got someone here who wants to talk to you," the nurse said gently, and then left the bedside.

"Hi." He brushed her hair aside and steadied himself as he stood at her bedside.

Someone had cleaned her face and washed her hair. Lacerations and bruises lay in places that his earlier glance had caused him to mistake for dirt and grime. He placed a gentle kiss on her cracked lips, taking her hand as she raised it slightly off the bed. He lifted her fingers to his lips.

"Tell me." A raspy whisper, sounding more like a rusty door hinge, rose from her throat.

"He didn't make it." Caleb locked his fingers around hers, feeling the strength drain from her body. "The plane went down over South Bend."

Tears streamed down Carrie's ashen cheeks, though her eyes remained peacefully closed. He pressed her limp fingers against his lips. "I'm so sorry."

Her breathing slowed to an even pace. She lay in a medicated sleep. Slipping his fingers from hers, he sat back and pushed his hair from his face. Total exhaustion encompassed his whole being as he closed his eyes and folded his hands, hiding his face. *Lord, I don't understand.*

Chapter 4

The monitors hummed and buzzed, making a constant racket that added to Caleb's headache. He hadn't realized how uncomfortable he was until the moment he sat up. The caustic cadence of the clock grated against his every nerve. Tick, tick, tick, tick. *Will it ever stop*? He glared in its direction. Almost two hours had passed. Carrie hadn't stirred since he told her of Gregg's death. He shifted uneasily in his seat, restlessness preventing any sense of comfort. It occurred to him that he didn't know the extent of Carrie's injuries, or even the reason she needed surgery. Her right foot lay in a plaster cast elevated by a contraption that reminded him of a circus trapeze. Her left foot looked entirely different. It was suspended by another machine, locked in place with metal rods and Velcro straps. The incision sites were bare and seeping a clear, tear-like fluid.

"I thought you were resting. Would you like some coffee or something?" asked the nurse who entered the room again.

"She broke her legs?"

"Her ankles," the nurse corrected him, pointing to the cast. "The right side was a clean break. The doctors were able to set and cast it. On the left side, she wasn't so fortunate." The nurse walked around the end of the bed and showed him several incision sites. "They call this a displaced fracture. It means that not only did she break it, but it moved out of place as well. The surgeon had to place a metal rod in her ankle along with some other hardware in order to stabilize it. We haven't placed a cast yet because we're watching the incisions."

"I don't know what all that means," Caleb responded, unable to wrap his mind around the information she provided.

"She'll be able to start using her right ankle in about six weeks; it will be the stronger of her two ankles. She won't be able to bear any weight on her left for quite a while. It's possible she may need a brace for the rest of her life."

"So she can't walk at all?"

"It will be awhile." She adjusted one of the monitors that was alarming and silenced the buzzing noises. "Her ankles were the worst of her injuries. I don't know how she managed to break both of them."

"The plane was too low when she jumped."

He lifted his eyes from Carrie and grabbed a notepad and pen from the table. Given the time the plane took off and the coordinates where she landed, he'd be able to calculate the altitude of the plane and determine approximately when the trouble began.

The nurse excused herself and returned to a small work station located just outside the door. Caleb busied himself writing a list of questions concerning the crash. He turned his head as a hand brushed his side.

"I was told to keep you busy." Carrie's voice failed as she reached for him.

"You're doing a great job of it." He squeezed her hand and brought her fingers up to his lips. "How are you feeling?"

"Really dizzy and kind of nau..." She tried to roll and vomited over the side of the bed.

Caleb moved out of the way as the nurse came in and cleaned up the mess.

"She has Zofran and Phenergan on her anesthesia orders.

Looks like she could use it." Padraic spoke to the nurse as he entered the room. "Nice slow, deep breaths," Padraic coaxed as he dampened a washcloth and wiped her face and neck.

She closed her eyes and returned to an exhausted sleep. The nurse pushed the drugs through her IV. Caleb waited for her to leave, then took his place beside Carrie again.

I didn't think you'd be here this soon," Caleb said, as he turned to face Padraic.

"Granddad called. Said you needed me here." Padraic moved to a chair nearby.

"He's right." Caleb sighed, resigned to the truth. "Thank you."

"I stopped by your apartment and grabbed some stuff. Here's your phone. Granddad said you left it with him." Padraic tossed him a backpack and placed the phone in his hand. "There's food."

"You didn't take your boards." Caleb unwrapped the sandwich Padraic handed to him.

"Someone canceled on Wednesday, so I took them then." Padraic unwrapped his sandwich. "It wouldn't have mattered. Tests can be retaken. Don't ever hesitate to call me."

"My head is a mess right now." Caleb looked at his food, unsure if he'd be able to stomach it.

"Did you tell her about Gregg yet?"

"She knows." He took a reluctant bite and surprised himself with how hungry he felt.

"She take it alright?" Padraic devoured his sandwich.

"As well as can be expected." Caleb picked at his food. "It just seems like it's been one crisis after another."

"Perspective is the primary difference between crisis and opportunity," Padraic replied after a brief hesitation.

Caleb finished his sandwich in silence.

Even in Gregg's wake, the animosity between his best friend and Carrie's father lived on. There would be no forgiveness, no healing for Padraic.

It was Gregg, serving as pastor of the Colter Bay First Baptist Church, who convinced the Talons to return Padraic to his tribe. There, the atrocities invoked upon a helpless six-year-old boy were enough to turn the gentlest spirit toward enmity. The total truth lay somewhere between what Padraic chose to remember and what actually occurred, but the transformation from innocence to darkness was blatant. It was a decision Gregg later regretted, but never had the fortitude to approach Padraic with directly.

"Are you okay? You have that look in your eyes again." Padraic cleaned up his mess and opened his coffee.

"I'm alright," Caleb sighed. "I really hoped that you and Gregg could have resolved..."

"Don't start." Padraic stood up and grabbed his jacket off the back of the chair. "You and Carrie can grieve his death, but don't expect me to."

"I just thought maybe it would have allotted you some peace." Caleb found himself standing between Padraic and the door.

"The fact he's dead, and I'm not responsible for it, allots me plenty of peace." Padraic donned his jacket and pushed past Caleb.

"Hey, don't go." Caleb grabbed his arm, but released the grip almost as suddenly as he reached for him. "I need you to tell me what's going on. I can't focus. I don't understand what people are telling me."

Padraic hesitated, and then motioned for the nurse to give him the chart. "Karen, can I see that chart, please?"

"Padraic." She met him on the threshold. "HIPPA?"

"She's going to be my patient next shift unless you plan to stay another twelve hours." He held his hand out and accepted the chart Karen placed in his grasp. "Thank you."

He opened the chart and showed Caleb the X-rays. "Clean break," he said, as he pointed to the first picture. "Nasty break." He pointed to a second picture. "It was probably a clean break to begin with. The second fall caused the displacement."

He turned the page and glanced at the swarm of numbers that consisted of her lab values. For a moment, his eyes left the page and met Caleb's, then returned to the chart. A few seconds later he closed the chart.

"What is it? What do all the numbers mean?" There was no doubt in his mind something in that chart spoke volumes to Padraic.

He handed the chart to the nurse and returned to the bedside, still not facing Caleb. "The surgery went as expected." Padraic placed his hands against the sides of Carrie's cheeks. Her eyes fluttered open. "I think the displaced fracture is from when I dropped you." He spoke directly to Carrie, offering a timorous grin.

"You dropped her?" Caleb felt as though he was being led from a pressing issue.

"Forgive me?" Padraic took her hands in his.

She gave a weak nod, then closed her eyes again.

Caleb pulled him aside once he was certain Carrie had drifted back to sleep. "What aren't you telling me? What do the numbers mean? What do you mean you dropped her?"

"I didn't tie her harness tight enough. It unraveled before I could get to her." Padraic kept his eyes trained on Carrie as he delivered his answer.

"Harness? What were you doing?"

"You'd have to see the terrain to understand."

"You can't just tell me?" Caleb drew in his lip, realizing his hostile tone.

"No." Padraic shook his head.

Caleb stared at him hard for a moment. *Okay, he doesn't have the words; that's not uncommon. But why won't he look at me?* He thought and then asked, "What about the numbers in the chart? What do they mean?"

"Those are her lab values." Padraic stopped short.

Caleb crossed his arms and continued to stare at him. "And?"

"She has a few labs in there that probably need to be redrawn. Some of her levels are just...not what they should be." Padraic released her hands and turned to face Caleb, but instead looked toward the empty chair across the room.

"Look at me and tell me what that means," he stated firmly.

"Her lab values will stabilize as she does." Padraic stood, looking fidgety. "Any idea of what may have caused the crash?"

The abrupt change of the subject was his warning not to press the issue any further. Caleb recognized it immediately.

"My gut feeling is that the fuel was contaminated."

"What makes you think that?"

Caleb surveyed the scene and knew full well there were words unspoken that were chastened by Padraic's soul. The lack of eye contact was a native custom that he'd grown to accept. It was Padraic's way of respecting an individual's privacy. The natives believed the eyes were like windows, and within each person lay many secrets that were not always to be shared. Caleb studied his friend's demeanor, wondering what newly acquired secret had suddenly spurned Padraic's native defenses. He let out his breath and relaxed, taking a seat near the bed again. He'd have to wait. Eventually he'd be told, but everything about the way Padraic was acting said it wasn't going to happen now.

"The burn wasn't right—didn't look right, smell right, taste right. I don't know."

Eeriness crept over him as he watched Padraic move toward the door.

"Are you headed back to the site or staying here?" Padraic asked. He shut off his phone as it started to ring.

"Everything kind of depends on her." Caleb sat up and stretched his arms out in front of him.

"At least your priorities are straight. I'll talk to Karen about getting you a blanket and pillow. You really do need to get some sleep."

"When are you coming back? We've still got a lot of stuff to sort out, including your paperwork for Carrie's rescue."

"Carrie was rescued by your ground team." Padraic tapped the door frame. "I'm working tonight. We can talk later."

"So you're not going to file a rescue report?"

"I wasn't with your ground team when they rescued her." Padraic slipped out the door before another word could be said.

Caleb slammed his body against the back of his chair. *He's going to do it again. He's going to make us all look like idiots.* Reports needed to be filed; questions needed to be answered. *Why does he always get to be the one who saves the day? Why does he get to ride off into the sunset and leave me here with the mess? Why can't I just once have an edge? I want to do something and not have him be a part of it. Is that*

39

too much to ask? He always has to be better at everything—be more, do more, know more—than everybody else.

"Hey." He hadn't noticed that Carrie had opened her eyes again and reached her hand toward him.

"You're awake." He stood and took her fingers, kissing them lightly as he sat down beside her on the bed. "How are you feeling?"

"Like I fell out of a plane." Her grin turned to a grimace as she tried to lift her head.

"It's more probable that you jumped." He brushed the side of her face with his hand, enjoying the softness of her skin.

"You always have to be so exact." She took his hand and held it in hers. "Is Padraic gone?"

Caleb answered with a nod. "Do you remember anything prior to the crash?"

"I remember not wanting to get on the plane in the first place. That trip was nothing but a stupid ploy to rack up brownie points in front of his congregation." She motioned for Caleb to give her the water glass. "He was so anxious to get back to Africa that he got himself killed and nearly killed me in the process."

"Carrie, your father is dead." His voice held a note of rebuke.

"At least something good came of this trip." She closed her eyes again, losing the battle against the sedative effects of the medication.

Chapter 5

Neither the window nor the clock provided clear guidance as to whether it was dawn or dusk. A dreary gray hue hung heavy over the parking lot. From her tinted window there wasn't much to see, other than street lamps and winter-washed vehicles. The scarcity of remaining parking spaces made Caleb guess it was early morning. Somewhere amid all the chaos, he must have fallen asleep. From the stubble on his face, awful taste in his mouth and soreness of his muscles, he knew he had slept long and hard. He placed his feet firmly on the floor and rubbed the back of his neck. He didn't remember the chair folding out into a bed or the acquisition of pillows or blankets. He glanced at the door where a pretty girl dressed in green scrubs closed the chart and stood to greet him.

"I thought she was Padraic's patient?"

"He was pulled to the OR about an hour ago. We are short a perfusionist. Padraic is the closest thing we have in the hospital at the moment." The nurse came into the room; her protruding abdomen indicated she was in her last months of pregnancy.

"My name is Jerica. I've been looking after Carrie. Padraic said you'd probably want to shower when you woke up. This is his key. The call room is through the double doors, and it's the fourth room on the right-hand side. He said to feel free to use his stuff. You'll find clean clothes in your duffel bag." Jerica placed a key card in his hand, and then went to

Carrie's bedside to check on her.

Carrie's eyes were closed in peaceful slumber, and Jerica assured Caleb that Carrie would remain in a sedated state for at least a few more hours. He grabbed his duffel and walked down the hall in search of the call room the nurse had described.

The room was tiny, containing a twin sized bed and a small flat screened television mounted to the wall. Just enough room to sleep. Caleb tossed his duffel onto the bed and dug out his toiletries and a clean set of clothes. A fresh set of hospital towels were folded at the foot of the bed. He turned on the television, then the shower. The bathroom reminded him of the water closets found at the trail stations. A shower barely big enough for him to stand in, a toilet and pedestal sink held its only claim.

The water scalded his skin as the steam awakened his senses. It felt good, and he didn't want to get out and face the turmoil that awaited him down the hall. It could be a few days before Carrie was even coherent enough to talk. In the interim a plan needed to be established. It didn't matter how much Carrie hated her father, Gregg's presence kept her from being sent away to one of those group homes in the city. Caleb hadn't tried to use the papers Helen had given him, and at this point, without Gregg's written approval, he was certain there was no validity left to them.

Caleb grabbed his sneakers from the duffel and put them on, thinking back to another fateful moment.

He was fourteen when he came home to an empty house. The Talons brought him home when his parents failed to pick him up from camp that year. It wasn't unusual for them to forget about him; everyone knew they were crack heads. He spent most of his time with Padraic anyway. He turned fifteen just before school started, and still no parents to speak of. That first year no one knew he was alone, except for Padraic. If the Talons knew, they never said as much. Then when Padraic burned the house down, swarms of do-gooders started coming out of the woodwork. By then it was too late. He already had his license and a decent job and was working on his GED. There was a circus of paperwork, and to this day he still wasn't certain if he had been legally emancipated or not. "I can't let her go through all that," he whispered to himself.

He gathered his things and started out of the room as his phone rang. He looked at the ID, recognizing his boss's number. He pressed the receiver to his ear and walked toward the unit. "Cohen."

Joe cleared his throat. "How's Carrie?"

"Stable." Caleb pressed the buzzer to unlock the unit doors.

"Yourself?"

"You could have told me it was their plane."

For a moment, Caleb could hear his younger self complaining over an unfair assignment. *Lord, help me.*

"You're leaving me to become a full-time ranger in less than two months, Caleb. You need to be prepared for this kind of assignment—even if it's personal."

"Joe, this is a little more than personal. Gregg is dead, and Carrie is in the ICU."

"According to word of mouth, you called in your twin for the rescue."

"The team didn't even want to look for her. Brileigh said she wasn't listed on the flight plan and Reyn said she'd been incinerated. Padraic at least listened and reacted," Caleb retorted. He stopped short of going into Carrie's room.

Strapped to the monitors, tucked under the stark white sheets, she looked like her mother. He diverted his eyes toward the foot of her bed, relieved to see the traction still in place. *It's not cancer; Carrie will come out of this.*

"Hunt down your friend today," Joe interrupted. "I need a good rescue report. Our funding depends on the media attention these things generate."

"You think you're going to get one from him?"

"No, but you will." Joe's voice resonated through the phone.

"I'll see what I can do. I'll stop in the office and pick up some report forms. If I'm going to catch Padraic, it will be here at the hospital."

"I need taggers at the site before we lose any more evidence due to weather."

"You can't be serious. You want me to tag?" Caleb failed to curtail his irritation before it left his lips.

Joe lowered his tone. "You're not a ranger yet. You still work for me."

"It sounds as though you're putting me on the investigation team. Isn't that a conflict of interest?"

"Conflict nothing. The evidence needs to be collected, sorted and itemized. I'll give the lead to Brileigh, but he'll need your help. We are already short a team, and no one has experience in the field like you do."

Caleb knew he should accept that as a compliment, but instead he staggered under the weight of being in the forefront of this investigation.

"If I can find someone to stay with Carrie, I'll tag."

"Fair enough. I'll call Brileigh and Reyn."

Caleb closed his phone and approached the bedside table, where a steaming cup of coffee and a breakfast bagel waited.

"Did he leave?" He turned from the gifts and looked at Jerica.

"Yes. He said to tell you he called Grandmother. She should be here in an hour or so to stay with Carrie while you're working. He'll try to catch up with you later today. He's gone home to sleep."

Caleb nodded a thank you toward the nurse. He removed the plastic lid from the coffee and unwrapped the bagel. Daylight had prevailed since the last time he looked out the window. The dreary haze had lifted, but it still promised to be cold and damp. He continued his gaze, mind adrift. *If Padraic wanted to sleep, he would have crashed right there in that call room. Instead, he had called his grandmother to watch over her. He's got something else going on. He doesn't want to talk to me; otherwise, he'd be here. He knows something, saw something in that chart that he's not telling me.* Caleb glanced down at Carrie and realized her eyes were open.

"Welcome back," he said, as he returned his coffee to the table and offered her a gentle kiss on the cheek.

She extended her hand toward his and relaxed as he folded his fingers around hers. "What day is it?"

"Monday." He sat down on the edge of the bed and faced her.

Her eyes glittered like flawless emeralds, the bruises and lacerations fading with each moment that he drank in her presence. A mass of unruly curls clung to her neck and fell in her face as she tried to sit up. He lifted his hand to her face and drew his fingers lightly over her skin, half believing that she was real.

"I'm okay." She caught his hand as it slid from her cheek and kissed his fingertips.

"I'm sorry." He meant it, for everything. She didn't want

to go on that flight. He was the one that convinced her to go with her father.

She pulled him down beside her. "I know you really wanted us to be one big happy family, but it was never going to happen. I told him when he sent Padraic away that I would never forgive him, and I meant it."

"What happened to Padraic was not Gregg's fault. He had no way of knowing..."

"It has nothing to do with what he didn't know. He didn't care. You don't get it, Caleb. Gregg never cared about anyone but himself. The only reason he came back here was because it made him look good in front of his church. You've always defended him, and there's no reason to. He was never a friend to you. Gregg had you charged you with statutory rape before we ever started sleeping together."

"Lower your voice." He placed a finger over her lips. "This is not the time or place."

"I'm sorry," she said, as she bit down hard on her weathered lips. "Even in his wake, the man still irritates me. Can we talk about something else?"

They did need to talk about their relationship. Things had gotten beyond their control for the past few months. The fact that they shared a bed more often than not disturbed him, but not enough to change his behavior. Waking up beside Carrie seemed almost as natural as breathing. Gregg stopped caring about where she was and what she was doing after the second accusation proved unsubstantiated. Caleb would have liked to believe it was because Gregg trusted him, but Carrie's interpretation was probably closer to the truth.

He had come home one night and found her asleep on his couch, an old movie causing flickers of light, just enough to offset her image in the dark. She came to life when he sat down beside her and showed her the acceptance letter. He was scheduled to leave for orientation. The position he'd been promised was as a full-time ranger in the National Park System, right in the heart of the Grand Tetons.

"I always knew I'd be a rangers wife," Her breath caressed his ear. It was the moment he could not control.

"Are you alright?" She stroked his hand.

"Yes, I'm sorry." He released his grip and grabbed the notes he'd made earlier. "Do you remember anything that happened before the crash? Were you struck by lightning or anything unusual?"

"No, the weather was clear." She closed her eyes and remained silent for a long moment. "It smelled funny, and then there was this popping, something was popping."

"Like gunfire?" He stretched and wrapped his arms around her as she nestled into him.

"No." She shook her head briefly then laid it against his chest. "More like popcorn." Her breath escaped her lips in a forced blow that lifted her bangs away from her forehead. "We really weren't high enough. The gauges weren't reading right. It just happened so fast."

He toyed with her fingers, feeling her relax against him. As the tension left her body, he processed the information she gave him in silence. "You said there was an odor. Any idea what it was?"

She maintained her silence for a long time, then shook her head. "It smelled like the cabin that Padraic brought me to."

"Musty?" he asked, as she lifted her head to look at him.

"No, I don't know." She lay against him.

"Do you remember what he was doing? He must have lit the stove because you had some tea."

"He did. My clothes were wet, and he said something about hypothermia, electrolytes, internal hemorrhaging. I really couldn't follow a lot of what he was saying. He did promise me that he'd come back and tell me about his date."

"His date, huh?" He could tell by her weight and breathing that she'd drifted back to sleep.

Leave it to Carrie to be more concerned with Padraic's love life than anything else going on around her. It was just her way of coping. He kissed the top of her head. *It was probably better that she had something else to think about, other than the plane crash.*

Padraic's grandmother, Sarah Talons, smiled at Caleb as she carried in her wicker bag full of beading supplies. She settled her petite frame into the chair beside the bed and shooed him out the door.

"You go, I'll keep vigil. I'll have her call you when she wakes."

Sarah's eyes shone like black diamonds, her skin worn like well-weathered deer skin. Anyone would have guessed her to be Padraic's real grandmother.

"Alright, let me just tell her that I'm leaving." He greeted Sarah with a kiss on the cheek, and then returned to Carrie.

"I'll be back in a little bit. Mrs. Talons is going to stay with you, okay?"

"Please," she opened her eyes as he released her hand, "Leave the light on."

"I will." He nodded at Sarah and turned on the bedside lamp.

Even as a little girl, Carrie was afraid of the dark. When they were kids, sometimes at church camp he'd take the batteries out of her flashlight. One time, he removed the light bulb from the flashlight since she'd taken to carrying extra batteries. That particular day the youth leader had decided to take the girls on an overnight campout on the south side of the gorge. When Carrie returned she was so visibly shaken and inconsolable, Helen had to come and pick her up.

It was then that Padraic introduced Carrie to ChemSticks and always made sure she had a pocket full of them. Padraic always made sure there was a light on for Carrie.

Chapter 6

Caleb tried Padraic's number for the fifth time. He wondered if he was asleep or just not answering his call. Caleb bit hard into his bottom lip, splitting it open. He cringed at the taste of his own blood. *I hate it when he does this. God, I need him to answer me.*

"Talons," Padraic answered with a disinterested tone.

"What'd you light the stove with?" Caleb let out his breath.

"What?" Padraic's annoyance radiated through the phone line.

"In the cabin with Carrie, what did you use to light the stove?"

"A flint lighter," Padraic answered, releasing a long sigh.

"You didn't use any type of gas or anything?"

"No, I didn't need to."

"Carrie told me the cabin smelled like the plane just before the crash."

"I did not use any gas."

"Are you sure?" Caleb hit his head with his fist. *Oh, why did those words come out?*

"There's a reason I don't take your calls all the time."

He did not need to wait for the dial tone to know Padraic had ended the call.

Of course Padraic was sure. *He wouldn't lie about something as menial as lighting a fire,* Caleb thought, as he slammed the door of his truck and tried to focus on the task ahead of him. First on his agenda was to check the maintenance ledgers. This would tell him if, and when, Gregg used the sumps to ensure the fuel was not contaminated with water. Caleb caught sight of the itinerary board and flipped through until he found Gregg's flight plan. It verified Brileigh's original point. Carrie was not listed as a passenger. He shoved the board back onto the shelf and walked toward the refueling station.

"Leave the light on." Her voice interrupted his thoughts. Caleb lifted his head and almost expected to see her at his side. His shoulders shrugged against the brisk November wind as he approached the owner.

"Dixon, did you fuel the Dareme plane?"

"I did." A heavy man in a jumpsuit and the early stages of balding ducked under the wing of a small craft and confronted him. "There was nothing wrong with my tanks. They all passed inspection this morning. I had a fresh shipment of fuel delivered the day before last. That crash was pilot error. I'm tired of getting shut down. It always turns out to be pilot error!" The man squinted as the sun scorched his face.

"Gregg was a good pilot." Caleb met the man's glance then turned toward the pumps.

"They're all good pilots. They all like to think that they can't make mistakes. Well, they can and they do. And I'm the one who loses business every time one of them wants to jerk around with the safety codes."

Caleb raised his hand to Dixon's hostile tone. "I'm not here to accuse anyone of anything. I just want to find out what happened and write the report so that I can go back and pick up the pieces."

"Oh man, Caleb, I'm so stupid. I'm sorry. Here I am going on. I heard you found Carrie. How is she doing?" The change in demeanor and attitude was abrupt.

Caleb looked at him, uncertain of his sincerity. "She's in the ICU at Mercy," he heard himself answer as he tagged the pump that Dixon identified as the one used to fuel the plane.

"Poor kid. First her mom, then her pop. What's going to happen to her now?"

The question stopped Caleb in his tracks. He'd thought about her situation, but to hear someone else voice it out loud brought it to full reality.

"Suppose they'll let you marry her a year early?" Dixon raised an eyebrow at him.

"Maybe." Caleb pretended to be preoccupied with swabbing the nozzles of the tanks.

"You are going to marry her, aren't you?"

"That's what she tells me." Caleb continued to collect soil samples from around the tanks and tried not to encourage the conversation any further.

"What is she, seventeen now?"

Dixon followed Caleb as he went in the office.

"She'll be seventeen at Christmas," Caleb replied, as he pulled the operations ledgers off the shelf and copied the last month's reports.

"She's young, but she'll make you a fine wife."

"We're trying to find out why a man was killed yesterday, not make wedding plans in his wake." Heat rushed to Caleb's face.

"It's all right, calm down. Your Injun pal will always step up to the plate if you won't."

The comment was enough to make Caleb come unglued. He bowed his head and prayed the next words spoken would not play into the trap that Dixon had laid.

"We need to shut the facility down. There's too much evidence here. I thought I could do a clean sweep for you, but it's not going to happen."

Caleb walked away, disregarding the verbal slander behind his back. When he reached his truck, he slammed the door and stepped on the gas.

He silently prayed, *Lord, what is going to happen with her now? She's sixteen; she's not even out of high school.* He wiped his face with his gritty hands and pushed back his hair. He cleared his throat, glanced at the clock. *I have to think about this. I need to review the laws for emancipation in Wyoming. I can't just let her be shipped to the city. I have to do something. She's expecting me to do something. Everyone is expecting me to do something. There is just too much. God, right now I really just need to focus. Help me concentrate on this case and not be distracted.*

The headquarters parking lot was nearly full when he entered the building, tossed his keys onto his desk and powered up his computer. He'd spoken with the police and the press at the station and at the hospital. Normally publicity didn't bother him; he had a good face for the camera. His solid appearance and solemn demeanor were just the right mix that the public wanted to see. Reyn was right, though. He looked like a grown-up Opie Taylor with his short strawberry blond hair, freckled face and dark brown, puppy dog eyes. Prince Charming he was not, but given the group, he was the most approachable.

Reyn plodded into the office and cursed at the empty coffee pot and everyone within a ten-foot radius of it. Reyn was the only black person Caleb had ever known to have an actual passion for orienteering. Most of the others were not brought to Colter Bay by choice. It was a forced adventure, intended to broaden their horizons past the city lights. A lot of them were given the choice to join the team or go to jail. Within a week, those guys gladly returned to their cells. City gang-bangers were no match for trail kids, especially out here. One bad turn always followed another. A hostile encounter or an idle threat was matched with a released belay line and a hundred-foot free fall. Trail kids turned their heads whenever a blood rake ran its course. Usually, the recipients were entitled to such an orientation.

Climbing and hiking were not Reyn's forte. His goal was to pilot one of the rescue helicopters. Piloting took more skill than Reyn had been able to prove he had, so for the time being he remained a foot soldier. Book learning did not come easy for a high-strung city kid with little aptitude for listening.

The only thing that surpassed Reyn's attitude was his mouth. Crude jokes, racial slurs, and name calling seemed to be his standard vocabulary. Too much time in the field together and Caleb often had to watch his own tongue. There was a twofold incentive in helping Reyn study: the first would be to get Reyn into flight school, but the most important would be to get a decent partner.

"So, Opie, what's the story?" Reyn threw himself down in one of the office swivel chairs and twisted.

"Haven't got one," Caleb heard his voice answer.

"Your girl?" Reyn wiped his nose and leaned forward feigning an interest.

"She's locked down in the ICU at Mercy."

He faxed a preliminary report and a summary of his findings at Dixon's place to the main office.

"I didn't listen to you." Reyn sounded almost apologetic.

"We didn't listen to each other. Lost a lot of valuable time." Caleb cleaned and filled the coffee pot then returned to his desk. "So, I spoke with Carrie. She told me the plane took on a funny smell, and there was a popping noise. She said it sounded like popcorn to be exact, then the gauges went crazy. Any ideas?"

"Popcorn?" Reyn laughed into his hand. "Are you serious?"

"Think like a pilot. What's going on with the plane? Popping, gauges going awry, some strange odor? Put yourself in the cockpit. What do you think is happening?" Caleb faced him.

"Dix said his pumps were clean if there's water in the tank that's Gregg's fault, not his."

"Not water, I'm thinking fuel. Either the fuel itself is contaminated, or someone put the wrong fuel in Gregg's plane." Caleb helped himself to a fresh cup of coffee and printed some statistical data for small engine plane crashes and malfunctions in the Wyoming region.

"Ain't no way in…"

Caleb interrupted. "When small-engine planes get just a little bit of jet fuel, they shake, then the gauges go crazy, pistons start popping and the plane goes down. Does that not sound like what Carrie said?"

"So is that your final answer, Einstein? You think Dix sabotaged the plane?"

"No," Caleb said, as he returned to his data screen. "It's possible this is specific to Dix, but I don't think so. Right now I'm running a check on all the single-engine planes that have run aground in this area. I think the data is going to point either toward the source or the distributor."

"Wow, Opie, them's some big apples you're playing

with."

"True enough, but it's *our* little people getting killed." Caleb saved the data on his thumb drive and shut down his computer. "I'm going back to the hospital for a few hours to see Carrie and try to catch Padraic. Hopefully he can fill in some of these blanks on the rescue report for me."

"Good luck with that," Reyn smirked.

"Brief Joe on our theory about contaminated fuel. I'll meet you at takeoff." Caleb checked his phone as the text came in. Tagging teams were scheduled to take off at sixteen hundred.

Caleb glanced at his watch, grabbed his coat and papers from the desk, and then headed out the door. Reyn followed him with a litany of curses concerning the forthcoming mission.

"I don't want to go any more than you," Caleb said, raising his hand in peace. "Joe said we go; that's it." He climbed into his truck and slammed the door.

Carrie was awake and sitting up when he entered the room. Sarah, on the other hand, was slumped to the side with her beading secure in her lap. Carrie's legs remained suspended in the mechanical devices, but otherwise all the other monitors had been removed. A single IV line remained in place with a pump that he'd been told was for hydration and pain control. She looked good—awake and alert. As he walked in, her eyes temporarily diverted from the Amber Alert that flashed across the television screen and met his.

"Hi." Carrie's smile sent genuine warmth through him as he set his things in the corner and greeted her with a kiss. "Is she all right?" he asked, looking toward Sarah.

"It's been a long day," Carrie sighed, as she replied. "See, she's making a jingle dress. She's been telling me all about it.

Makes me wish I was Hopi."

"You don't have to be Hopi to wear it. Shoot, half the girls at the Pow-Wows aren't even Native American," he said, as he settled himself around her. "I can't remember where it all originates from, but I think the dress and the dance have something to do with healing."

"Mrs. Talons told me, it was a Midewinini legend. The dresses as well as the dances were passed on to the Lakota Sioux. She says the stories are an important part of who Padraic is." Carrie lay herself against him and he could feel the tension drain from her body as she tucked herself into his arms.

"I don't think dresses of any kind are all that important to him." He tickled her ear with his breath.

"Of course they are. His culture sneaks out all the time! Look at how he prioritizes. Everything is done on Indian time, always by situation, never by appointment."

"He's a Lakota Sioux raised by a Hopi/Mexican woman and an Irishman. At best, I'd say he's culturally confused."

"I call it cross-trained, but confused may be more accurate," Padraic piped in.

"Where have you been?" Caleb lifted his hand as Padraic swung and gripped it in a firm greeting.

"He's been here most of the day, except when he went out looking for you." Carrie sat up, beckoning Padraic to come in. "Listen, Padraic's been telling me all about Gail. She's from Michigan. She's the one who finally convinced him to apply for medical school. Isn't that great?"

"What?" Caleb nearly fell off the bed. "You said you wanted to work the trails. What's this about medical school? Don't you think you've been in school long enough?"

"Gail wants me to try medical school. She thinks I'd

make a good doctor." Padraic shrugged.

"Where is your focus, man? You're never going to get anywhere following someone else's dream."

"All I did was apply for the program. I don't think I'll get in." Padraic pulled a chair to the bedside.

"Then why bother doing it?" Caleb let out his breath, throwing his back against the pillows.

"It makes her happy just to know that I've applied." A sly smile crept across Padraic's lips as Caleb fell silent.

Closing his eyes, Caleb shook his head, gathering all the information. This was insane. This was stupid. This was...he jumped off of the bed and pointed at Padraic.

"You lit a kerosene lamp!" His mind raced forward.

"What are you talking about?" Padraic helped Carrie recover from the abrupt movement.

"To make Carrie happy, there had to be light. You lit a kerosene lamp and didn't tell me!" He tried to speak over the rush of air in his lungs.

"So?" Padraic held a lost look on his face.

"'So?' What do you mean, 'So?' Carrie smelled kerosene in her dad's plane! That's jet fuel. It doesn't belong in single-engine planes." Caleb turned to face Carrie as Padraic pointed in her direction.

A pale look of shock had replaced her smile. Sarah, now awake, stood up and offered her some water.

"Do you know what kerosene smells like?" Caleb started to take a step toward her, but felt Padraic's grip on his shoulder.

"Enough." One word spoken was all he needed to put himself back in check. "That's further than she needs to go right now." Padraic's tone was low, but harsh.

What does he know? Caleb drew in his breath trying to

look him in the eyes. *He's not telling me something.* Padraic's grip remained firm, but his eyes stayed focused somewhere in the distance.

"Anything Carrie remembers..."

"Can wait," Padraic interrupted.

"What if this was intentional?"

"Shut up before I shut you up." The hold switched. Caleb felt the pressure placed on his shoulder joint; the slightest move on his part would slip his shoulder out of the socket.

"Okay." He placed his free hand on Padraic's chest and pulled out of his grasp. "I'm sorry, sometimes I get ahead of myself."

"It's okay. I'm all right. What did you mean by intentional?" Carrie took his hand and had him sit beside her on the bed. "Like someone was trying to kill us?"

"No." Caleb chose his words carefully. He knew Padraic would be true to his aforementioned remark. "Intentional is the wrong word; responsible would be more accurate. If there was jet fuel in your father's plane, then the crash was definitely not pilot error."

"Dix put in the wrong fuel? Is that possible?" Carrie asked, as she scratched her legs, trying to remove the sleeves that were constantly squeezing and releasing her calves.

"Leave those on," Padraic commanded, then quickly refastened them and pushed her hands away.

"They're so uncomfortable."

"So are blood clots." Padraic lifted her chin.

She forfeited the battle and offered a weary smile as Padraic slid into a chair beside the bed.

"Do you know what kerosene smells like?" Caleb chose his words carefully, and watched Padraic's reaction more than Carrie's.

"I think so. It smells like gas, right?" Carrie tucked a curl behind her ear, meeting his stare for a moment.

"No, different fuels have distinctive colors and odors. Otherwise, it would be quite difficult to tell them apart." Caleb took her hands in his. "So, I guess where we need to start is to make sure it was kerosene that you smelled."

"You still have that swatch test you were using on Reyn?" Padraic asked. He leaned forward in his seat while Sarah readied herself to leave. "I can bring them to you after I drop Grandmother off."

"Yes, but Reyn has them. You'll have to stop at his place. I'll call him. He likes to be warned if you're coming." Caleb grabbed his cell phone as Padraic and Sarah said goodbye and headed out the door.

"Is everything okay?" Carrie beckoned him back to her side.

"I'm not sure. Did you notice he didn't look at me once the whole time he was here?"

"He's like that sometimes, especially when he thinks you're trying to scare me."

"Did I scare you? I didn't intend to."

"A little bit, but then I saw that look you get." She turned her face away from his.

"What look?" He placed a finger under her chin.

"When you start figuring stuff out, your eyes shine, and your mind is ten miles farther than anybody else. It's why you're going to be the best ranger Wyoming has ever seen."

"I can't believe you've been through so much, and you're offering me encouragement. What's this about you trying to send Padraic off to medical school behind my back?" His hand caressed her cheek.

"It's his gift, and you two are the only ones who can't

see that." She lay back against her pillows and offered him her hand. "You need to keep care of him. Padraic's going to wander off too far one of these days. Then, you'll have to have to go out and find him—because you'll be the only one who can."

"Padraic doesn't get lost." He kissed her fingers.

"He just doesn't let you know when he is."

"You've really put a lot of thought into this."

"I've lost everyone else. All I have is you and Padraic." She bit her bottom lip to keep it from quivering and turned her head away as her eyes welled up with tears. "It hurts so much inside me right now. Why did God have to take my mother? I really need her."

He held her and accepted the tissues and washcloth the nurse brought to him. Words escaped him. "God's plan…"

"Stop. I really don't want to hear about God's plan right now." She pushed away from his arms and wiped her tears. "God is not my friend."

He stopped himself from answering too quickly. *She's hurting, Lord. How do I help her? She's turning away from You when I need her to go toward You.*

"I've felt that way, too." He poured some water and held the cup out to her. "It's then I remember that even though my feelings may change, His don't. God is good, a refuge in times like this, and He cares for those who trust Him."

"You can tell me how to trust him, how he's my refuge, after I bury my father." Her voice pierced his ears with stilled defiance.

"Okay." He caught her chin before she looked away. "I will." He placed a gentle kiss on her lips and felt the tension drain from her limbs. "I can also talk to Mrs. Talons. She took care of your mother's funeral. She'll know what to do for your dad."

"I want to see him."

He moved beside her, taking both her hands in his. "No," he stated firmly. "You don't need that picture in your head. It's enough that it's in mine."

She withdrew her hand from his and stared at him for a moment in silence. "Okay, will you go get my stuff for me? I want to brush my hair, my teeth."

"I will do that."

"And my clothes." She motioned the sign for clothing, bringing a smile to his face.

It had been a long time since any of them had used sign language with one another, but she reverted to it so easily. Padraic had been taught sign language because the adult world had deemed him autistic. The truth lay in the fact he spoke Sioux, not English, and was raised in the tradition that speech was meant for those with something to say. Idle chatter was unacceptable.

"Did you hear me?" She raised her voice and brought him to her side.

"Yes, I'm sorry. Your clothes, and I do have a key. Did you want me to go now?"

"If you don't mind. I really just want my own things." She tilted her head and offered a teasing smile that he couldn't resist kissing.

"I wish you had called me when I was out. I don't like leaving you alone."

"My cell was on the plane. Caleb, are you all right? You seem a bit distracted."

"Just a bit? I'm a whole lot more than distracted, but I'm okay. I'm just trying to sort through what I'm supposed to do. I want to know what happened to your dad's plane and justify his death. But I also want to keep you safe. You have no parent or guardian now."

"I haven't had one since my mom died." Carrie picked at her fingernails and kept her eyes toward her lap.

"I know you didn't think Gregg was much of a father to you, but it was his presence that kept you from becoming a ward of the state and getting shipped to the city. Now we really need to sit down and make some tough decisions." He took his place on the bed and reached for her hands.

"Can't we just revert back to our original plan from before he showed up and ruined everything?" She set her hands down and met his stare.

"I don't think so. I had your mother's permission to marry you if your father did not come home. I don't think the paperwork is still valid." He let out his breath and sat down opposite her.

"You didn't get sent away."

"That's different," he replied. "I had already been living by myself for a year. I had a driver's license, a job, and my GED. Our situations are very different."

She lifted her eyes to look at him for a moment then shook her head. "It's because I'm a girl."

He grinned and tried to disguise a chuckle before he nodded his answer. "Well, I'm not going to lie to you. Judges do tend to protect girls a little bit more."

"Even the ones who don't want to be protected?"

"Especially the ones who don't want to be protected. This is not a bad thing. These people are not our enemies. The systems are in place to make sure you're safe and that no one takes advantage of you."

"You can do that." She lifted her chin and placed a curl behind her ear.

63

"Not legally, not yet anyway. You're not quite seventeen. We haven't only disobeyed God's laws. We've gone against man's as well. If the social workers, counselors, judges found out about us, I could end up in jail." The seriousness of his tone brought shivers to his skin.

"I'm not going to tell anyone," she said softly.

"This is not just about protecting me. It's about us doing the right thing. We need to get our paths straight and face God. Find out what he wants us to do. I think I know, but I'm not sure you are ready."

"I'm ready for anything you ask of me."

"Do you know what emancipation is?"

She shook her head. "Do you mean like what Lincoln did with the slaves?"

"Sort of, but in this case instead of freeing you from slavery, it frees you from being considered someone's child." Her quizzical look brought a smile to his lips.

"I like being someone's child," she stated under her breath.

"I can't marry a child." He withdrew his touch as she sat up and looked at him.

"You'll marry me now?"

"Not unless you're ready. Marriage is..."

"I am ready. I have been ready," she interrupted.

"You need to pray about it, and so do I. We need to pray about it together, maybe go see Pastor Mike and get some counseling first."

"I don't need all of that. I've always known I wanted to be married to you."

"Yes, but things are different. We need to make sure this is what God wants us to do right now, because if it's not part of His plan, it won't work."

She turned from him, tossing a tissue in the trash bag beside her bed. "Do I need to be emancipated in order to be married?"

"I'm not sure; every state is different. I need to research Wyoming's laws governing emancipation."

"My father shouldn't have come back. He hated it here almost as much as I hated him being here. Now he's dead, and I'm not sorry he's dead. I just wish he'd never come back. If he'd never come back, he wouldn't be dead now, and we wouldn't be in this mess."

"Your dad did the right thing. You were his responsibility, not mine. What I did to you was wrong."

"Why can't you just let me hate him?" She pushed his hands away and grimaced, reaching for her calves.

"Are you all right? Should I get the nurse?" He looked toward the door, but the nurses were well engrossed in report.

"I'm okay. What I'd really like you to do is to go and get my stuff. I want to get out of this bed, take a shower."

"I'll get your things, but I don't think showering in your condition is an option right now."

"Stop telling me what I can't do, and go get my stuff." Her biting tone lit through him like a burning wick.

"I'm on my way. Is there anything else I can bring you while I'm out?"

"No, just go." She turned away from his kiss.

"I'll be back as soon as I can." He seized her chin and forced her to face him. "I love you."

"I love you, too." She bit her quivering lip and held the tears that welled up in her eyes.

Chapter 7

Caleb glanced at the living room as he unlocked the door. Helen Dareme had always kept an immaculate house, cluttered only by her whirlwind of a daughter. Gregg could not have begun to compete with his wife's competence for order. Caleb opened Carrie's bedroom door. Her closet was wide open and was witness to a mad dash toward packing. Except for a few stray items, her vanity had been emptied. Caleb realized all her comfort possessions would have been on the plane with her.

"Thought I'd find you here," Padraic said, as he walked in and tossed a pile of mail on the kitchen table.

"Carrie asked me to get her things." Caleb abandoned the bedroom and picked through the letters.

"She keeps a bag under the bed. It's got her extra hairbrushes and stuff in it. Just grab it. Here," Padraic handed him a pink cell phone. "I had their phones turned off and added a line to yours."

"To mine? How did you do that?" Caleb brought the bag to the living room and placed it on the couch.

"It's a small town. Bethany likes to do favors for me." Padraic filled two glasses with water and handed one to him.

Caleb accepted the drink. "You have issues."

"You have more." Padraic lifted his glass in a toast-like fashion.

"Amen." He felt his breath escape his lungs as he collapsed beside the bag. "How did you know this was here?"

"How did you not know?" Padraic slapped his shoulder and took a seat opposite him. "She's been ready to run since Gregg came back."

Caleb watched and waited. *He's come here with the intent of finding me alone. He's here to tell me something that he doesn't want anyone else to know.*

Usually waiting him out worked, but today he wasn't budging. "Is everything alright?" Caleb disrupted the awkward silence.

"No." Padraic stared at the wall.

Caleb leaned back on the couch and waited. "Are you going to tell me, or do we need to play twenty questions?"

"You really don't know?"

Padraic couldn't seem to sit still. His feet tapped in a constant rhythm. He started to pace.

"Come on, man, don't play this game with me. There's too much drama going on right now. You're just adding to it." Caleb followed him with his eyes. The rage on Padraic's face was evident. He was ready to come out of his skin.

Padraic turned an eerie glare straight at him. "She's pregnant."

"Gail?"

"Carrie."

Pregnant? There was no air left in his lungs, no voice, no words. Caleb gulped hard and then dropped his hand over his face, certain he was going to throw up.

He fought against the acid erupting in his throat. "Are you…" He stopped himself. *Don't even say it.* Caleb drew back in a defensive posture as Padraic withdrew a folded piece of paper from his back pocket.

He ran his finger down a list of numbers. "This HCG level, it should be zero or less."

Fifty-nine thousand. Caleb couldn't move his eyes from the paper. "She never told me."

"If you didn't know, then she probably doesn't either." Padraic threw the lab sheet at him and collapsed in the leather recliner.

Caleb grabbed the back of his neck and lowered his head so that the world could not see his face.

"I'm not sure if in the emergency it just got missed, but it isn't mentioned at all in her care plan." Padraic sat forward with his arms resting on his knees. "I pulled the labs as soon as I noticed."

Caleb managed to find his voice after a half hour of silence. "Did Carrie say anything to you about us?"

"I didn't know until I saw the labs." Padraic sat forward and stilled his presence.

"I'm sorry," Caleb said, as he shook his head in disbelief.

"I'm not here as your judge." Padraic stood and fended off the restlessness. "Besides, if Carrie loved me the way she does you, we'd have a litter by now. That's how we Injuns do things." Padraic grabbed a white box from his pocket and tossed it to Caleb. "It's the ring she wants. She showed it to me so that I would know when you were ready."

Caleb lifted the lid and saw the glitter of a five-cut engagement ring with a band enmeshed with diamonds and tiny sapphires. "You'll always give Carrie whatever she wants." Remorse poured through his body almost as the words came out of his mouth. "I didn't mean that the way it sounded." Padraic walked to the door, and Caleb followed.

Padraic turned to face him but didn't speak for a long moment. "I don't know what you want me to do."

"I don't know what to do. I can't believe she's pregnant."

"What were you using for birth control?" Padraic gathered Carrie's school bag and suitcase.

"I didn't ask. I thought she'd taken care of it."

"Really? You didn't ask her? She's sixteen." Padraic's sarcastic tone rubbed against the grain.

"Everything just happened so fast. I was planning to put the brakes on when she got back from Oregon." Caleb rubbed his forehead, following Padraic out to his truck.

"You should have put them on before she left."

"Listen to you! It's not like you don't have a different girl in your bed every week!"

"I'm not you." Padraic loaded the bags into Caleb's truck. "You should be thankful that Gregg is dead instead of trying to resurrect him." He dug his keys from his pocket and opened his truck. "Gregg would have you charged with rape." Caleb couldn't tell if Padraic was being facetious.

"I didn't rape her."

"Legally, you did." Padraic slid behind the wheel of his truck. "That's how the state is going to look at this, too."

"Don't just drop this in my lap and walk away!" Caleb grabbed the door before Padraic could close it. "What am I supposed to do?"

"You should have asked yourself that before you started sleeping with her." Padraic yanked the door and freed it from Caleb's grip. "There are plenty of precautions you could have initiated to protect her."

"I didn't plan it!"

"Not the first time, but what about the second? Or the third? Or how about the tenth time? Did it ever cross your mind that she was way too young to be doing this?" Padraic slid out of the truck and approached him with a clenched fist.

"Yes, it did. I just didn't know how to stop it. You know what it's like telling her no." Caleb breathed a sigh of relief as Padraic dropped his fist and turned from him.

"All I can do is buy you time until you figure it out." Padraic faced him, tension draining from his face. "No one else has to know right now."

"Why did you tell me?"

Padraic kicked the ground and sucked in his cheeks. He diverted his eyes to the cloudless sky overhead. "Because I knew."

Caleb released his breath. A beating from Padraic was definitely deserved, but not something he wanted to experience. "I guess I need to tell her."

"Let her tell you." Padraic reached inside his truck and started the engine. "This is going to be just as much a shock to her as it was to you. It might be a week or two before she even contemplates it. Maybe by then all this stuff with the funeral and social services will be over with."

"Shouldn't she know? With everything that's going on, what if she gets the wrong medication or something?"

"It's a little too late to be going down that road now. All I can do is manage what she gets from here on out. I can't do anything about what's already happened." Hostility returned as he turned around and raised an open hand toward Caleb. "We're lucky Carrie even survived that crash. If it wasn't for the medical attention she received, she wouldn't have."

"I'm not doubting that." Caleb raised his palms forward, warding off the threat. "I'm talking about now. If the doctors don't know she's pregnant, might they give her medications that she shouldn't have?"

"I will do everything I can to protect Carrie and her baby." Padraic climbed in behind the wheel.

"I know you will." Caleb stood in the way so he couldn't close the truck door.

"I didn't want to know this alone."

"It's okay. You made the right decision. My judgment is more in question than yours." Caleb clenched his keys and looked at the imprints on his palms. "Do you still want the swatch test from Reyn?" Padraic stated as he gripped the steering wheel and kept his focus forward.

"Yes it's the only lead we have." Caleb heard himself answer.

"Joe shouldn't have you on this case." Padraic shoved Caleb out of the way, slammed his truck door and drove away.

Caleb wiped his face. A light snow had started to fall. He glanced down at the flashing text on his phone and noticed a message from his boss with the departure time for the tagging mission.

His thoughts raced with panic. *I can't just leave her here, pretend I don't know anything. We can't have a baby! I'm leaving in January! How am I supposed to take care of her and a baby and complete ranger training? We're just not ready for this.*

He dashed into the house and made it to the bathroom just in time. Stomach acid singed his throat and nose. The cool tiled floor offered little comfort from the continuous onslaught of bile erupting into his esophagus. Sweat poured from every orifice of his body. *I can't do this. I need You to forgive me, show me what I need to do.*

Caleb returned to the hospital and found Carrie in a different room, out of bed and in a wheelchair. Her left ankle remained bound in a black metal casing attached to a portable pulley system, which had allowed her to move to the window. Her right leg remained in the cast and slightly elevated by the wheelchair appendages.

"You moved," he said as he set her stuff down on the windowsill.

"This is a step-down unit. Padraic says it's a good sign—it means I don't have to wear all those monitors."

"He was here already?" Caleb spied the swatch test on her bedside table.

"He said he's going to pick up a couple extra shifts so he could be close, in case I needed something while you're tagging." She looked up at him.

Caleb bit hard into the side of his mouth and stifled the jealousy that crept up inside him. *How does he stay one step ahead all the time?*

She picked up a sample from the bedside table. "It's this one. Is it kerosene?"

Caleb opened the bag and inhaled the scent. "No, it's jet fuel." He closed the bag and set the test aside.

"Do you think someone killed my dad on purpose?"

"Your dad had no enemies." He frowned at how tired and pale she appeared. "Let me put you back to bed." He turned down the sheets and placed her on the bed before she could object.

"Don't baby me." She lifted her head off the pillow. "The more I do for myself, the better it is for the both of us." She adjusted the pulley and fixed the pillows under her casted foot.

"You look a bit tired, though, and there's no sense in overdoing it." He sat down on the edge of the bed, drinking in her presence with a pleasure that embraced him. "I'm still trying to recover from the thought that we almost lost you."

He slipped the engagement ring onto her finger. "There's some paperwork I need to go through. While I'm gone, I'm going to pray about this. I want you to do the same."

"When are you leaving?" Carrie twisted the ring he had placed on her finger.

"An hour or so. Where's Padraic now?"

"There was a code in the ICU, and he said something about being a perfusionist. Said he'd come check on me when he got out of the OR." She held up her hand and admired the ring.

"What's a perfusionist?" He scratched his head, glancing up at the clock.

She shrugged. "I have no idea."

"He's a jack of all trades when it comes to anything medical."

"That's why he'd make a great doctor."

"He has technical skills," corrected Caleb, "but he's lacking in the social graces it takes to be a good doctor."

"His wife will take care of that," she stated nonchalantly.

"His wife? Do you know something I don't?" She shrugged again as he reached for her. "Medical school, now a wife? Tell me, does he know about any of this?"

"Maybe." She offered a passive smile.

"I hate to disappoint you, but Padraic approaches his love life the same way he does everything else." Caleb took her hand in his, "He's with a different girl every time I see him. He will never be satisfied."

"Maybe when he finds the right girl," Carrie smiled lifted a steaming Styrofoam cup from her table and inhaled the sweet scent of vanilla.

"That's the issue. He thinks he already has." Caleb stated as he caught her eye before she could look away. "I forgot to stop for your latte, but I see you got one anyway."

She pointed at a second cup on the counter, "There's a coffee and a bagel for you to take with you. He didn't think you'd have time to stop before the flight."

"He's right. I don't." Caleb retrieved the coffee and opened the lid. "Cell phone," he said, as he reached into his pocket and placed the pink case in her hand.

"Will I be able to reach you?"

"Not when I'm at the site, but I'll call you when I get to the station. What's your number?" He opened his phone.

She powered up her phone and looked at him with a grin. "It's the same as it's always been."

"Far be it from Padraic to change anything." He snapped his phone shut. "I do have to go. I want you to think about all the things we've talked about. Pray, maybe do your homework."

She steered her eyes away from him and chewed her bottom lip. "I'm not going back." Her raspy whisper challenged him.

Air built up so fast in his throat that he found it difficult to breathe, much less muster up an audible response. He stood, backed away from her bed, and closed the door. School would be the furthest thing from his agenda. "Let's not make any life-altering decisions right now."

"You're not going to try to talk me out of it?"

Her look of surprise caught him off guard. "You have enough on your plate without having to worry about school." He took her hands and looked at the ring he'd placed on her finger. "I talked to Sarah Talons earlier. She's made all the funeral arrangements. Calling hours and remembrance services will be Sunday. The funeral and graveside service is Monday."

"Will I be out of the hospital by then? That seems so fast."

"It is. It's November—if we're going to have a burial,

we have to do it before the ground freezes." He sat beside her. "I trust Mrs. Talons. She knows about these things. She also mentioned that they still have their foster care license. Padraic's agreed to move out, so you should be able to stay with them."

"No! I thought I was staying with you." She sat up, breaking her hands away from his.

"We need to have a plan in place for you until we can work out the details. You're a minor, Carrie, and our relationship isn't legal. The Talons can legally house you until we figure something out."

"I don't want…"

"It's that or go to a group home in the city. I wouldn't be surprised if the social worker has already picked one out for you."

Padraic stood on the threshold. "You're supposed to be discharged to Kendel on Tuesday, with follow up in the rehab center. It's on your care plan already."

"No, they can't do that! I won't go!" She struggled to move and became more entangled in the bed sheets.

"I spoke with Grandmother. She's calling the powers that be to see if she can get temporary custody. We just need to stay calm, especially you." Padraic placed a gentle kiss on her forehead.

"I'm scared." Her tears christened the tips of his thumbs as he held her face in the palms of his hands.

"We're all scared." Padraic's focus lay completely on Carrie. His voice was earnest, but laden with hope. "Let's put our faith up front. We're going to get through this." He fastened the leg sleeves to her calves and turned on the machine.

Caleb diverted his eyes from the encounter. "Carrie's identified the fuel." Caleb pointed at the swatch test, filling the awkward silence.

Padraic backed away from the bed. He looked tired, dressed in royal green scrubs with his hair hidden under a surgical cap. "Good. Now that that's over, we can focus on recovery."

"I still need a rescue report from you." Caleb settled Carrie, then stood beside Padraic.

"Good luck with that," was Padraic's only response as he removed his cap and tossed it on the windowsill.

"Just write something down." Caleb grabbed his jacket. He knew he was fighting a losing battle.

"No pen." Padraic shrugged, giving Carrie a quick wink.

"You'd simplify my life if you did." Caleb fished his pockets for his keys.

"I wasn't put here to simplify your life."

"Amen." Caleb grabbed the bagel and lifted his coffee in a toast fashion. "I have to go. It's already three-thirty and takeoff is at four. It will probably be a few days, no more than a week." He gave her a quick kiss and then reached in his pocket and tossed a pen at Padraic. "Blank reports are in the folder by the window. Call dispatch if anything changes."

"Wait, are you going to be back for the funeral?" Carrie asked, grabbing his sleeve as he tried to leave.

"I plan on it, but I have to do this, Carrie. This is my job."

"I know, I just..."

"I'll call you as soon as I can. Do what the doctors and nurses tell you to do."

"I will." She dropped her hand to her lap.

"I'll walk you out." Padraic followed him.

Caleb stopped at his truck and faced Padraic. "She didn't say anything to me about the pregnancy, so you're probably right about her not knowing. Any idea on when she might know?"

Padraic shook his head. "It's the last thing on her mind right now." He grabbed the door before Caleb could open it. "I can tag for you."

"Thanks," Caleb pushed his hair back and looked up toward the hospital, "but I need do this. Maybe getting back to the scene will put a clearer picture in my head." He took his keys out of his pocket and opened his truck door. "I trust you. Call dispatch."

"Are you sure you don't want me to tag?"

"I can deal with the dead. You specialize in the living. Take care of my family." Caleb extended his hand and felt Padraic's strong grasp.

"I will." Padraic released his grip and walked back toward the hospital.

Chapter 8

A thick blanket of snow fell from the sky, forbidding the sunlight to touch the windowsill of Carrie's dreary hospital room. Three days had already come and gone, and still there was no word from Caleb.

That's not unusual, there isn't any reception up there, she thought, as she chewed her bottom lip and adjusted the pulleys that ensnared her useless left ankle. Knowledge brought little solace. The room remained warm, almost too warm, as she watched the frigid blizzard continue its intent. Tomorrow would be Friday, and the thought of having to go through the calling hours and funeral without him left her hollow inside.

Why did You send my father back here in the first place? I didn't need him. If You wanted him in Africa, You should have left him there. Now everything is a perfect mess. Caleb would be upset if he knew she was addressing God so informally. *If it weren't for Caleb, I wouldn't have addressed God at all.*

A twinge of guilt interrupted her anger for a moment. Truly she believed that there was a God and that her mother was waiting for her just inside the gates of heaven. Even now, she wondered what her mother was saying to Gregg. She wiped the smirk from her lips and arched her back as another wretched cramp ran its course.

She adjusted herself in the bed and turned on the news. In just the few days that Caleb had been away, autumn had given way to winter. Six inches of heavy wet snow blanketed the ground. An eerie wind echoed outside her window. The plows were busy. She could hear the scraping of their blades, the sharp warnings of their alarms as they backed up and the defining thud when the drop of the plow hit bare ground.

She was comforted in the knowledge that some things were pretty dependable in northern Wyoming—like a white Christmas. She'd never experienced a Christmas without snow. It would be too weird, she decided, and arched her back as another cramp stole breath.

She glanced at the television screen in an attempt to distract her mind from the agony within her body. Every muscle ached, and her head hurt. There was no peace from the pain. Every intricate repair that was naturally occurring within her body, she felt with a vengeance—even breathing was almost too much to bear. She wiped her eyes before they could tear.

"You need to stay ahead of the pain." Padraic had explained the PCA to her earlier. "There are no prizes for the person who endures the most pain. Instead of suffering, save your energy for healing."

She looked at the black button that he'd attached to her bed. Her mother had the same button those last few weeks in the hospital. Padraic had told her mother the same thing. The only painless rest her mother received was under Padraic's watch. It was attending to her mother that sent him to anesthesia school. Of that, she was certain.

Unlike Caleb's, Padraic's attention had never been exclusively hers. Padraic's adoration for her mother had been just as complete.

She had been glad when the nurse removed the tubing for the PCA pump earlier in the day. One less cord to have to contend with, and possibly by the time Caleb returned, she would be cleared to leave the hospital. She'd endure any amount of pain in order to do just that.

She turned her attention to the television and realized she didn't even know the date. According to the tiny white lettering at the bottom of the screen it was November 7, six more weeks until she could officially call herself seventeen—not that age mattered to her, but Caleb was obsessed with it.

It just sounded better to be seventeen. Sixteen to him, and everyone else, was so young. Being seventeen meant she was close enough to eighteen to make her own decisions, to know her own mind, to no longer be considered a child.

If her father had stayed in Africa, she'd be married, maybe even thinking about having babies of her own by now.

She couldn't get comfortable. Whether it was the constant ache of Caleb's absence or the burning and twisting of her healing muscles, she found no relief.

She was surprised when the dry heaves began. They led to an onset of chills that rotated hourly from extreme cold to sopping sweats. Cramps ripped through her lower back and abdomen as she tried to put on a good front for her visitors.

Sarah Talons spent most of the daylight hours at her bedside and ran interference with the pretentious social worker. The visits from the worker frightened Carrie. She was thankful Mrs. Talons kept vigil over her.

I just won't say anything to anyone until Caleb gets back. If I don't speak, I can't get anyone in trouble, she resolved within herself.

Sarah defended Carrie's silence and stated she was exhausted, grief-stricken and in pain. The social worker defined it as defiance.

Padraic's presence was enough to send everyone home at the end of the day. He'd check her chart and adjust the settings on her pulley equipment. He didn't seem to mind her silence. *He doesn't have much to say either,* she pondered as evening shaded her vision to the outside world.

"Oh, Lord have mercy," Carrie said, as she cringed at the scarlet stains left on the bed sheets.

"It's all right. I'll help you get cleaned up." Joyce, her dark-haired nurse, spoke with an ever-present smile.

"I should have known all this achiness wasn't just from the accident." Carrie tried to help Joyce remove the sheets from the bed.

"How about a good shower while you're up, then I'll get you some Motrin and chicken noodle soup. Those are my creature comforts during the curse." Joyce tossed the sheets into a nearby hamper then opened the bathroom door. "Would you like some help?"

Carrie pushed her wheelchair into the bathroom and looked back toward Joyce uncertain of her next move, but unwilling to admit her dependence.

"I'll finish up with the bed. Holler if you need me." Joyce remade the bed and turned down Carrie's sheets.

"I just came to check on Carrie." Padraic tapped on the 'No Visitors' sign posted on the door and went straight into the room.

"She just went in the shower, so it will be a few minutes." Joyce's voice waned as Padraic paid her no mind and walked right past her. She laid the pillow down and watched him.

He rapped on the open bathroom door with his knuckle and knelt beside her. "Carrie, are you okay?"

"I'm okay." She tried to turn the shower on.

"Takes forever for the water to heat up in this place." He moved the handle and allowed the spray to soak the sleeves of his scrub top. He grabbed a fresh set of towels from the top shelf and ensured all of her amenities were within easy reach.

"What else do you need?"

She grinned and caught her breath as another wave of nausea permeated through her. "I don't feel good."

"Nausea or pain?"

"I just feel like I'm going to throw up all the time."

"Joyce, has she had Zofran today?"

"She hasn't asked for anything." Joyce came to the threshold.

"She's asking now. Are you all right in here by yourself, or do you need help?"

"I can do this. I just want to feel better." She held back her tears, wrapped her arms around his neck and placed her head on his shoulder.

"The medicine should help. Let me know if it doesn't." He rubbed her back. "I'll come back at ten and watch Jeopardy with you." He broke away from her embrace and lifted her chin.

"Bring chocolate," was her only response.

A grin overtook his face. "Hot chocolate or candy?"

"You mean I have to choose?"

"No, Kimimela." He kissed her forehead and stood. "I'll see you at ten." He gave a slight wave to Joyce and left.

"Joyce, I really don't feel good. I hurt all over." Carrie waited until Padraic was out the door.

"Your body has been through an awful lot these past few days." Joyce helped her into the shower.

"I just ache all over. I feel awful, and this bleeding is..." Carrie cringed as the water pummeled her body.

"Is there any reason to believe you may be pregnant?" Joyce crossed her arms, taking a hard look at Carrie.

If anyone found out about us, I could end up in jail. Caleb's words forced her to bite down hard on her tongue. "I may not be a nurse, but I do know you have to have sex in order to get pregnant. With Padraic serving as a self-appointed warden, my opportunities are pretty limited in that department." She felt her cheeks flush and ducked her head under the running water.

"I can see he's a bit overprotective of you." Joyce secured the waterproof wrap around her cast and released the pulley from her right leg. "He seems quite smitten with you. Are you two a couple?"

"No. We're just friends. I wandered off the playground in preschool. Padraic found me and brought me home. I think I've been his pet project ever since." She washed her hair and turned her face up toward the spray. "He found me this time, too, so I guess I have no grounds for complaint." Carrie turned off the shower and grabbed a towel.

"He found you? I heard it was the ground team." Joyce helped her over to the toilet and gave her fresh underwear and pads.

"That's what everyone heard. It doesn't make it true." Carrie grabbed the trashcan and heaved her stomach contents. "I'm sick, I'm on my period, and my ankles are broken. I don't think I can feel any worse."

"If I were you, I wouldn't tempt fate." Joyce helped her finish in the bathroom then brought her to bed. "I'll check and see if you have some IV meds. Oral stuff is futile if you're throwing up." Joyce placed a damp cloth on Carrie's forehead and dimmed the lights. "I'll be back in a few minutes."

What if I am pregnant? What if I am losing the baby right now? If I try to stop it, then everyone will know, and Caleb will go to jail! If I don't, I'll lose my baby. There might not even be a baby, and I'll get Caleb in trouble for nothing!

Silent tears burned crimson streaks down her cheeks. She

choke down some of the water Joyce had left at her bedside and reached for her phone. I need Padraic, the fear invaded her ability to breathe. She managed to control her fingers long enough to text him.

Joyce was the first to her bedside. Carrie could hear her speaking, but lacked the air to answer her.

"Carrie are you okay?" Joyce's voice seemed so distant.

"She's having a panic attack." Padraic crossed the threshold and grabbed the oxygen mask off the wall. "Slow deep breaths," He took her phone from her hands and guided her through a relaxation exercise. The text had simply read, 'Come now.' "What can I do?"

"I brought you some Zofran for nausea and some Toradol for your pain," offered Joyce.

"She doesn't want Toradol. Call her doctor for a morphine cocktail and some multivits." Padraic placed his hand over the IV port and refused to relinquish access. "Please, do as I asked."

Carrie met Joyce's eyes and gave a slight nod of agreement. Joyce stepped away from the scene and walked out of the room.

He placed the oxygen mask over Carrie's face and pulled her blankets to her shoulders. "Tell me."

"I'm afraid." She pulled the mask away, unsure if she had the strength or courage to speak.

"I'm not going to let anything happen to you." He stood as Joyce came in with the new medicine in hand.

"Dr. Anchorage wants to know if you plan on managing all his patients this evening." Joyce handed him the syringe pump and cleaned the open port.

"What are we giving her?" He secured the pump to the IV pole and hit the start button.

"Everything you asked for plus a prophylactic antibiotic."

"Which one?" Padraic took the small IV bag from her and read the label.

"Unasyn." Joyce stepped aside as Padraic spiked the medications and hung them on the IV pole.

"Unasyn is a broad-spectrum antibiotic. I think it's okay." He grabbed his phone and checked his medication app. "Yeah, that's fine. I'm going to stay with her until she goes to sleep." He followed Joyce to the door.

"I think she'd like that." Joyce pressed the dimmer switch once again and said good night to Carrie.

"Are you awake?" He returned to Carrie's bedside.

"The pain is going away, but I'm so scared. It's all my fault. Caleb's going to go to jail, and it's all my fault." She set the face mask aside and grabbed some tissues.

"Caleb is fine. I talked to him this morning. He's walking it in, said he needed some one-on-one time with God. I expect him tomorrow."

"No, you don't understand." She gulped a big breath of air. "He said he'll go to jail if anyone finds out and I—" the words stuck in her throat, unable to pass her lips.

"And you're pregnant."

She looked at him in stunned silence. "Then it's true? I am?"

"According to your labs, it's true." He washed her face with a cool cloth.

"Does Caleb know? Does everybody know except me?"

"Not exactly." He checked to make sure her door was closed. "Caleb knows." He refilled her water glass and brought it to her. "I purged your lab results and replaced them with one that didn't have a HCG reading."

"Are you going to get in trouble?" She fought against the medicine that made her entire body feel heavy.

"Not nearly the trouble you and Caleb would be looking at if anyone else found out." She sat up and grabbed his arms.

"I'm bleeding. It's really bad. The cramps have been so painful in my back and stomach." She tucked her hair behind her ear and tried to face him in her shame.

"Do you mean spotting, or actual period bleeding?"

"Like the worst period of my life bleeding." She dabbed her eyes.

"You're miscarrying." He breathed into his hands. "We need to move you to labor and delivery."

"Can you stop it? Can you save my baby?"

He shook his head. "Maternity is not my thing."

"Do you think my baby can be saved?"

"No, not if what you're telling me is true. You're just not far enough along for any interventions." He wiped her tears with his thumbs.

"Then I've lost my baby, too." She laid herself against the pillow and allowed the medicine to cloud her thoughts.

"Let me take you to labor and delivery. The people there may be able to…"

"No," she stated firmly with her eyes closed. "Both you and Caleb would be in trouble."

"If it means saving the baby, neither of us would care about the trouble." He lifted her head and positioned her pillow.

"Do you think my baby can be saved?" She opened her eyes ever so slightly and saw his gaze avert toward the floor. "You're right about this, Padraic."

"I'm not a doctor."

"It doesn't matter. I know you're right." She sniffed one

last time and released his hand. "What happens next?"

"I don't know. I'll tell you what, you get some rest. I'm going to go up to labor and delivery." He arranged her blankets and turned on the bathroom light, leaving the door slightly ajar.

"What for?" She winced as the leg sleeves squeezed her calves.

"Cross-training." He kissed her forehead and walked away from her bed.

Chapter 9

"Padraic Talons, where are you supposed to be?" An older, heavyset nurse greeted him at the desk of the labor and delivery unit.

"I'd be at your house if you were there, but since you're not, I'll take advantage of you right here." He leaned down on the desk, meeting her at eye level. "What do you have good to eat up here?"

"You need to go find yourself a wife and leave us honest working women alone," the nurse hollered over her shoulder as she led him toward the break room.

"I like working girls," he stated nonchalantly as he poured himself a cup of coffee.

"If your grandmother heard the things that come from your mouth ... I have a mind to give her a call about you." She pulled a Tupperware dish from the refrigerator and a plate from the cupboard.

"You'll feed me first, right?"

"Half the girls in this hospital would be glad to fill your plate, and you come to me!" She dished him out a hefty portion of meatloaf and set the plate in the microwave.

"None of them cooks as good as you, Ms. Leticia." He helped himself to the cookies already on the table.

"You've always been a player, Padraic, since the day I laid eyes on you. You only want what you can't have."

"True enough." His smirk just added more venom to her recourse.

"Lettie, the epidural in room six is alarming again," Wendy said as she came into the room. He recognized her immediately. They had graduated from the same nursing program over two years ago.

"That good for nothing Charles is on for anesthesia." Leticia snorted and kicked Padraic's chair, "Go fix it."

"I'm just here for dinner." He picked up his fork, only to have her snatch it from his hand.

"You'll get your dinner after you fix that blasted machine. Now go."

He pushed away from the table and looked at Wendy, then followed her down the hall. "What room is it?"

"Six, and she's a fetal demise patient, so please…"

"I'll be nice." He glanced down at Wendy. She fidgeted with her glasses and cleared her throat.

He greeted the patient and silenced the alarm. "Has the medicine been working okay for you so far?"

The young woman nodded, maintaining a sullen demeanor.

"The site looks okay. Sometimes these machines are a little overly sensitive." He took a syringe from the drawer, withdrew some medicine from the epidural bag, capped it and tossed it in his pocket. In the same moment, he slid the cassette from the pump and detached the line from the patient. Squeezing the epidural bag he purged the line, ensuring it was free from air, then reattached it to the patient and restarted the pump. "Hopefully that will keep the alarms at bay for a while. You're not in any pain at the moment?"

The patient shook her head.

"If the alarms start again or you have any other questions or concerns, just let Wendy know." They watched the pump for several seconds to make sure they were alarm free.

He left the room and waited while Wendy resettled the patient.

"Thanks for doing that for me," Wendy said as she led him back to the break room. "I heard you were taking your boards for anesthesia."

"I should be receiving the results soon." He pulled out a chair from the break room table and motioned her to sit with him. "Are you hungry? Leticia's made dinner. We can eat, and you can tell me about your patient."

"Padraic Talons, you leave my nurses be. There's enough drama on this floor without you adding to it." Leticia raised a crooked finger toward him and pulled Wendy out of the chair. "Don't listen to a word he says. It's not your patient he's interested in."

"Leticia, I'm going to be doing anesthesia up here. A little insight from Wendy about these fetal demise patients, that's all I'm after, really." He tapped the chair beside him.

"Well, I reckon I have about twenty-seven years of labor and delivery experience. I'll tell you everything there is to know about failed pregnancies. Wendy, you go on back to the desk. I'll tend to this quest for knowledge." Leticia pulled his plate from the microwave and placed it in front of him, then proceeded to tell him everything he wanted to know.

He gulped his food, but drank in every piece of information she offered. "So this retained placenta, is this something you need to worry about if the patient is like only a few weeks into the gestational period?" He rinsed off his dishes and placed them in the drying rack.

"In any pregnancy retained placenta or products of conception can be an issue, but the earlier she is in the pregnancy, the less likely she is to have a problem. Most don't even know they are miscarrying. They think it's a heavy period with a lot of cramping." Leticia stroked her chin and gave him a hard stare. "Why all of a sudden all this interest in L&D?"

He threw a side glance toward Wendy, who was busy typing on the computer at the nurses' station. It was a quick glance, one he was sure Leticia would see and interpret as a predatory appraisal. "I'm interested." He kept his tone low and seductive, and then offered an innocent grin toward Leticia. "I'm always interested in acquiring knowledge about potential patients, especially after this little conversation. I don't want to take up your time, though, or keep you after work with my questions. Wendy, she might not mind if I keep her after hours."

"Why do I waste my breath on you? Stay away from my girls, and get off of my floor!" Leticia pulled him toward the desk and slammed a bin of unused medications into his chest. "Take those back to the pharmacy on your way out."

"Do you work tomorrow?" He spoke to Wendy, but kept his voice loud enough to elicit a response from Leticia.

"You get off this floor this instant, or I will call your grandmother."

"It was a scheduling question. I'm not being promiscuous." He grinned, meeting Leticia's glare. "Fine, I'm off to the lab." He grabbed the bin and picked through it.

"Pharmacy! You are going to the pharmacy. Quit flirting with the girls long enough to at least figure out where you're going. What are you doing?" She slapped his hands away from the contents of the bin.

"Just checking to see if there's anything good that I might want to keep."

Leticia picked up the bin and thrust it hard against his chest. "So help me!"

"Alright, I'm leaving. Thank you for dinner." Padraic took the bin and walked off the floor toward the pharmacy.

He pocketed a vial of Pitocin and an ampule of Methergine. From Leticia's impromptu class, he knew he might need both—the Pitocin to help bring on the necessary contractions to clamp down the uterus and lessen the chance of a postpartum hemorrhage, and the Methergine just in case there was any excessive bleeding.

Carrie was awake with her full attention on the television when he slipped back into her room and closed the door. Side by side, a picture of six-year-old twins—a mousy-looking, brown-eyed girl and an adorable black-haired, freckle-faced boy—stared out with forced smiles on their faces.

"They're missing." She spoke without averting her eyes from the television.

"Where are they from?" He placed a cup of hot chocolate in her hands and a candy bar on her bedside table.

"Somewhere in New Hampshire. It just came on about an hour ago." She sipped the cocoa.

"How are you feeling?" He could tell, even in the dimly lit room, that the color was returning to her face.

"Do you think they'll find the twins?" She kept her eyes glued to the screen as the reporter recapped the story.

"They may." He placed all the medications and supplies he'd collected in the tray of her bedside table. "I really need to know how you're doing." He squeezed her free hand and was able to capture her attention for a moment.

"I...I had the baby. She's in the bathroom." She kept her eyes on her fingers and displayed an unwillingness to face him with her trembling lips and tearing eyes.

"I'm so sorry. I shouldn't have left you alone." He held

her face in his hands and leaned his forehead against hers.

"She was so real, not just a bunch of clots. It was like she was a real little person." Carrie cupped her hands as though she were holding the baby.

"I need Caleb." She took a deep breath and lifted her head toward him.

"I'll meet him at the trailhead in the morning," he stated, unsure of what else he could do.

"Will you take care of my baby?" she asked in a hoarse whisper.

"I will."

He located the washcloth and unwrapped the fetus. Tiny stubbed fingers reached out toward him in what could only be distinguished as an arm. The remainder of the body was little more than a collection of clots. He uncapped a specimen cup from the vanity drawer and contained the baby.

I wish Caleb was here, too. At least he'd know what to say, what to do. He'd know how to talk to God and Carrie about this, he thought.

"What are you going to do?" She wiped her nose and cheeks as he came back into the room.

"What would you like done?" He sat on the edge of her bed and brushed the hair out of her eyes.

"I'm not sure," she said, as she placed her hands over his and freed herself from his attention.

He looked toward the medicines he'd brought. "Are you still bleeding?"

She nodded her answer. He laid her back on the bed and placed his hand on her abdomen and located the firm, rounded surface of the fundus.

"Are you still cramping?" He continued to massage her abdomen.

"Yes, but not as much. That really hurts when you push on my stomach, and it's making me bleed more." She tried to block his efforts.

"Put your hand here." He took her hand and placed it on the top of her uterus. "Feels like the top a baseball kind of, doesn't it?" She nodded in agreement. "That's the top of your uterus. It needs to stay firm. That's why we need to massage it. See how high it is?" He placed a gentle touch just above her umbilicus. "It belongs down here." He moved his hand over her pelvic cavity but did not touch her. "Massaging it will help the uterus return to its rightful size and place, and lessen the bleeding." He drew up the Pitocin and attached the syringe to a port in her IV. "This will make the cramping a little worse, but we need those contractions to help firm things up." He pushed the medicine, removed the syringe and disposed of it and the vial. "I have pain medicine if you need it."

"The nurse gave me some of that morphine cocktail you ordered not too long ago." She continued to massage her stomach.

He drew up the Methergine. "I don't want to give you this unless I have to. It has some side effects."

She had turned her attention back toward the television as he tucked her in and handed her the cocoa. "My baby?"

"I'll bury her underneath the lilac tree we planted on your mother's grave." He opened his coffee and glanced up at the news. "Did you name the baby?"

"Rebecca." She winced and guarded her abdomen.

He watched her as many thoughts went through his mind. *My hands can heal physical needs, but I can do nothing for the real pain. I'm not Caleb. I'll never be Caleb. I'll never see things the way he does. I'll never be as close to God as he is. I want to be committed, but You made me a player. No one will take me seriously—not Caleb, not Carrie and certainly not God. I can't reach You, Lord, so why do I try?*

He snapped open his cell phone and stared at it. The only one he really wanted a word with was way out of his range.

"Hey." She waved a hand in front of his face.

"I'm sorry." He closed the phone and shoved it in his pocket.

"Are you going to tell Caleb?" A haunted expression filled her emerald eyes.

"Maybe you should." He averted her stare.

She touched his face and brought his attention fully toward her. "Thank you for everything you do for me, for us."

He removed her hand and kissed her palm. "Get some rest." He tucked her in, and then settled in a nearby chair. "I'll be here if you need me."

"Don't you have to go back to your floor?"

"No, I worked day shift today. I just keep my scrubs on to ward off evil." He turned off the television.

"Please call your grandmother to come stay with me when you leave." He could hear her yawn.

"I will."

Chapter 10

Caleb watched as the team prepared to board the aircraft that would take everyone back to the station. Evidence had been collected and sent ahead of them. He shrugged his pack onto his shoulders and stepped away from the team. Relief from Reyn's mouth and time alone with God were the two things he needed now, especially after spending the past forty-eight hours in the presence of Carrie's father's ashes.

"Get on the plane." Reyn grabbed his shoulder.

"I'll bring myself in." Caleb backed away from him.

"Get yourself back to the collection site so we can go. I don't aim to be crawling rocks all the way back to Colter Bay!" Reyn raised his hand in an attempt to snatch Caleb's belay line.

Caleb leapt off the overhang and slid his caliber into a pin before Reyn could reach him. It was a risky maneuver. If the pin and the caliber didn't meet at exactly right moment, he would free-fall, and Padraic wasn't there to catch him.

"Get on the plane. I'll bring myself in." Caleb lowered himself faster than he normally would and escaped the tirade of curses that echoed above him.

Caleb lowered himself to the trail and gathered his gear. He looked back toward the rendezvous site and saw that Reyn was gone. Brileigh could endure the abuse for a while. Reyn lacked the skill to follow him, and everyone knew it. Caleb blew on his hands and started down the trail at a pace he knew the team wouldn't be able to follow. Brileigh would understand. Caleb and Padraic often opted to bring themselves in. It would give them a chance to debrief and settle the demons before entering their social roles again. Today, though, the demons were Caleb's to tame alone. He turned off his radio. It was evident that the battle ahead of him at his Lord's feet would be more exhausting than the terrain.

The words of David consumed his thoughts as he locked in for his second descent: "You know my sins; my guilt is not hidden from You. May those who hope in You not be disgraced because of me. May those who seek You not be put to shame because of me. Shame covers my face." He stopped in the midst of the woods and looked at the darkening sky.

Silently he prayed, *Rebuke me, Lord. Let the shame, guilt and retribution fall fully on me. Carrie would not be here if I had not led her. I am the one who is weak. Forgive my transgressions against You and against her. Tighten Your grasp around me that I will respond to Your discipline in a manner that pleases You. I have disgraced You, but You blessed me. Lord, help me to make my own path straight that I may lead Carrie and our unborn child closer to You. Give me the strength and the fortitude to follow Your will and not my own.*

He finished a third rappel. Evening had fully enveloped the landscape as he tried to gain his bearings of just how far he'd wandered. Clanging metal and rustling nylon directed his attention away from the trail that led to Ben's Lair. When he saw Carrie's chute, he stopped and allowed the scene to open around him. The only thing Padraic took was Carrie; everything else lay untouched. This site, too, contained evidence for the investigating team.

Caleb plotted the coordinates and radioed dispatch of his discovery. He judged the incline; this wouldn't be an easy assignment. Oh Lord! He stepped back from the sudden death drop off. No one in their right mind would have attempted this rescue alone in the dark! It's suicide!

He looked toward the havoc below and then above toward the top of the rock. It was possible there were alternate routes. No, there are no alternate routes for Padraic. He doesn't look for them. Caleb drew in a deep breath and swallowed a squall of snow. He glanced toward the trail; weariness fell over him that made his bones ache.

The wind picked up, and his cheeks felt as though they were being rubbed with sandpaper. He turned off the radio, but it didn't clear his head of the static that was going on around him. Rubbing his temples, he realized he needed sleep.

He directed focus toward Thurmond's Mound. Somehow his legs carried him to the woebegone shelter. There on the door hung the kerosene lamp—the one Padraic had neglected to tell him had been lit. So much time in the investigation had already been lost due to the delay of that minute detail. Caleb wondered why Padraic didn't think it was important.

He pushed open the door to the shelter, tossed his pack on the floor and sat down on the cot. He unlaced his boots, kicked them off and freed his weary feet from the entrapment of his hunter's socks. The cool air caressed his toes, which convinced him to dress down to his t-shirt and boxers. Overwhelmed with fatigue, he grabbed his poncho liner and lay down on the cot, closing his eyes.

Seventeen refueling sites and two major distributors served the Northwest region. In the past year, there had been three small-engine plane fatalities. Gregg's death made number four.

Caleb pulled the blanket over his head, unable to stop the churning of information in his mind.

Eighty-one reports of engine problems and gauge malfunctions. Thirteen of those, logged in the past six months, had received fuel from Dixon's station. That was over sixteen percent of the total number of incidents, and now, with Gregg's accident factored in, it was too much of a coincidence to be pilot error.

Stop! he thought, and forced himself to turn over. *Lord, please do not let me be consumed by this investigation. Please, I need to sleep. Don't let me preoccupy my mind with this information. Don't let me be distracted from Your will for my life and Carrie's. Take control of my thoughts and my dreams, and give me rest.*

Eeriness crept through him as he gazed upon the unforgiving terrain. Sheer slate rock faces with little to no veins, no valleys, no plateaus; only vertical assents of an unnatural nature. Goosebumps formed on his skin, and he felt himself shiver. He felt more disturbed by the hollowness that engulfed him than the stifling breeze that disheveled his hair. *God, this is not where I am.* He squinted as the sun seemed offensively bright in all directions. *I'm asleep. Lord, please wake me up. You would not bring me here. This is not where I am.* He rubbed his eyes and pushed his hair back. One lone climber was making slow but viable progress. *What kind of idiot would attempt this alone?* He didn't get the words out of his mouth before he could answer his own question. *Padraic.*

"You're going to have to go out and find him—because you're the only one who can." Carrie's voice tickled inside his ear.

Me? He shouldn't even be here. He knows better than this. How did he even get here in the first place?

He was led.

The answer burned his chest, making it difficult to breathe. *I can't save him. Not here! He's stronger, he's faster, he's smarter, he's better. God, no!* He dove toward the dangling belay line. A loud bull whip crack penetrated his eardrums as he lifted his eyes and watched Padraic's body rake against the rock face, leaving a twenty-foot blood mark. Padraic said nothing. He steadied himself with his climbing line, wiped his face and restarted his quest.

Don't let him do this! Without that belay line, he's got nothing! No safety, just sudden death! Stop climbing! God, do something! He shouldn't be here alone. What is he thinking? Why is he here?

He was led.

Oh, my God!

Caleb felt his feet hit the floor of the cabin. He wiped his face with his hands and tried to steady his breathing. *Oh God, I hate it when You do that to me!*

Pastor Mike had told him the dreams were visions from God, a sixth sense that he'd been gifted with, in order to see potential problems or dangers that lingered in the background of people's lives.

Caleb dumped his canteen over the back of his neck and let the icy water soak his face and hair. Most of the so-called visions seldom made enough sense for him to do anything about. Important things like cancer and plane crashes, he was never forewarned about, just stupid stuff like Padraic climbing alone.

I know he climbs alone, I know he takes risks. That's who he is. There's nothing I can do about it. I can't stop him from being who he is. This has nothing to do with me.

Caleb finished packing his gear and headed down trail toward Ben's Lair, unable to shake the uneasiness that came with every vision. *Gift? How can you call it a gift? It's a beguiling curse.*

His feet hit the ground after a solid rappel down to Wilderness Falls. He stumbled back, feeling a strong grip on his shoulder.

"I'm going to use your gear," Padraic said, as he steadied Caleb and unhooked his lines.

"What are you doing here?" Caleb grabbed the ropes and pulled them out of reach.

"Reyn didn't get on the transport. They think he tried to follow you." Padraic freed the ropes from Caleb's grip and tethered in.

"I told him to go with the team. He knows he can't follow me. He can't even rappel independently." Caleb locked the belay line so that Padraic couldn't move.

"He'll go where you lead him." Padraic snatched the line. "I always did."

"You're different. I don't have to worry about you getting lost. Man, get down. He's my responsibility. I'll go get him." He let out a deep sigh. "This is not what I needed to hear right now."

"I'll bring him in. Carrie needs you." Padraic gripped the lines just below Caleb's hand and twisted counterclockwise, forcing their release.

"No, he's my responsibility." Caleb lacked both will and strength. It was a battle he'd rather forgo.

"Reyn, I can handle. Carrie needs you." Padraic released the lock on the belay line and ignored the gesture to stop.

"I can do both," Caleb insisted.

"I can't."

Padraic's low undercut tone rattled his very being. Silence followed for more than a moment as they stared at each other.

"It's not right." Caleb stepped back and watched Padraic prepare to ascend.

"A lot of things aren't right, but they're still done." A slight wave and Padraic jerked the rope, climbing faster than Caleb could respond.

"Don't kill him," Caleb called after Padraic.

"It's not my intent," was the only promise Padraic would make.

Chapter 11

Carrie didn't even lift her head to acknowledge Caleb when he opened the door to her room. He adjusted the shades, allowing the sunshine to christen the sills and spill out over her beautiful golden hair. Still, she offered only silence and looked as though the past six days had emptied her soul.

"Let's go outside. There's nothing like a little sunshine to warm you up." He helped her into the wheelchair and took her to the hospital solarium. "I can't help you unless you talk to me." He knelt down beside her and saw the tear streaks down her ashen cheeks.

With trembling hands, she gave the ring back to him. "They won't emancipate me." Her voice cracked and barely broke above a whisper.

He returned the ring to her finger. "I don't need your social worker's permission to marry you. I only need your consent." He placed her mother's Bible on her lap and opened it so that she could see the paperwork neatly filled out in Helen's script.

"My mom did this? Did you know?" Her eyes watered as she handed the papers to him.

"She gave your dad the option of fulfilling his mission in Africa or coming home. We didn't know what his choice would be. I promised her to let him choose." He opened the packet to the last page and pointed to her father's signature. "I didn't know about this."

"My dad signed it, too?"

"Two months ago." He pressed his finger against the date.

"The social worker won't let them discharge me from the hospital. She said that there are plans already in place for me to go to the group home in the city. She said that's where the doctors want me to go because the physical therapy center is there, too. She said—"

"Did you tell her about the baby?" Her stunned silence gave him his answer. "Padraic told me."

"He said I should tell you." She tried to turn her head, but he caught her chin and forced her to face him.

"I wish you had told me. I need you to stop relying on him and start trusting me. You're going to be my wife and the mother of my children." He gently pushed her curls aside and teased her lips with a kiss. "With all things, you need to tell me first, okay?"

"Okay." She let out her breath as she leaned her forehead against his.

"You must be Caleb." A well-dressed, heavyset black woman cleared her throat as she approached them.

"I am." He stood, extending his hand.

"Amanda Restley, hospital social worker." She smiled politely and accepted his handshake. "Maybe now that you are here, we can go forward with our plan of care."

"I'm going to take you back to your room," he said, as he turned Carrie's chair and caught the look of fear in her eyes. "I want to talk through some things with Mrs. Restley."

"Without me?" Carrie grabbed the brakes before he could push her forward.

"Yes." He took her hands away from the brakes and kissed her fingertips. "Trust me?"

She slowly nodded her answer. He brought her to the room, Mrs. Restley following close behind. He tucked Carrie into bed, then handed her the remote.

"Promise me you won't tell." Her whisper caressed his ear as he settled her.

He offered little more than a grin and a gentle kiss on the cheek before facing Amanda Restley. "Would you like to talk in your office?"

"Yes, actually that would be preferred." Mrs. Restley smiled at Carrie and beckoned him to follow her down the hall. "I suppose Carrie has already mentioned her treatment plan?"

"Yes ma'am." He followed her into a dingy gray office that contained an old, functional metal desk and walls lined with filing cabinets.

She offered him a seat in one of the wooden guest chairs in front of the desk as she settled her robust frame in the office chair. "What are your thoughts concerning the course of action we've initiated?"

He hesitated and tried to choose his words carefully. "She's really never recovered from the loss of her mother. Now with her father's death and her physical injuries, she's having to cope with a lot more than she's used to."

Amanda lifted her pen and began writing some notes. "I have thought about getting her into therapy once she's settled."

"She's never lived outside of Colter Bay. She has a lot of friends here. She's never missed a Sunday at the First Baptist Church. She's a senior at the high school. This is her home. She doesn't want to be in the city."

"Colter Bay does not have the services she requires for her recovery."

"She has a solid support system in Colter Bay. We would make sure she receives all the treatment she needs." He paused, feeling the tension build. "Pulling Carrie from the community she grew up in, from everything she knows, that just doesn't make sense to me."

She raised her head and locked her gaze on him. "What does make sense to you?"

Caleb hesitated at the question. "Carrie's not ready to think long term. We have to take things day by day. Tomorrow, we bury her father. I can't really prepare her for anything else right now."

"You plan to take responsibility for her?" She sat up straighter in her chair, placing the pencil down on the desk.

"She wears my ring." He kept his frustration buried as he pushed his hair back.

"That, I've noticed." She broke eye contact. "She's very young to be wearing a ring."

He shifted nervously. "I believe that staying in Colter Bay would be the best thing for Carrie."

"For her sake or yours?" Amanda's crisp comment felt like a slap.

"Both." He chewed the inside of his cheek and forced himself to swallow the anger building inside him.

"Your relationship is not platonic." She kept her parental tone as she pushed away from her desk.

"I never said it was." His breath escaped his lungs as he tried to sit still under her guise. "All the interventions that you introduce now won't change what has already happened. If we truly have Carrie's best interest at heart, we need to work together."

"I'm not entirely sure we both have her best interest at heart."

He sat back, unsure of how to respond.

"Ma'am, how much cooperation have you received from

Carrie since her admission?"

It was Mrs. Restley's turn to pause as she looked down at her notes. "Truthfully? None. Her nurse has been almost as impossible as she has. Her chart keeps disappearing, and the computer keeps changing her patient number so the documentation of her care is sketchy at best."

Caleb hid his smile, shaking his head. "Tall Indian guy?"

"Yes. You two know each other?"

"He's very good to his patients." Caleb wiped his mouth, regaining his composure.

"A bit gestapo-like, if you ask me." She grimaced, and then looked back at him.

"I don't mind him being a bit overprotective. It means I don't have as much to worry about when I'm working." Caleb shifted in his seat, thankful for the slight detour in the topic so he could regain his thought process.

"What is it that you are concerned about that she may need such an overprotective nurse?" Mrs. Restley asked.

"The crash is still under investigation, and it's looking suspicious at best. There's a lot more evidence that needs to be taken into consideration before a determination can be made as to the nature of Gregg Dareme's death."

"You're the officer in charge of the investigation?"

"No, I'm not in charge of anything, but I know suspicious when I see it."

"As do I." She picked up her pencil and scribbled down a few more notes. "Given what you've told me, it looks as though the city may be the safest place for Carrie after all."

He folded his hands and tapped his lips, praying that his temper would hold and not be as evident as he felt. "You may be right, at least until after the investigation. I'll talk to her about it. She'll be less likely to fight me over the decision."

"I've signed a release for her to attend the services for her father. Other than that, she needs to be in her hospital room."

Caleb nodded at the decision and walked toward the door. "I'll tell her." He closed the door and shook the barrage of thoughts from his mind.

His phone disrupted the tension as he walked back toward Carrie's room. "Cohen."

"Hello, Caleb, it's Donald Trombley calling from City Hall. How are you doing today?" The voice sounded jovial in the midst of all the chaos in his mind.

"Fine."

"The reason I'm calling is that we've received all the paperwork we needed for your license a few days ago. We were wondering when you are going to pick it up?"

"License for what?" He stopped on the threshold of Carrie's room.

"Your marriage license. You haven't gotten cold feet already, have you?" Donald laughed into the phone.

Caleb froze at the sound of the information. Marriage license? He hadn't even considered the paperwork involved in getting the license.

"No, no, it's just really crazy here. What do I need to do?" He smiled at Carrie and greeted her with a kiss on the cheek.

"I just need you and your bride to be able to sign a few papers in front of me. It really shouldn't take that long."

"Alright, I'm going to try to get there before five. Will you wait for me?" He looked at his watch, then dropped his wrist.

"Of course. The whole town has been waiting for this day, son."

"We won't have time for a ceremony right now. We just want to get the paperwork in and signed."

"Totally understand, we all know what's going on with Carrie—this whole thing with her parents is a terrible tragedy. She needs the stability that you can provide her. I just need signatures, and we'll be done."

"Thanks, Donald." He closed his phone and turned off the television.

"What was that all about?" She tilted her head as he sat down beside her.

"Did you apply for a marriage license for me?" He looked down at his phone, still befuddled about the whole conversation.

"I didn't know that was an option; otherwise, I'd have done it last year," she teased.

"That was Donald Trombley, the town clerk in Colter Bay. He says he's been waiting for us; our license is there."

"That's just weird." Carrie offered a crooked smile.

"I couldn't talk your social worker out of sending you to the group home." He tapped his phone on the palm of his hand, trying to make sense of the thoughts that raced through his head.

"Carrie, you have physical therapy this afternoon. Do you want me to take you down?" The nurse tapped the door frame.

"I thought they were closed on Fridays." Carrie pushed her blankets aside and slid herself into her chair.

"I can call to verify, but the computer says that's where you are supposed to be for the next two hours." She handed Carrie a brush and waited for her to straighten her hair.

"I'll take her down." Caleb took the handles to her wheelchair.

He pushed her to the elevators, stepped off on the ground floor and looked at the 'Closed' sign on the door of the physical therapy lab. "I guess you were right." He turned, seeing his truck in the parking lot out the side door.

"This is really weird," she sighed, looking up at him.

"Do you trust me?" He knelt beside her and felt his heart pound, as he contemplated his next move.

"Of course."

"Wrap your arms around my neck." She did as she was told, and before he could clarify his thoughts he carried her out to his truck and buckled her in.

"This is not our wedding. It's just a paperwork issue. We don't have time for a proper ceremony." He pulled the truck onto the highway and looked at his watch. It usually took forty minutes to get back to the bay. He'd have to hurry. "Legally you've been kidnapped."

"Cool." She reached for the radio.

"Not so cool. If we're caught before we get these papers signed, I'm going to jail."

"Let's not get caught." She laid her head on his shoulder and tried to get comfortable.

He was sure the police would be waiting for him at city hall, but they weren't. He carried her into Donald's office, set her in a nearby chair and grabbed the folder that had been set out for him.

"Caleb sign here and here, Carrie right beside him. I'll notarize it. Call Beverly in for a witness, and we're done." Donald handed him a pen and called for the secretary. "As soon as everyone is done signing, I'll fax it, and sir you can kiss your bride. Oh yes, rings—Beverly, where are those rings?"

"Right here." The gray-haired woman scooted around the desk and unlocked the top drawer. She pulled out the satin white box and opened it.

Carrie's band was simple but beautiful: a thin platinum ring with tiny inset diamonds and sapphires. Caleb lifted it from the box and placed it on her finger. Beverly then presented the box to Carrie. She placed a plain platinum band on Caleb's finger. He knelt down beside her.

"I know this isn't what you wanted."

"You're wrong." A single tear spilled down her cheek. "I never wanted the Cinderella wedding." She placed her hands over his and drew his touch away from her face.

"I love you." His lips pressed firmly against hers until he heard Donald clearing his throat. "Oh, we'd better go."

"Yes son, there's only so much that can be done at City Hall." Donald accepted Caleb's handshake and walked them to the door.

"Where are you taking me now?" Carrie fastened her seat belt as he shifted the truck into drive.

"We need to get you officially discharged from the hospital." He turned onto the highway, still controlled by the chaos that surrounded his thinking.

Her wheelchair remained parked beside the physical therapy lab. He settled her into it and brought her back to the hospital room where Carrie's night nurse Joyce and Amanda Restley were involved in a heated conversation.

"Where have you two been?" Mrs. Restley demanded as they entered the room.

"We were told to go to physical therapy," Carrie answered before Caleb had a chance to speak.

Amanda Restley drew in a long breath and looked at Caleb. "Have you had an opportunity to discuss the care plan?"

"I've told her," he answered, "but she doesn't want to go

to the city, and I can't force her."

"This decision is meant to protect you, Carrie. I'd hoped that you'd be able to understand that." Amanda drew in her breath, crossing her arms in front of her.

"I feel safest when I'm with Caleb," Carrie interrupted as Caleb handed her a drink of water.

"Staying with your boyfriend isn't an option for you." Amanda answered too quickly.

Caleb scratched his head, then took Carrie's hand. "I don't think staying with your boyfriend is an option either."

Carrie cocked her head to the side and offered a passive grin that made him smile. She released his hand and let out a sigh. "I'll go where you want me to, Caleb."

Amanda Restley was about to respond when her pager interrupted. "I have to take this call. Carrie, all the arrangements have been made for you to attend your father's service tomorrow. Do you have any questions for me before I go?"

Carrie shook her head as Mrs. Restley backed out the door. Joyce paused for a moment and looked at both of them as though she wanted to say something.

"Is there anything I can get for you before I go?" Joyce asked as she checked the call light and handed Carrie the TV remote.

"I have a question." Carrie pushed her curls behind her ear and glanced up, catching Joyce's attention. "Is the only thing keeping me here tonight the social service issue?"

Joyce eyed both of them before responding. "If you're asking me if you have been medically discharged from the hospital, the answer is yes."

"What does that mean? Medically discharged?" Carrie placed the remote on the bedside table.

"It means that the doctor has written and signed your

discharge orders. Legally, if you were old enough or had a guardian, you could go home." Joyce chewed the inside of her lip as she delivered the information.

"If her spouse wanted to take her home, he could?" Caleb felt his heart race as he dug in his jeans pocket for the marriage certificate that Donald had given him.

"Absolutely." Joyce glanced down at the paper he presented. "I'll bring your discharge papers."

"She knew." Caleb spoke after Joyce stepped out of the room.

"It does seem so, doesn't it?" Carrie shifted in her chair. "Will you help me with my stuff?"

It took only a few minutes to gather the few things she'd unpacked. Joyce came in with the papers to sign and handed Caleb a script with Carrie's prescriptions.

"I remind you, Carrie, you are just a few days post-op, and with your ankles broken, you are at risk of developing blood clots in your legs. You need to take your Lovenox and try to stay as active as possible. If you develop a fever or have pain in your legs or if they feel hot to touch, you need to come back to the hospital right away. Do you both understand?"

"Yes," they answered in unison.

"Well, if you have no more questions of me, then you are free to go." Joyce dismissed herself with a congenial smile.

"Let's leave the flowers for the nurses," Carrie suggested as Caleb placed her bag on her lap and heaved his onto his back.

The evening air chilled his lungs as he tossed the bags into his truck, and then lifted Carrie into her seat. "We have to leave this chair here. It belongs to the hospital. I'll try to find one for you before the service tomorrow." He brought the chair back to the entrance and returned to the truck. "Where to?"

"Home," she answered as he started the engine and shifted into drive.

"Whose home?" He turned onto the highway as a steady rain-snow mix began to fall against his windshield.

"Ours." Her head rested on his shoulder as she snuggled as close to him as she could get.

Except for the soft hum of the radio, the ride to his apartment was quiet. Her eyes were closed, and her body lay heavy against him as he pulled into his parking space and looked toward his apartment. The snow was coming down steadily, adding to the foot or so that had fallen in his absence.

How quickly everything had changed. Two weeks ago the lawns were green, and people were still walking around in lightweight jackets and sneakers. This evening told a different story—not a bad one, just a different one. Staring at the door of his apartment, he swallowed hard. Today, he'd changed his future.

There would be no ranger school. None of the dreams or plans that he'd worked so hard to achieve would ignite into the career he'd so desperately wanted. Instead, he'd become a father.

I don't want to be a dad. I want to work for the National Park System. I want to do something with my life. Why did you let this happen? He held back his tears as Carrie shifted her position, remaining in a peaceful sleep. *Why did I have to choose? One more year, that's all we needed. One more year. Lord, I need Your help. I need to face this role with as much passion as I did forestry. Please allot me peace with this decision.*

He wiped his face with his free hand, closing his eyes and leaning his head against the back of the seat. *Lord, I want to listen, I want to be obedient. Make your will my own.*

"Caleb, your phone." Carrie sat up, shaking him awake.

Opening his eyes, he grabbed the wheel of his truck in full panic.

"It's okay, it's off. We're parked." She placed her hand on his chest.

"Oh my word." He closed his eyes and shook, heart pounding against her touch. "I'm sorry."

"It's okay. Do you know where we are?" She asked.

The windshield was covered in a thick blanket of heavy white snow. He opened his door and looked toward his apartment building. "We're right outside my apartment. I'll go unlock the door and come back to get you." The fresh coat of snow licked his mid-calves as he propped the door and carried her inside. A second trip brought in all their stuff.

"Who was on the phone?" Carrie asked from her position on the couch.

"Oh, I don't know, I didn't look. What time is it?" He turned on his coffee pot and collapsed on the couch beside her.

"It's almost four in the morning." She placed herself on his lap.

His hand slid under her shirt, his fingers gently caressing her abdomen. "It's hard to believe I'm going to be a daddy." A renewed excitement filled his being as he nuzzled her neck. "If I get started I may not stop."

"I'm not asking you to." She reached behind his head and turned out the lamp.

Chapter 12

"I don't need you, you rock-hugging timber nigger!" Reyn yelled. He backed away as Padraic finished the climb, dropped his harness and stretched out to his true size. At six-three and two hundred pounds of muscle, Padraic didn't need his God-given steel eyes or reputation for rage to intimidate Reyn. Padraic threw his canteen toward him and gathered the gear.

"Your boyfriend send you out to get me?"

"I sent myself." Padraic surveyed the site. There wasn't much left, except a charred indentation marking the path of destruction.

"Yeah, right. Since when do you make an independent decision?" Reyn winced as Padraic stood too quickly.

"I could just tell everyone I couldn't find you." Padraic started further up the trail.

"Lie to Opie?" Reyn scoffed, as he grabbed his gear and followed him. "You sure you want to do that?"

"Where was Gregg's body?" Padraic opened a new canister of tobacco and spread the contents in the area where Reyn pointed.

"What are you wasting good smoke on?"

Padraic turned abruptly. "Let's go."

"What? No chant or prayer? No Indian voodoo or nothing?"

"No point in praying for the dead." Padraic didn't look to see if Reyn followed him; he just kept a steady pace that he knew would be difficult for Reyn to keep up with.

"You're the poorest excuse for an Injun I've ever known! Caleb went the other way." Reyn collapsed on a fallen log.

"Caleb didn't know you were following him." Padraic retraced his steps.

"How could he not know? I'm his partner." Reyn coughed.

"He told you to get on the transport." Padraic tossed him a granola bar.

"Would you have done that?" Reyn unwrapped the bar and hesitated before taking the first bite.

"He wouldn't have told me to get on the transport." Padraic shrugged and sported a know-it-all grin.

"You crazy wood nymph! You think you're so special. Always finding the lost people out here, when the one who's lost the most is you. You don't dare move from Opie's shadow. That's why you're still here!"

"I'm here," Padraic stood, determined not to let the sting of the accusation surface, "because you didn't get on the transport." He tightened his shoulder straps and started trailward again.

Reyn shrugged on his pack and followed Padraic. "Shut up, you feather nit. So I'm not a rock crawler. If I could fly..."

"If your brain worked half as hard as your mouth you *would* be flying." Padraic raised his arm, stopping their progress. "Trail's washed out. We'll have to take the ledge." He led Reyn farther south than he really wanted to go.

"If we're going to rappel anyway, we might as well go the same way Caleb did." Reyn's tone grated like an open blister inside a new pair of boots.

Padraic faced him. He bit the inside of his cheek, drew in his breath and shrugged his shoulders. *Fine, if you want the whole experience.* He led Reyn to the overhang where Caleb had abandoned the team.

"Have at it." Padraic dropped the lines and stepped back, waiting for Reyn to set up.

"I don't set the ropes, Caleb does." Reyn stepped back keeping a guarded stance.

"Caleb isn't here." He tossed his pack on the ground and turned his eyes toward the sky. Clouds were moving in tight from the north. The air felt dry against his tongue, as a cold breeze crept close to his skin.

"I can't set the ropes," Reyn repeated, lowering his pack.

Padraic opened his canteen, taking a long drink. He crossed his arms and blocked the tirade of obscenities Reyn launched in his direction. *Just words*, he heard Caleb's voice, *don't take on someone else's anger, you've got enough of your own*. He steadied his breathing, maintaining a stoic outward presentation.

"Neeche! Set the damn ropes!" Reyn's dark skin flushed and his eyes bulged.

Padraic pushed off the rock and stepped forward. Reyn backed away, swallowing any words he may have been preparing to say. Padraic kicked the pin that Caleb had used for an anchor; it held firm. "Anchor pin is good," he confirmed, and then looked over the drop-off. It was a straight shot with only one lip, something even a novice climber would have little difficultly maneuvering. "Are you about ready?"

Reyn gave him a hard stare, but for the moment held his tongue. He reached toward the lines, sorted them and locked them into place, then looked up at Padraic.

"Go ahead, it's your setup." Padraic glanced down at the locks, ensuring the lines were safe, but not long enough to allow Reyn to feel confident.

"Without a belay?" Reyn harnessed himself in but made

no attempt to start the descent.

"Belay yourself." Padraic kicked Reyn's feet and pushed him over the ledge.

"Son of a—" Reyn's face scoured the rock's surface as his arms and legs sprawled, searching chaotically for a stronghold.

"Better grab your line." Padraic cut down a side slope that left him at the base of the ledge.

Reyn stopped his fall, pushed his upper body away from the wall and steadied himself, wiping the blood and gravel from his face.

"You are so not my friend!" Reyn screamed.

Padraic grabbed the belay line and knocked Reyn off balance, leaving him with an unsteady hold.

"Never claimed it." Padraic launched a fierce pull and locked Reyn into an immobile position.

"Knock it off, Neeche!" A yelp escaped Reyn's throat as a quick release from Padraic's hand left him to free fall for a few seconds.

Padraic jerked the rope with a slight twist, tossing Reyn off balance again.

Reyn grabbed the rock face and steadied himself. "Talons! You best never sleep."

"Seldom do." Padraic released the belay line, giving Reyn the opportunity to move unhindered.

"When I get down there I'm going to pound one of these pistons through your skull." Reyn edged his left foot forward in an attempt to get a better stance.

"First, you've got to get down." Padraic locked the belay rope again, eliminating Reyn's freedom of movement.

"Stupid ditch pig brother of yours knows better than to let you out alone!" Reyn released his belay line. Padraic stepped out of the way as the rope fell to the ground beside him. "What was he thinking sending you after me?"

Dangling without a belay line isn't optimal. Padraic squinted as the sun pierced through the trees, warning him that it was getting close to dusk. *He's thinking. He knows I can't stop him, and if he falls, he'll be all right. He's just going to have to get back up.*

Within ten minutes, Reyn had completed a near perfect rappel and stood on solid ground facing him. "You're a bastard." Reyn released the ropes and took off his harness.

"That's already been determined." Padraic grabbed the gear and repacked, checking the equipment for any gross damage. "Weather's changing. We need to move."

He kept his pace fierce and cut a direct path toward Ben's Lair. Darkness engulfed them as they stood at the edge of an incline. Reyn backed away from the ledge.

"You've lost your mind if you think I'm going to let you belay me in the dark."

"I'm not against a tandem. I've got Caleb's gear." He set up the ropes. "Lock in or I'll throw you over."

"I'm not climbing with you! You're a lunatic." Reyn backed up, raising his hands in an attempt to ward Padraic off.

"Caleb climbs with me." Padraic grabbed Reyn and locked him in.

"Caleb's an idiot!" Reyn's voice echoed across the canyon as Padraic tossed him over the side. "I swear to God I'll kill you, Talons!"

"You told me there was no God." Padraic leapt from his position and dropped Reyn's feed faster than need be.

"Godforsaken son of a…"

"I can't be forsaken if there is no God," Padraic answered, taking such another enormous bound that he felt the jolt through his ankles and knees as he planted his feet against the surface. Adjusting his stance, he walked the remainder of the rock face until solid ground lay beneath his feet.

"You were born forsaken, you imbecile!" Reyn crashed to the ground as Padraic released the rappel ropes.

"True enough." Padraic gathered the gear and pointed east. "Thurmond's Mound is that way; Ben's Lair is over there. The choice is yours."

Reyn hesitated and looked longingly toward Ben's Lair, but realistically to Thurmond's Mound. "We're quite a ways off." Reyn stepped past Padraic and opted toward the east trail. "Thurmond's Mound. Is that where you took Carrie last week?"

Padraic didn't stop to answer him. A distant rumble of thunder under a light mist of snow decided their fate. It would be safest to take up refuge in the hut. Even without the handicap Reyn provided him, exhaustion claimed most of his strength. He had little energy left to manage the remainder of the trip tonight. Spending the night with Reyn didn't appeal to him, but given the weather, it was better than trying to push forward. Reyn was talking. *If he'd just shut up and move with a purpose!* The constant chatter grated against his last nerve. *Just move faster.* Padraic picked up his pace. *There has to be some peace somewhere. I just have to get away from him! How does Caleb stand it?* Padraic stopped momentarily, giving Reyn a chance to catch up. The hut was less than a click away, but the hike seemed an eternity with this incessant noise box beside him.

"So, do you and Opie share Carrie like you do everything else?"

Suddenly, Reyn lay sprawled on the ground, covered in a

sheer blanket of fresh snow. Padraic shook the tightness from his hand, realizing what he'd done. A fast, mean blow just below the temple brought the silence he craved. His body shook as he threw down his pack and tossed Reyn's body over his shoulder. He carried Reyn to the hut and laid him down on the cot. Slamming the door behind him, he kept a steady pace back to where he'd left their gear and then returned to the hut. There were things he needed to do: ensure there was fuel, make a fire, check their equipment, make sure Reyn was breathing. Throwing their gear in the corner, he opened the stove and grabbed the flint lighter.

"You broke my jaw." Reyn sat up, placing his feet on the floor.

"Don't talk to me." The harshness of his tone was enough to make the hair stand up on the back of his own neck.

Reyn lowered his face into his palms but kept his eyes on the Indian across the room.

Padraic's body shook with a vengeance that was erupting within him. Steadying his hands, he lit the stove and faced the window as an icy rain-hail mixture attacked the hut. It sounded as if they were under attack by a machine-gun-wielding militia. Reyn jumped to his feet as the door flew open and a flurry of wind and precipitation peppered the room. Closing the door, Padraic tossed his pack against it and pushed Reyn back down on the cot. Returning to the stove, he restarted the fire and filled the kettle with water from his canteen. The storm took on a vengeance of its own as it clawed against the hut, hurling ice, stones, limbs, and whatever debris it could muster.

"Storm came up fast." Reyn lifted his head as Padraic handed him a cup of tea.

"They always do." He grabbed a bagel from his pack and

tossed it at Reyn. He wasn't referring to the maelstrom bombarding them from outside, but the internal inferno that kept him from any peace.

"Espied with hellacious demons, he'll never be right," Gregg Dareme had spoken openly in front of him as a child. Joseph Talons wrapped his strong arms around Padraic in an effort to conceal the fit of rage that consumed him. "It's best that he is returned to his tribe." Greg had followed Joseph and Sarah out of the church. "Sarah, I know you've been praying for a child. Believe me when I tell you, this is not God's will for you. He's a distraction from your faith."

Returning to his tribe shattered whatever innocence Padraic had managed to maintain in his six years of life. Most of the details were lost in his memory, but he knew whom to blame for his anger.

At eight years old, he managed to walk away from the tribe unnoticed and return to the Talons by a route that to this day he was still unable to remember. Seizing a baseball bat from the garage, he went to Gregg Dareme's home with full intentions of bludgeoning him to death.

It was Helen who opened the door, her belly swollen in the final stage of pregnancy. She wiped her glassy green eyes in attempt to disguise her tears from him. Gregg had left her. He'd gone on a mission trip to Africa and discovered his true calling from God. Padraic listened as Helen sat on the step. She wept and read the letter over and over. Dropping his bat, he sat down beside her.

"You're just a little boy. I shouldn't be out here crying like this. I just—just don't know what to do. Who will ever love my baby?" She had said.

"I will." He had placed his thumbs on Helen's cheeks and

wiped away her tears.

Padraic stirred the fire as the storm launched another front at their sanctuary. The medicinal tea had worked its magic, easing the swelling and pain in Reyn's face and luring the oaf into a forced slumber. Padraic tossed a blanket over him and returned to his corner on the floor beside the fire. Closing his eyes, he allowed his mind to wander into memories.

Search and rescue teams, police dogs, air teams, even the National Guard had been involved trying to tame Sarah Talons' wild child, but he managed to evade them and found refuge off trail in the Tetons. Sarah would feed him, keep his bed, and provide him with clothes and shoes when he wandered in, but made no attempt to hold him there.

The winter he turned thirteen, Sarah Talons fell and was hit by the mail truck, dislocating her hip. She never asked him to stay, but there were chores to be done and Joseph had to work. Joseph taught him how to drive, plow, and chop wood; Sarah focused on reading, writing and math. By fall, she'd enrolled him in high school. He wasn't prepared for the rules and could have cared less about their schedules. It took Sarah almost a month to antagonize him enough to go back. A little effort on his part was all it would take to make her happy.

He should have paid more attention to the gang of boys that followed him through the gym and out the back door of the school. About a fourth of a mile down an unmarked trail, the first fist was raised. Nothing else was clear; he pulled himself up into a sitting position, hearing the faintest of crying.

She stood dressed in a sparkling blue and violet butterfly

costume, clutching a silver wand. A baby? He tried to make sense of the sight. No, a little girl with soft cascading ringlets that looked like waves of honey was crying. He had taken the beating, but it was the butterfly who was weeping.

She took his hand as he led her back to the schoolyard. Gregg Dareme stood on the grounds, talking to the police. Helen paced the parking lot, tears streamed down her cheeks. The butterfly flashed a sensational smile, dropped his hand and ran to her mother.

He disappeared as quickly as he had arrived. The site of Gregg Dareme ignited a rekindling for blood within him. He kept himself off trail. Two days became two weeks before he resurfaced at home. He was ready when the boys jumped him the second time—four of them went to the emergency room and one went to intensive care. The rest decided it was best served to leave him alone. Charges weren't pressed, because he didn't start the fight. The kids at school kept their distance.

Brileigh and Brody Sweftner had changed everything. They were sophomore twins who knew more than their share of trouble, but enough so that they steered clear of him. On the ground lay the red-headed kid from church. The twins had taken taking turns kicking and punching him, as a group of spectators egged them on. It wasn't a fair fight, but that didn't bother him. What bothered him was the sight of Kimimela in the midst of the fight. Brody had her by the hair. He pulled her off the boy and offered a quick fist toward her face for interference.

The impact was a broken wrist. Padraic had winced at the defining snap. He didn't remember all that transpired. Brody lay unconscious when he felt Kimimela's hand on his face.

"Stop," she had pleaded with damp eyes.

His hands were in tight fists pummeling Brody's skull

into the ground. There was no way of knowing how many times he'd hit him.

"Caleb's hurt pretty bad this time. Please help him." A tiny hand turned his face, and that ginger gesture drained the vengeance that had encased his soul. "He's not waking up." She moved to the red-headed boy.

"You broke my shoulder! Brody? Is my brother breathing?" Brileigh had hollered until they locked eyes.

Carrie quickly grabbed Padraic's hand and turned him toward Caleb. "I need you to help me." Her direction had been enough to refocus him.

Caleb, Brileigh, and Brody were brought to the emergency room. Padraic and Carrie had been taken into police custody.

"No, Daddy. You will not make a liar out of me! The only evil going on here is in you!" Gregg Dareme's daughter's voice had echoed through the hallways.

The officer spoke to Padraic, but no words would form in his mind. Silence seemed his only ally. Gregg's voice reigned over everyone's as he demanded Padraic to be locked up and evaluated.

"He's my friend! He helped me! You can't do this! It's wrong!" she had yelled. "Brileigh and Brody started it! They jumped Caleb and when I tried to get them to stop, Brody was going to punch me! He stopped him, Daddy! That's why Brody's wrist broke! It's not his fault! He was trying to stop them!"

Gregg Dareme had pushed his daughter aside and stood over Padraic, shaking his finger. "You can't control what's within you." Turning to his daughter, he continued, "He's already put eight of our schoolchildren in the hospital—two in intensive care now! It doesn't matter who started it, he has no conscious for what's happened here, and no self-control." Gregg presided over him with absolute authority.

Padraic didn't remember going to detention. He only remembered the day Sarah and Joseph brought him home. The red-headed boy sat perched on his bed, looking as though he was ready to bolt almost out of his own skin if the need arose. Carrie showed no fear, jumping into his arms, hugging him and talking incessantly.

"Carrie, stop it." The boy stood, pulling her away. "I'm Caleb," he said, as he turned to Padraic and offered his hand.

Padraic ignored the gesture and went straight to the bedroom window. It only took a moment to pull himself onto the roof. With a little momentum, he was able to jump to the hillside that claimed his path into the safety of the mountains. He didn't stop. It was eleven miles to his refuge. The sun bowed down as he sat waiting for peace. He hadn't noticed that Caleb followed.

"This place is beautiful. How did you ever find it?" Caleb had said as he sat beside Padraic. "Takes the sin right out of my soul. How about you?"

After a long silence, Padraic answered, "I have no soul."

Caleb kept his eyes glued on the sunset and his tone unaltered. "You're wrong."

Sarah had taken him to church. He'd seen and heard all about a Christ, someone who supposedly loved him enough to be crucified on his behalf. *Crucified on behalf of people like Caleb, not like me,* Padraic had thought.

Caleb laid on the rock pointing out the constellations as they had appeared. Silence was granted when needed, and how Caleb knew when to speak and when to listen, Padraic didn't know.

After an hour, Caleb's voice broke the silence. "You can't

control it, can you?" Padraic kept his eyes locked above, unwilling to answer. "It's called rage, that feeling where you just are outside of yourself, and you can't stop whatever it is that's happening," Caleb had said.

A coolness had settled around them, but not so much that either offered up a complaint. The wind stirred the trees as night noises had begun their lullaby. Caleb had become so quiet that Padraic wondered if the redhead had fallen asleep.

"Do you know where it comes from?" Caleb's voice countered the quiet.

"Some," was the only answer Padraic could muster, but Caleb didn't ask for any more than what was offered.

"Have you ever prayed about it?" Caleb had remained motionless as he offered up the question.

"I don't pray," Padraic stated quietly, but his voice was clearly audible.

"You might want to start thinking about it. You can't be enraged and in submission at the same time, at least that's what makes sense to me."

It was the beginning of a conversation that had left them both in the mountains all night. Dawn approached, as did a settling of Padraic's spirit. Whatever it was that Caleb had, he knew he needed it. It took until spring before he accepted Christ, and still today, it was a relationship he wasn't completely comfortable with. He could submit to and love a God who could heal his mind, but reciprocated love wasn't fathomable.

A loud crash of thunder shook the hut and brought Padraic to his feet. Reyn lay undaunted by the havoc happening around them. Purple and black bruising settled around Reyn's eyes and the right side of his face. His black skin camouflaged the worst of it, but the strike was unmistakable, the rage as present as it ever was, despite all efforts to disguise it.

He deserved it. Padraic shook his head at the thought. *It doesn't matter what he does, what he says. I need control of me.*

"It's getting worse." Reyn's voice echoed above the storm's wrath.

"It is," Padraic confirmed, speaking of the storms within himself as well as the weather.

"You don't look so good, Tonto." Reyn sat up and grabbed Padraic's canteen taking a long sip of water. "All right. Fess up, Indian. I know you've got something stronger than water here."

Padraic grabbed a second canteen, from his pack and tossed it in Reyn's direction. Reyn opened it and lifted it to his mouth, and just as quickly spit the contents all over the floor, tossing it back over to him.

"What is that, like thousand proof or something?!"

"If you can't handle whiskey, you shouldn't ask for it." Padraic tilted his head back and downed the entire canteen, then tossed it aside. "You just don't know how to drink."

"Maybe you've been drinking too much." Reyn rinsed his mouth with water and resettled on the cot.

"True enough." Padraic drew in a long breath and continued to stir the fire.

Reyn had dozed off in self-defense or self-preservation. Padraic really wasn't sure which, but was glad in either case. He watched the fire.

Padraic was seventeen when he burned Caleb's house down. To this day, Caleb thought it an accident. Only when facing God would Padraic ever admit that there was an altogether different truth. *Lord, I don't want to relive this,* he silently told himself, shaking the thoughts of the past. Standing too quickly, he felt his head swim and legs sway in response to the ingested whiskey.

He made a point of not drinking too much in front of anyone, certain his taste for whiskey and his Indian blood would just invite unwelcome comments. A thousand prayers couldn't touch what a single shot of whiskey could do for his untamed mind. The more he consumed, the less he remembered, a sure combination for maintaining his sanity.

He and Caleb had been drinking together since they were teenagers. It didn't take much for Caleb to pass out. It was then that Padraic would forgo the beer and open the whiskey, unbeknownst to Caleb and the rest of the world.

"Are you sure you're okay over there?" Reyn tossed on the cot, facing him.

"I'm just tired." He sat down and removed his boots, feigning the idea of sleep.

"Then go to bed. The last thing we need is you sleep-deprived." Reyn switched to his back and stared up at the ceiling.

"Why aren't you a pilot? If that's your calling, why aren't you doing it?" asked Padraic.

"Shut up and go to sleep." Reyn faced the wall as another rumble of thunder shook the hut.

"You're just going to get sucked into doing something you don't want to do, become someone you never wanted to be," Padraic said, tossing the stick he was stirring the fire with onto the flame and grabbing another one.

"That's you, not me. I *will* fly." Reyn faced him for a moment, then turned back toward the wall.

"You ain't proved it yet." Padraic stirred the flame, allowing himself to be drawn in by the warmth and light. "You're just talk; you don't move."

"You're not moving all too fast either, Tonto."

"I," Padraic threw a few more sticks into the flame, "haven't been called."

"Stupid Christians! Always trying to save everybody. Well, I don't need saving, and I don't need you."

"You going down Ben's Lair yourself tomorrow? And if you manage it, there's Wilderness Falls and Columbine."

"You're such a cretin." Reyn pulled his blankets over his shoulders and faced the wall again.

Padraic stretched out, lacing his hands behind his head, waiting for the weariness to overtake him. "I'm deciding whether or not to tie a rope and throw you down, or if I should just teach you to rappel."

"I'm going to destroy your white brother when I find him," Reyn stated in a monotone voice riddled with fatigue.

"Leave me unleashed?" Padraic asked, closing his eyes as the warmth of the fire blanketed his body.

"No worries, you'll self-destruct," Reyn finished abruptly.

Padraic chuckled, unwilling to open his eyes as the warmth and humor lured him toward sleep. "True enough."

Chapter 13

Whiskey was only a temporary blessing. Its effects were fleeting, like the weather that brought them to the hut. It allotted Padraic the sleep necessary for survival, but nothing more. It was rest devoid of memories, emotions and chaos—just a step shy of peace. If it wasn't for his knowledge of the negative effects of alcohol, there would be peace. *I can do without it, I'd just rather not.* He glanced at his watch. The two hours he'd been able to escape into the void of non-existence was worth the price.

The reeling of his mind was beginning again. Constant chaos permeated his very being, leaving him with no focus, no purpose and no form of control. *I can't keep this up.* He dropped his head in his hands. *I need to be outside.* He grabbed the gear and his boots, checked to ensure Reyn was still asleep, and then closed the door behind him.

Ben's Lair was slick and muddy with the night's washing. It could be a difficult slope on a good day. He set the ropes for a double-man rappel, and then looked toward the early dawn. *Today is not going to be a good day.*

Why am I not satisfied? Why do I feel incomplete? God, I can't please You because I can't reach You. Padraic's hands and arms began to shake as he walked away from the edge, trying to grasp onto any semblance of reality. He hadn't realized that he'd free-scaled the incline that they'd rappelled the night before, but at least while climbing, his mind could be nowhere else.

"What the! Nechee! We are going down, not up, you crackhead!" Reyn stood at the base of the trail, ready to go.

Padraic descended quickly. "Did you reset?"

"It didn't reset itself." Reyn adjusted his pack and followed Padraic toward Ben's Lair. "Listen, Talons, I want to know exactly what your plan is. I really didn't like yesterday's antics." Reyn raised a distancing hand as Padraic faced him.

"This is an anchor pin." Padraic knelt down, moving the ropes aside. "I've used it several times. I'm almost positive Caleb used it the other day." Padraic sorted the ropes and pointed at the belay line. "This is your belay line. There are two ways you can do this: you can go it alone, or you can have someone watching your back." He stood up and pushed his hair out of his face. "Cutting a belay line is a serious decision. Once it's done, it can't be undone."

"You were messing with me yesterday. I had to do something," Reyn countered with a defensive tone.

"Sometimes it's necessary to cut your belay line, especially if it isn't working."

"Mine was definitely not working."

"You're wrong. It was working. Just not the way you wanted it to. I know how to be on belay."

"You sure didn't act like it yesterday." Reyn set down his gear and took out his harness.

"We don't always do things the way we should." Padraic tied himself in and waited for Reyn to do the same. "Just because your belayer isn't doing what you want or expect him to doesn't mean you're justified in cutting your line. It's a matter of trust." Padraic leaned back, placing his hands in a locked position.

"And there's some reason I should trust you?"

"No," Padraic shook his head, "I guess not."

"Even Caleb would have cut that line. Face it, Talons, you are a psycho."

"True enough." Padraic kicked Reyn's feet from underneath him and pushed him over the edge.

For the next two rappels, Padraic savored the silent treatment he received from Reyn. *Caleb would have cut...* The thought penetrated him like a toothache.

You should cut it, so he doesn't have to. The thoughts were coming back to him. Padraic tried to dismiss them as quickly as they came, but lately they were getting more difficult to ignore. The voices knew exactly what he needed. Peace would come when he closed his eyes and never opened them again.

Suicide was wrong, and he lacked the strength and courage to follow through, but there were other options, things he knew he wouldn't survive. Once things were settled, and he knew for sure that Carrie was taken care of, he would sever the belay line. Caleb didn't need him. In fact, life would be a lot less complicated if he could fade out of existence.

By noon they were at the bottom of Columbine facing the Colter Bay Nature Trail, only four miles from the trailhead. Reyn sat down on a boulder, appearing exhausted but satisfied with the day's efforts. Padraic washed his hands and head in the running water of the falls, then joined him for a break.

"That water is frigid." Reyn finished a granola bar and downed the rest of the contents of his canteen.

"Feels good," Padraic answered, pushing back his hair. "We're done. It's all trail from here; you know your way back."

"No, don't make me chase you through the woods, too."

"Caleb is a good partner. He's just distracted right now." Padraic collected all his gear and stood, bidding Reyn to do the same. They started down the trail at a slow pace, weighted down with their equipment and more than a day's worth of fatigue.

"Have you thought about the Air Force?" Padraic asked. He hated this part of the trail. This four-mile stretch meant he'd soon be out of his safety zone.

"Are you still trying to get me killed?" Reyn stepped up his pace.

"I'm just looking at all the options to make it look legal."

"Quit worrying about my life and tend to your own," Reyn stated, ending the conversation.

Padraic and Reyn were greeted with hot coffee and sandwiches at the ranger station. Brileigh had filled out all the necessary reports and only required their signatures.

Padraic checked his radio, wiped it down and placed it in the charger. Reyn tossed his on the desk and berated Brileigh's ability to lead. Padraic opened Caleb's gear.

"Do you want to take it home with you?" Brileigh walked away from Reyn's tongue tirade. "You like to be pretty thorough with your gear. I know I can trust you."

Padraic secured the backpack and walked out the door without speaking. The encounter left him on the verge of exploding. *I can trust you…really?* Ironic words coming from Brileigh's lips. *The man can scarcely carry a ruck on his shoulders due to the injuries I've inflicted on him.* Padraic tossed his gear into his truck and drove to his apartment. Within an hour, he'd gone through all the ropes, chains, calipers and clips. He had cleaned each item with surgical precision and then repacked.

His answering machine was blinking with more messages than he could endure. Pouring himself a tall glass of whiskey, he locked his door and turned on the television. CNN was replaying the story concerning the missing twins. Carrie's earnest look of concern filled his mind as he tipped his glass to his lips.

Maybe you could help those kids, God, because you certainly are not helping me.

Chapter 14

Caleb slid out of bed, careful not to disturb his new bride. Watching her for a moment, he understood. *I am blessed. Lord, I'm so thankful she survived that crash. I can't imagine life without that little green-eyed pest.*

Tiptoeing to the bathroom, he closed the door and started the shower. It had been a long weekend.

Amanda Restley had called him early Saturday morning. Her tone conveyed contempt, but it was not unforeseen. During the entire conversation they both shared a commonality: Carrie's best interest.

At the graveside, Carrie tossed roses onto her father's coffin as it was lowered into the ground. Well after everyone left, she stayed on the bench beside her mother's grave, caressing a lilac bush that was blooming out of season.

"It's beautiful." She lifted the petals to her nose, breathing in their fragrance.

He knelt in front of her, taking her hands in his. "Let's go home."

He hadn't expected to have to return to work so quickly. He wanted the week to get things settled and to establish some sort of normalcy for her. She needed to see a doctor. He'd noticed a lot of spotting, especially after they'd been intimate. Their first night as man and wife, he discovered all too late that she was bleeding.

Truthfully, he wondered with all that her body had endured over the past week, if she was even capable of tolerating the pregnancy.

I'm not wishing anything ill on our baby, Lord, but if something is going to happen, please let it happen sooner rather than later. He towel-dried his hair and body, then slipped into his jeans and work shirt. Checking his watch, he grabbed his coat and leaned over the bed to give Carrie a kiss goodbye. Feeling a warm stickiness between his fingers, he lifted his hand off the bed and pulled back the covers. A large dark red patch of blood outlined her lower body.

"Wake up, Carrie, you're bleeding." He grabbed her arms, forcing her into an upright position. "I'm calling 911. I think you're losing the baby."

"No, I'm not." Her body trembled as she pulled the covers, concealing her body.

"Yes, you are. You've been spotting since I brought you home. And this," he pulled back the blanket, forcing her to look at the bloodstains, "this is more than spotting. We can't ignore this."

"You said Padraic told you. You said…" She grabbed her cell phone and pushed speed dial.

"Told me what?" He grabbed her wrists, making her drop the phone.

"I thought he told you. You said he told you." She released herself from his grip and covered her face.

"Told me what?" His voice snapped with an unnatural sharpness.

"She died Thursday. I thought you knew." She grabbed her nightshirt from beside the bed and slipped it over her head.

"How could you possibly think that I knew?" He stepped away from her, unsure of how to respond. "Every decision I've made for the past week has been based on the fact you were pregnant." He grabbed the sides of his hair, knowing he was losing control.

"I was." She slid out of bed, redressing herself in a long flowing skirt with an elastic waistband, and then adjusted her casted ankles.

"But you're not, and you deliberately didn't tell me!" He paced the room. "The only reason I married you was because I thought you were pregnant." He followed her into the bathroom, backing out as she raised her hand.

"I thought you knew," she insisted.

"Don't lie to me! This whole thing is nothing but a way to get me to do what you wanted me to!"

"I honestly thought you knew. When you came back, you said Padraic told you about the baby." She finished cleaning herself up and joined him in the bedroom.

"I've been talking about being a dad now for four days! That didn't clue you in?" His tone clawed his own soul.

"I thought you were talking about our future." Her tears stifled his response.

After a moment, he drew in his breath, unable to look at her. "I'm taking you back to the hospital."

"The bleeding is normal. Padraic said I'm going to bleed off and on for a few weeks." She wheeled herself into the living room.

"Padraic said? What was his hand in this? Why does he always know everything before I do?" He turned too quickly, knocking her right leg off its sling.

"You weren't there. He was the only one I could trust!" Carrie shouted, and then regained control, repeating herself. "He knew about the baby before I did. When I told him what was happening he went to labor and delivery to find out what to do."

139

"And?"

"It was too late. I miscarried while he was gone."

"Why didn't he take you straight up to L&D?" He knew the coldness in his tone was uncalled for, but couldn't shake the grasp it had over him.

"He wanted to. It was my decision not to go. I didn't want anyone to get in trouble." She faced him.

Caleb retreated to the kitchen, grabbing his wallet and keys off the counter. His mind was churning so fast, there was no control of his tongue. "I don't believe you. Let's go. Get in the truck." Grabbing her chair, he directed her toward the door.

"Where are you taking me?" She drew her hands in as he forced the chair out into the icy parking lot.

"You need to see a real doctor." He unlocked the truck. "Then, I'm giving Donald a call at city hall. If I can't stop the paperwork from going through, then I'm asking for an annulment."

"No!" Her shriek sent shivers down his spine, only adding fuel to his fury.

"Yes! We are not ready to be married, Carrie. This whole thing was based on lies. We can't start our lives together with a foundation of deceit. Where do you think that will take us?" He lifted her into the truck and slammed the door without buckling her in.

Control, Lord God. Get a grasp on me! He sat on his tailgate, trying to catch his breath. His body trembled with anger as he tried to piece together the web of prevarication with which he'd been ensnared. He had been betrayed by both Carrie and Padraic. He pushed his hair away from his face, refusing to succumb to the tears welling up in his eyes. *Why didn't I see this?* He drew in his breath and forced himself to the driver's seat.

"Don't do this. Please don't do this." She kept her face hidden in her hands as he tried to focus on his driving.

"What choice do I have? I'm nothing but a puppet between you and Padraic. Neither one of you have respect for my beliefs or my feelings!"

"That's not true." She winced as he slammed his hand against the steering wheel.

"Then tell me what is true, Carrie? Because for the past week I've been making life-altering decisions based on a fallacy created by both of you."

"I'm sorry."

"It's too late for I'm sorry." He turned the wipers on as the snow began to fall. "Don't talk to me. I'm trying to drive. Buckle your seat belt."

She remained silent with her head bowed for the remainder of the trip. *She's praying. She should have been doing that long before we ever got this far.* He wheeled her into the emergency room and signed her in at the triage desk.

He paced nervously, waiting for the triage nurse to call her name. *I'd better call work, let them know I'm not coming.* He took out his cell phone, and as he tried to dial, he noticed there was no signal inside the building. *Great.* He snapped his phone shut and looked over at Carrie. She wasn't crying anymore, but she kept her gaze to her lap, unwilling to look at him.

"I need to call work." He didn't expect her to acknowledge him.

Stepping outside, the gust of powdery snow was more refreshing than quarrelsome at that point. He kept an eye on her. She sat unmoving, appearing almost as though she were in a state of shock.

"Joe, listen, I'm back at the hospital with—"

"We need to talk about this case," Joe interrupted.

"I'm worried about Carrie."

"So am I. That's why we need to talk. You've built a pretty strong case for investigation, and these people are not pleasant to work with. Their witnesses are prone to accidents or disappearing. You know the twin case that's all over the news right now?"

"Yeah." He turned away from the doorway, hoping for some privacy from a couple who were coming out of the hospital.

"Their father was a driver for their northwest route." Joe's voice stated with a nervous quake. "I've been watching these people work for years. You shouldn't have pushed this report up without me seeing it first."

"You think Carrie's in danger?" He felt his heart almost leap into his throat.

"I'm saying she's more at risk than I like to see. Never fax a report up without talking to me. There's a lot more to playing this game than climbing ropes. The hospital may be the safest place for your little girlfriend right now. At least she's under constant observation. As soon as she's settled, get here."

Caleb closed his phone, pushing his hair back as he breathed in a thick squall of snow. Shaking off the dusting, he stomped his boots on the mat and reentered the emergency room. The anger that had consumed him dissipated as he scanned the waiting room. Fear replaced it. An empty spot remained in the place where he'd left her.

Don't panic. His whole body started to shake.

"Where is she?" Padraic grabbed his shoulder and turned him around.

"I—I don't know." He stepped back as Padraic pushed passed him, flashed a badge across the ER doors and disappeared.

Caleb stood at the receiving desk as the receptionist assured him that Carrie wasn't taken into any of the treatment rooms. Padraic resurfaced, grabbed Caleb by the arm and forced him outside.

"Just tell me she's back there. You've seen her?" Caleb regained his footing as Padraic released his grip. "Tell me."

"She's not." His answer was short and cold.

Caleb tried to get past him, but Padraic would not allow him back inside. "Joe just called me. The distributors are corrupt. Carrie's a liability. I have to find her."

"What are you talking about?" Padraic growled.

"Carrie's life has been threatened, and now she's missing," Caleb stated, trying once again to get past him.

"How long has she been missing?" The impassivity of Padraic's tone just added to the panic that Caleb felt inside.

"Ten minutes. I was on the phone."

Padraic grabbed his phone from his pocket and hit speed dial. "Voicemail." He sent a quick text. "Does she have her phone with her?"

"I don't know." Caleb shoved his hair back.

"Sue, see if there's anyone in the women's bathroom. Check handicapped and family one as well." Padraic spoke to the triage nurse, and then went to the receptionist. "Call a code Adam, sixteen-year-old female, blond hair, green eyes, wearing… what was she wearing?"

"How should I know? She can't be far. She's in her wheelchair." Caleb swallowed hard, unable to think past the panic.

"Call the code." Padraic dialed another number. "I'm calling the cell phone company. If we can locate the phone, maybe we can locate her. The phone has a GPS tracking chip."

Security blocked the doors and parking lots, elevators came to the lobby, opened and remained locked in position. Within minutes the hospital staff began checking rooms, stairwells and offices. Padraic scanned his badge and started back toward the old OR.

"Call the police. If I find her, I will let you know." The words were direct, without feelings of earnest or fear.

Caleb watched him walk away. *He's talked to her. How much has she told him?* Carrie was in danger, and having Padraic's help was essential. Nothing else mattered.

The police sought him out as the code was lifted and people started filtering back to their duty stations. Caleb checked his phone. No word from Padraic or Carrie.

"Unfortunately we can't launch a full-scale search for twenty-four hours. The code you're trying to call is reserved for children." The officer finished writing and closed his notepad.

"She's sixteen."

"Once she's married the law no longer recognizes her as a child. We'll do all we can to get the ball rolling. Is there any reason to believe that she may have left of her own free will? Did you two have an argument or anything like that?"

"Yes, but no, Carrie would never leave me, not of her own volition."

"Have you called her friends or family?" the officer asked as Caleb shifted from foot to foot. "Why did you bring her to the hospital today?"

Caleb bit his tongue. She hadn't wanted to come. She said there was nothing wrong. He was the one who insisted she be seen. If he'd kept her home and just gone to work like he'd planned, none of this would have happened.

"She started having some symptoms that we were told need follow-up. She was just discharged less than a week ago after a pretty bad wreck." He was being evasive, but the officer accepted his answer.

"What I'd like you to do is start calling her friends and family. Maybe someone has heard from her." The officer gave Caleb a patronizing pat on the shoulder then walked over to his partner and began talking.

"Walk with me." Padraic came from nowhere and pushed him toward the door.

"Did you find her? You spoke to her?" His breath left his lungs as the November air nipped his face.

"No." Padraic was known for his elusiveness, but today, in this situation, Caleb could afford him no mare patience.

"Just tell me what you know!" Caleb seized Padraic's arms, and then released his hold and stepped away. "Is she okay? I know you've talked to her. You're acting like you've talked to her."

Padraic opened his cell phone, pressed a few buttons, and on speaker for the world to hear was the conversation he and Carrie had before leaving for the hospital. After a minute, Padraic snapped the phone shut. "The cell phone company tracked her phone to your apartment."

"I didn't know that call went through." He felt the blood rush to his head.

"A year ago Carrie lost her mother. A few months ago she lost her innocence, a week ago she lost her dad, five days ago she lost her baby, and today you walk out on her."

"I know!" Caleb stated between clenched teeth.

"Do you really know?"

"None of this would have happened if you had minded

your own business. I know you set up that bogus appointment with physical therapy, and you filed for the marriage license. I also know you altered Carrie's medical records." Caleb felt the anger wash over him, losing control of his temper and tongue. "You forged Gregg's name." The words came out as Caleb tried to process the thought. "You did! Didn't you?"

Padraic stood stoic, unwavering in the storm of accusations. A few seconds passed before he spoke. "I'll find Carrie, and when I do, I'll remove her from this equation so that you can have your Isaiah six moment."

"What's that supposed to mean?" Caleb grabbed Padraic's shoulder as he tried to walk away.

"Figure it out," Padraic stated, breaking the hold, unscathed by the encounter.

"Where are you going? You haven't answered me." Caleb followed him through the waiting room. "Did you forge Gregg's name?"

Padraic scanned his badge and opened a door leading to the OR. Hesitating only for a moment, he looked straight into Caleb's soul.

"Does it matter?"

Chapter 15

We married on the premise that both Gregg and Helen agreed. The whole foundation for that decision is gone! Caleb got into his truck and slammed the door. He held his head in his hands, unsure of what to do, where to go, who to start with. *It's just too much. I can't focus. I can't even manage coherent thought right now.*

Bowing his head over the steering wheel, he waited. *Please, I need to be able to think. I need to know that Carrie is okay. Lord, I know You know where she is. Please let me know where she is.* He struggled against the tears welling up in his eyes. *To know she is safe, God, just that much is enough.* He drew in his breath again, feeling the air shudder against his lungs.

He opened his truck door and stepped into the parking lot. Large snowflakes polished the ground. The majority of the vehicles lay beneath four inches of fresh powder. He followed the walkway around the building. It was evident that most of the traffic filtered through the ER. He glanced back toward his truck and realized only his steps had christened the newly fallen snow.

She's still inside. He looked again at the ER doors. The absence of wheelchair imprints renewed his spirit. *If she's in the building, Padraic will find her.* He lifted his face to the sky, seeing the slightest bit of sun through the wintry weather. *I don't know how much more of his interference I can take. What he's doing, what he's done, what he's asked others*

147

to do, it's wrong—and he doesn't even see it. Does he not see where he's headed? This is just going to keep escalating. He's out of control.

Caleb walked back to his truck and climbed into the cab. *Would he even listen to me at this point?* His phone vibrated. A text from Padraic's phone filled the display. The sight of it brought mixed feelings. Padraic never texted anyone except Carrie, which meant that he found her, and she had his phone. *So now what?* He looked back toward the building. *Getting passed Padraic's defenses when he isn't guarded is an insurmountable feat; and now that he is?* Caleb wiped his brow and blew his breath out in frustration.

Be grateful. He bit his tongue, not allowing his thoughts to snowball out of control. *She's safe; now all three of us need to recover.* Responding to the text would be futile; there would be no dialogue. It served its purpose. He started the engine, tossed the phone aside, and drove to range control. *The least I can do is go to work.*

Joe met him as he turned on his work station. The look on his boss's face was enough to tell him he was in for a lot more than a scolding. Joe motioned for him to follow and closed the door once inside the office.

"You're getting ahead of yourself, Cohen. You are not a ranger yet," Joe stated in a calm low voice, thrusting a folder toward him. "Stunts like this get people killed. Review that file. You are off this case."

"So the preliminary findings for this investigation are…" Caleb looked up as Joe's voice interrupted.

"Your investigation and findings were professional and well thought out with supporting evidence. There's no doubt in my mind that there was more to this plane crash than pilot error." Joe pointed to the thick file that Caleb held in his hand. "With that being said, we are fortunate enough that you are just a trail kid. Hopefully, the report you sent without my approval never lit the radar of the giants above you."

Caleb felt his face burn as the blood rushed to his head. "If we are right, we need to report it. Gregg Dareme is dead."

"Being right isn't going to resurrect him." Joe retorted.

"So, we do nothing?" Caleb shifted his weight, looking directly at his boss.

"We continue to build our case."

"How many people are going to have to die before something is done to correct the problem? If we can find the source of the contamination…"

"You're so adamant about being the hero. It doesn't matter how right you are if you're dead, and that is doubly so for your little girlfriend. Hasn't she been through enough?"

"Let's not bring her into this." Caleb threw himself into a chair.

"I'm not the one who wrote her name all over the affidavit. Did you really think it was an oversight her name wasn't on the itinerary? There was a reason I asked for the rescue report. There is a lot more at stake than just funding." Joe raised his hands and paced in front of his desk.

"I didn't know." Caleb felt as though the wind had been knocked from his lungs.

"It's not your job to know. You're supposed to listen and do as I say." Joe sat down and crossed his legs, casting a stern look toward Caleb. "Where is she now?"

"She's safe." He turned his eyes toward the folder in his hand.

"Injun's got her?" Joe leaned on his desk. "Good, only safer hands are God's."

Caleb held his tongue, feeling the blood burn up his neck

and his face flush. "What do you want me to do?"

"You and your brethren located Carrie's parachute. Tag it and bring it in," Joe stated calmly, leaning over his desk. "And I still want a rescue report from Padraic. He was first on the scene. He knows more than he thinks he does."

Caleb hesitated before pushing himself out of the chair. Another trek up Ben's Lair was not what he wanted to do right now, and enlisting any type of assistance from Padraic was out of the question. He remained silent as he walked back to his desk and tossed the file down. Helping himself to a cup of coffee, he returned to his chair. *She's all right, she'll call me*, he told himself as he opened the file and skimmed the reports concerning Verchante Distributors.

He reached for his cell phone, placing a pencil mark to hold his place in the report. "Cohen."

"Mr. Cohen, this is Barbra Dertzel calling from Verchante Distributors. We understand that there has been a query put through concerning a possible link between our company and the recent increase of single-engine malfunctions, including the Dareme plane last week, where a man was killed."

"We are looking at possible connections between production, distribution and transportation," he stated as he grabbed his pen and wrote down her name and number.

"May I ask why you think this was a fuel-related incident and not pilot error?" Her voice resonated authority that sent shivers down his spine.

"The evidence at the site clearly indicates a fuel-related crash. Where the actual safety breakdown occurred has yet to be determined. The investigating team will establish which avenue to pursue." Caleb snapped on his voice machine and began recording the call.

"You're making some pretty steep accusations based

solely on the charred remains of an airplane." Her voice faltered for a moment then came back with a forced challenge.

"Ma'am, I just collect and process the evidence. I don't make any decisions." Caleb tapped his pencil on his desk, taking a deep breath.

She continued, "I've spoken with the owner of Dixon Fuel. He says you closed his operations down last week. Isn't it possible that this is a local problem?"

"The investigation will look at all possibilities." Caleb sorted the files on his desk and found the report concerning the Dareme plane.

"So you're determined to launch this incident into full investigation? Do you realize the implications of this process? This is going to turn into a lot of bad press for everyone, and most probably a long and costly court case. Maybe we could settle this whole ordeal without all the drama?" A shuffling of papers followed.

Caleb stiffened. "All crashes will be investigated regardless of…"

"I'll speak with your supervisor concerning the investigation. We would like to arrange a meeting with Carrie Dareme."

"For what reason?" Caleb felt the blood rush to his face.

"Settlement."

"Settlement?" Caleb heard himself repeat.

"Ms. Dareme needs stability. We're sure she is frightened and grieving at this time. We are prepared to offer her a substantial settlement to protect her from a lengthy and unnecessary adjudication."

"This isn't about protecting Carrie. This is about protecting a company." Caleb sighed, knowing he wasn't ready for a battle, nor would Carrie be.

"Negative publicity is not something either of our organizations need right now, especially in lieu of all the recent budget realignments." Ms. Dertzel sounded less cutthroat and more weary.

"Determining the safety breakdown would not only save lives, but also save the company money. Is anyone interested in that perspective?" Caleb tossed his pencil down as Reyn came in.

"We plan to launch our own investigation internally. The settlement is primarily to secure the company from outside recourse while we try to resolve this issue."

Caleb took a second look at Reyn's battered face. "I'm going to have to call you back." He hung up his phone. "What happened?"

"What do you think, Ragweed? Your blood bro bashed my face in." Reyn threw himself in a chair. "You ever send that sorry excuse for a human being after me again, there will be retribution."

"Man, I shouldn't have let him go." Caleb pushed back his hair and let out a loud sigh. "He seemed stable when he offered."

"When have you ever known Neeche to be stable?" Reyn scoffed at that remark and swiveled his chair around to face Caleb.

"Are you pressing charges?"

"No, I'm not pressing charges! The dumb prairie nigger will shake tobacco on me and start praying or chanting or whatever. I don't need that headache in my life."

"Dumping tobacco?" Caleb sat back, swallowing against the sinking feeling in the back of his throat.

"At the crash site, Neeche dumped a whole lot of fresh smoke right where we found Gregg's remains."

Whenever Padraic's native customs surfaced, there was some kind of major inner turmoil brewing. Padraic wasn't always stronger than the demons that plagued him. No one knew that side of him better than Caleb.

The Indian boarding school where Padraic had been corrupted into believing lies, forced to comply with unthinkable demands and stripped of his innocence before he could complete kindergarten was responsible not only for the demonic battles within him, but also for the protective mechanism he used against himself and the world around him.

Caleb drew in a deep breath and sighed, looking at Reyn's battered face. There was a God-sized struggle waging inside his best friend. *Am I the cause of it?*

"He's a freak. You know that, right?" Reyn kicked Caleb's chair.

"No more than the rest of us," Caleb sighed and picked up his pen.

"Whatever." Reyn lowered his voice. "He knows his stuff though. Climbs like something I've never seen. Taught me a lot."

"He taught you?" Caleb sat up. Padraic was not known for his teaching ability. On a rescue, he preferred not to have help, and at best tolerated him.

"Said someday I might be out there rescuing him." Reyn swiveled in his chair, staring at his hands. "I like this job, but I know I'm meant to do it from the sky. It's in my blood."

Caleb watched silently, noticing a significant change in Reyn's demeanor. "Are you ready to test again?"

Reyn shook his head. "I can't learn from a book. I need to just do it."

"Do you have a plan?" Caleb sat back in his chair.

"Neeche mentioned the Air Force." Reyn let out a nervous laugh, covering his upper lip briefly with his forefinger.

"I was thinking Coast Guard, but either is good experience," Caleb answered in a serious tone that Reyn accepted.

"Coast Guard? I've never even seen the ocean." Reyn picked up Caleb's pen and began tapping it absentmindedly on the desk.

"Yeah, but they fly predominantly choppers and small planes. Search and rescue is what they do. It'd be easy to transfer that experience." Caleb chewed his bottom lip as Reyn scratched his head.

"That dumb feather nit said you'd know what to do five times over."

"So you guys did some talking between the punches?" Caleb stifled a smile as Reyn fidgeted in his seat.

"Neeche only had to hit me once for me to know I didn't want him to do it again." Reyn rubbed the side of his face.

"I don't have to live through the experience to know I don't want it to happen." Caleb offered a quick smirk.

"You two deserve each other." Reyn stood, taking his keys out of his pocket. "He climbs the same way he drinks—with reckless abandon. And you," Reyn shook his head as he started to leave, "you're no better than he is."

"True enough." Caleb coughed into his hand, trying not to show a reaction to the information he'd received.

Padraic was drinking on trail again. Caleb sighed and grabbed his cell phone. He needed to touch base with his best friend. He needed to do more than that. He needed to ground him.

Was it this whole thing with Carrie? Or did I miss something? Why is everything coming unglued right now? I need You now, Lord. Help him, help her. Lord God, help me.

"Opie, I asked you a question." Reyn hit Caleb's chair,

forcing him back into the conversation.

"You're right, he's not stable. I better go find him." He grabbed the file and his jacket and headed for the door. "Tell Joe I'll be back later."

Caleb went straight to the ICU, but Padraic wasn't there. *Of course he's not working; he's with Carrie.* He turned to leave and caught a glimpse of him walking into the break room.

"Can we talk?" Caleb followed him.

"I'm working," Padraic stated, not bothering to take his eyes off the chart he was holding.

"It's important." Caleb stood in front of the door, unsure if Padraic would attempt to leave.

"I'm at work." Padraic lifted his eyes from the chart and stared hard toward him.

"You won't talk to me?" Caleb held his ground until Padraic backed down, looking away from him. "After work, then. Are you going to be home?"

Padraic remained silent. Caleb turned, leaving the room. He'd have to accept the silence as a non-committal compliance. Sometimes it worked; other times it was anyone's guess.

Caleb drove back to his apartment, battling the anger welling up inside him. *I need to be satisfied that he is at work. That means he knows Carrie is safe. He wouldn't be there unless he was sure she was safe.* Caleb slammed his apartment door, throwing his keys and wallet on the kitchen counter.

My Isaiah six moment? What is that supposed to mean? He tried to recall the reference Padraic had spoken earlier. He grabbed his Bible off the coffee table and flipped through the chapters of Isaiah. He had read the book several times, and the reference from Padraic made no sense.

He doesn't know his Bible half as well as I do. You never see him in church. He doesn't pray. How dare he accost me with scriptures?

Isaiah six. Padraic's voice resonated in his mind. Caleb turned to the verse. "In the year King Uzziah died, I saw the Lord."

Waste of time. What in the blazes is that supposed to mean? Like I said, little to no sense.

A loud knock forced Caleb to look away from the pages. He opened the door and pushed his hair back, facing Joseph Talons.

"May I come in?" Joseph was a mountain of a man, but the epitome of gentleness as he waited for Caleb to swing the door open wider. "Have you seen my son today?" he asked as he stepped inside.

"He's working," Caleb heard himself answer, then quickly went about making a pot of coffee.

"Good. That's a good place for him. Perhaps he'll stay out of trouble for a few hours." Joseph relaxed on the couch, accepting the coffee Caleb brought him. "His test came back, perfect score."

"He always gets a perfect score, and I've never seen him crack a book," Caleb stated as he brought his own coffee to the living area and settled on the couch. "Just once I'd like to see him work for something. I mean, really struggle."

"He struggles daily." Joseph set his coffee mug down next to Caleb's Bible.

"Most of his trouble he brings on himself," Caleb stated. He swallowed a gulp of coffee, allowing the liquid to singe his throat.

"Don't we all?" Joseph laid his fingers at the top of the chapter and glanced up at Caleb. "Isaiah six?"

"It's some random reference Padraic spouted off at me today. I thought I'd look it up to see if it had any bearing." Caleb reached over and closed the Bible. "It doesn't."

"Don't be so sure. There is nothing random about that reference, son." Joseph motioned for Caleb to hand him the Bible and reopened it to the passage. "Do you remember who King Uzziah was?"

"Honestly?" Caleb shook his head. "No, and if I don't know, he doesn't either."

"Uzziah was a good king." Joseph ignored Caleb's comment. "I think his story is in Chronicles somewhere." Joseph thumbed through pages of the Bible for a few seconds, then gave up trying to find the story. "Uzziah was a good king, except he would take on responsibilities that were not his. He made choices and decisions that were not his to make, and in doing so, many of his people turned away from God."

"So, you think Padraic was trying to make some kind of analogy?" Caleb wiped his face with his hands, unwilling to accept guidance from someone as spiritually depleted as Padraic.

"I'll never understand how my son thinks. I'm just telling you what the book says." Joseph lifted the Bible slightly before placing it back on the coffee table.

"I'm not responsible for the decisions made by other people. I'm having a tough enough time dealing with my own." Caleb grabbed his coffee cup, retreating to the kitchen for a refill.

"Anything in particular?" Joseph sat back, settling in his seat.

"I married Carrie this past weekend. She lied to me. She and Padraic both lied to me. They had me believing–well, I just made the wrong decision. Her social worker was going to send her to the city. I didn't know what else to do. Things just started lining up. It seemed like the right thing at the time. I told her this was just paperwork to keep her here." Caleb paced, struggling to get the words out of his mouth.

"Before you married, you explained to her why you were doing it?" Joseph recounted.

"I did." Caleb returned to the couch sinking into the cushions.

"Any reason Carrie may think of the marriage as anything but a contract?"

"If you're asking me if we are sleeping together, the answer is yes." Caleb let out a sigh and set his coffee cup down. "We have been for a while now."

"Then, it's no surprise that she's confused." Joseph scratched his chin as Caleb rose from the couch and began pacing again.

"I know, but I really just can't take a lecture on morality right now. I was trying to get us back on track before the crash." Caleb settled in the kitchen, filling a glass with water. "Everything just got away from me. We're just not ready to be married."

"I concur." Joseph entwined his massive fingers, bringing his clasped hands to his lips. "Do you have a solution?"

"Everything done was pure reaction. I look at it now and maybe this was God's way of resolving this whole morality issue for us. I go and do this, completely messing up God's plan."

"Son," Joseph chuckled, laying a hand on Caleb's shoulder. "None of us can mess up God's plan. He already knows what we are going to do before we do it. Even Judas's kiss." Joseph led Caleb back to the couch and reopened the Bible to the passage in Isaiah. "I think it's interesting this passage was placed on your hearth. Let me tell you why. There's a twofold message here, speaking volumes in this one sentence." Joseph's finger underlined the first verse in chapter six. "The first I've mentioned: every decision you make influences the decisions made by other people.

"This scripture is infamous for a different reason. It's about Isaiah's heart." Joseph read the words aloud. "'In the year King Uzziah died, I saw the Lord.' At this point in the story, Isaiah realizes he was so caught up in the wrongs of King Uzziah that he had neglected to examine his own heart, his own misgivings." Joseph's fingers left the page and closed the book. "Once Uzziah was removed from the picture, Isaiah was forced to look upon himself and see how much he himself truly needed God."

Caleb's demeanor shattered as Joseph continued to explain the passage. *I'll remove Carrie from the equation so you can have your Isaiah six moment.* Padraic's voice sent a chill through him that made the hair stand up on the back of his neck.

Maybe he was trying to help in his own obscure way. Is that even possible? God doesn't speak through Padraic. The idea stopped his thought process cold. *Oh my God, I'm so stupid.* He let out his breath, feeling the walls he'd built between himself and God begin to crumble. *Lord, You speak through rocks. Of course You could use him. Why did I think You couldn't use him?*

These were my decisions, all of them. Maybe they were influenced by others, but ultimately I am responsible for the decisions I made.

"Caleb, are you still with me?" Joseph shook Caleb's knee, trying to get his attention.

"Padraic believes so adamantly that God will never use

him, so much so that I guess I believed it too. Granddad, I didn't even know I believed it until just now." Caleb slammed his back against the couch. "I don't even know why he calls me his friend."

"He, meaning whom? God or Padraic?" Joseph lifted his coffee mug from the table.

"At this point, both." Caleb released a gasp of air. "It's almost like I don't have any control of my own thoughts. Everything is just happening around me, and I'm reacting as fast as I can."

"Ah." The older man settled as a broad smile appeared across his face. "Spinning plates?"

Spinning plates. Caleb thought for a moment then nodded his head in agreement. Joseph Talons had long ago explained to him the spinning plate theory. It was an analogy to help him understand what it was like living inside Padraic's head. A thousand plates spinning like tops, with more being added by the minute, all required attention from their one attendant.

"It's just never been me before." Caleb rested his elbows on his knees.

"I think it's possible that you are being prepared for something, but if all you're seeing are the spinning plates, you're not ready." Joseph placed his hand upon the Bible. "When you get a chance, ask my Padraic why Isaiah six. It must have been laid on his heart for a reason."

"I'm glad you came. I needed you."

"I'm glad I could help." Joseph stood, taking his coffee cup to the sink. "Where is your bride this afternoon? Sarah would have my head if I didn't look in on her as well."

"We had an argument, she left. I don't know where she is." Caleb followed him to the kitchen, placing his cup in the sink as well. "Padraic won't tell me."

"Oh." Joseph let out a deep sigh. "Now that you and Carrie are married, you may want to establish some boundaries with my son."

"Easier said than done," Caleb answered too quickly.

"If you want to keep your wife and your friend, it needs to be done."

"I don't know what I want." Caleb scratched his head, facing the truth.

"It's time you found out, isn't it?"

"Yes, sir." Caleb gathered his breath, taking in all the insight that had been spread before him. *I've planned my own path, walked without Your guidance. I have misled my family and friends, and now we are all wandering. Lord, I just don't know how to get us back to where we should be.*

"When you see Padraic tonight, tell him he's got a stack of mail at the house, and we keep getting calls from some medical administrator from a university in the city."

"Medical administrator?"

"Know anything about that?" Joseph asked as he prepared to leave.

"Maybe. Something was said the other day about him applying for medical school. I didn't think he was serious." Caleb followed him to the door.

"Well, this guy on the phone is pretty serious, something about early admission and a whole lot of other stuff I really don't understand."

"I'll tell him, but I'm not sure he's all that interested. He only applied because his girlfriend wanted him to." Caleb held the door open as Joseph crossed the threshold and turned around.

"Gail? What do you think about her?"

"I haven't met her, but I know she's not a Christian." Caleb grimaced as Joseph shook his head.

"I'm concerned." Joseph retrieved his keys from his pocket.

"Don't be; it's not serious. He likes to play, but that's the extent of it. I've never seen him satisfied."

"Only because he chases the wrong things." Joseph shook Caleb's hand, then drew him into a hug. "I'll be praying for you boys."

"Thanks, Granddad."

Chapter 16

"I want something from you." Joyce slid into the seat beside Padraic and reached into his front pocket.

"Hold on, sunshine. This is a cafeteria, not a playground." He grabbed her wrist as she withdrew his cell phone.

"If you let me have what I want, I'll make it worth your while." She offered a seductive smile as he released her wrists.

"Really?" He kept his tone low in search of Joyce's motive.

"After work, your place or mine?" She dropped his phone in her breast pocket.

"Mine." He sat back, perplexed at her sultry tone.

"You'll be alone? No friends?"

"If you want to bring a friend, that's fine with me." He watched as she stepped away from his table.

"I may just do that. I'll see you at midnight." She left him, taking his phone with her.

Mercy nurses were known for their promiscuity, but Joyce didn't hold a reputation for being so bold. He returned to the ER and checked the schedule. Her name was listed as a float beginning the shift at 7:00 AM. *She has Carrie.* He tapped her name. *Of course! She was Carrie's nurse last week.*

He opened his apartment door after his shift. *This is the first place Caleb will come.* He started the coffeemaker and pressed the blinking light on his answering machine. He straightened up his apartment. For a bachelor, he kept his things surprisingly neat. Caleb and Carrie often accused him of OCD when it came to his possessions. The answering machine droned on as a knock at the door jolted his attention toward the clock. It was only eleven-thirty. Joyce wouldn't be here yet.

Caleb pushed past him, not waiting for an invitation. "She's not here." Padraic left the door open.

"You know where she is." Caleb's voice shook.

Padraic grabbed two bottles of beer from his refrigerator, popped the top from one and slapped it into Caleb's hand.

"You probably need this more than I do." Padraic took the chair that looked straight out the door, forcing Caleb to the couch facing the opposite direction.

"This company is dangerous," Caleb began. "Joe says they're responsible for the missing twins in New Hampshire. Walter Ross is the father of those twins. He drove a fuel truck for Verchante Distributors for almost ten years. According to Joe's file, six months ago Ross blew the whistle on some unsafe fuel carrier procedures. When he turned state's evidence, his twins disappeared.

"Gregg's death was no accident. It was negligent homicide on the part of the fuel distribution company. Carrie is the only witness in this case. That makes her a liability. Someone has already contacted me wanting to buy her off." The sweating bottle cooled Caleb's palm and dripped water onto his pants. Taking a long swallow, he wiped his hand on his jeans and then placed the bottle on the side table. "I know I'm a jerk, and we can discuss that later. Right now the only thing that matters is Carrie's safety. I need to talk to her."

Padraic kept his eyes on the door as Caleb continued speaking. He finished his drink, rinsed the bottle and tossed it in the recycle bin.

"You're not listening to me." Caleb stood, following him to the sink.

"No, I'm not," said Padraic, unsure of his next move. "Can we talk about this later?" Padraic met Joyce as she came to his threshold.

"I thought we agreed no friends?" She lifted her hand to his cheek, drawing him in for a welcome kiss.

"He's leaving." Padraic smiled, returning her gesture.

"I'm not leaving," Caleb answered just as quickly.

"How about," she stood between them, "you finish up with your friend here and meet me at my apartment?" Withdrawing his phone from her purse she tucked it into the front pocket of Padraic's jeans. "I've texted the directions. Don't be long."

"I won't." He closed the door behind her and looked at Caleb.

"Tell me where Carrie is." Caleb stood firm. "She needs to understand what's going on and that she's not safe."

"When I see her, I'll tell her."

"She's my wife, Padraic! Let me take care of her. I can't fix what's happened if you won't let me. I need to make the decisions."

"I've seen your decision-making abilities." Padraic grabbed his wallet and keys. "I'm not impressed."

Padraic walked toward his truck and opened the door only to have Caleb push it shut.

"Carrie knew I didn't want to get married. She used the pregnancy to change my decision. She never told me about the miscarriage until this morning."

"She violated you, she tricked you, she lied." Padraic folded his arms across his chest. "Do you have any responsibility in all this?"

"We are not ready." Caleb drew in his breath and steadied his voice.

"You were ready enough to take her to bed with you." Padraic kept his voice low as Caleb's face flushed.

"You have a different girl in your bed every other week!"

Padraic kept his lips tight, not affording an answer. Reaching for the door of his truck, he pulled it open and pushed Caleb out of his way.

"Look what you're doing! How is it any different from what I've done?"

Padraic slid into the driver's seat, started the engine and then opened the window. "I will never be loved the way Carrie loves you."

Shifting his truck in drive, he pulled out of the parking lot too quickly for Caleb to follow him. He checked his phone for Joyce's address and knocked on her door ten minutes later.

"Are you alone?" Joyce glanced out toward the parking lot.

"I am. Where's Carrie?" He waited for her to bid him inside.

"I'm here." Carrie opened the bedroom door and wheeled herself across the threshold.

"Kimimela." He wrapped his arms around her, lifting her from the wheelchair onto his lap.

She curled up within his embrace.

"I'm going to change while you two talk." Joyce excused herself to the bedroom.

"Caleb doesn't want me." Fresh tears washed her cheeks, leaving an aftermath of scarlet streaks.

Padraic wiped her tears with his thumbs and kissed her forehead.

"I wish I'd never jumped from the plane. I'd rather be dead." She tucked her face into his chest.

Wrapping his arms around her, he rested his chin on top of her head. "What can I do?"

"Please, take me to my mother." She answered after a long hesitation.

He carried her to his truck and buckled her in. Joyce followed him with the wheelchair.

"Thanks for calling me." He loaded the chair in the back of the truck.

"She says you've always been her hero." Joyce watched him climb into his truck.

"I'm not a hero. I don't think I even qualify for being one of the good guys."

Joyce stepped away from the truck as he slammed the door and started the engine.

It was a cold night, and Carrie didn't have a coat. The bench beside her mother's grave lay covered with the day's snowfall. He brushed it off, glad it was a dusty snow and not the heavy wet stuff that could chill to the bone. He carried her to the bench and sat down beside her. It was one of those nights that, if he were here, Caleb would point out all the constellations and tell them stories. She blew the snow off the lilac closest to her and took his hand.

"Thank you for taking care of Rebecca." She shivered as he draped his coat around her shoulders.

"I need you. I need you to take care of me." She laid her head on his shoulder, releasing a solemn sigh.

"I will." He wrapped her in a firm embrace.

"Will you always love me?" She lifted her eyes and captured his gaze.

"With my last breath," he assured her.

She laid her head against his chest, and stayed quiet for what seemed like an eternity. He sat empty of ideas to ease her pain. Too much had happened to undo the damage that she had sustained.

"Do you believe in God?" Carrie's voice broke his train of thought.

"I do." He knew how he was supposed to answer.

"I'm not sure what to believe anymore." Carrie drew in her breath.

The God questions were far from his domain. He believed in God, that much was the truth. He just wasn't certain that God believed in him.

"I want to go to Heaven. I want to see my mom again. But," she sat up facing him, "if Gregg went to Heaven, I would rather burn in Hell."

Padraic listened to her words; brushing the curls from her cheeks, he grinned. "My sentiments exactly."

"No, you're supposed to say something like forgiveness or that's just anger talking." She gave him a playful punch.

"You asked me. I'm telling you. I want to go to Heaven about as much as I want to go to Hell."

"So I guess we're both screwed?" Her face twisted into a confused, downtrodden look.

"We are in a quandary." Padraic drew her into a hug.

"A what?"

"A situation with no real answer." He accepted her hand as she entwined her fingers with his.

"So, what do we do?" She adjusted the jacket around her, shivering as the temperature started to drop.

"I don't know." He stood, drinking in the coolness of the evening. "How about we get some hot chocolate and call it a night?" He knelt down in front of her, awaiting her response.

"I'd like that." She wrapped her arms around his neck, accepting his strength as he carried her to his truck.

Winding down the overshadowed hallways in the old hospital building caused most people unrest, but for Padraic it was like his second home. The plan was to renovate these floors after the addition was built, but the money ran out and the project had been on hold for many years. The hallways now lay homage to broken equipment, outdated electronics and various other items that just had no other place to be. The equipment had not outgrown its usefulness, it was just that the hospital had upgraded to a point at which very few staff members were familiar with how to work with it effectively. Padraic enjoyed toying with the vintage machines found in these halls—to the point he almost preferred some of the equipment to that on the unit.

Carrie kept silent as he wheeled her into a corner room. "These are sleep rooms for anesthesia residents and students."

"What if someone sees me?" He could see that pain controlled her movements as she reached down and rubbed her legs.

"They'd be more concerned about you seeing them. As long as you look as though you belong here, no one will bother you. Do you want to take a shower or use the bathroom before I put you to bed?"

"I took a shower at Joyce's apartment. But I need to use the bathroom. Are you going to stay here with me?" She wheeled herself around, trying to orient to the room.

"Go to the bathroom. There are towels and stuff already in there. Put the blue scrubs on. You'll see them by the sink." He turned the light on and closed the door behind her.

She wheeled herself from the bathroom, dressed in a pair

of scrubs that were obviously too big for her.

"You'd make a cute nurse," he teased, settling her into bed.

"You're already the cute nurse. I'm the one who serves no purpose." Her face became sullen.

"We all have purpose. Figuring out what it is, that's the tricky part." He lifted her chin with a single finger, looking into her tear-filled eyes.

"I just don't know what to do with me anymore." She wrapped her fingers around his and pulled it away from her face so that she could escape his gaze. "Caleb hates me."

"There's a lot of stuff going on right now, and I think before you go to sleep we should talk about it." He uncovered her legs and placed his hands on her calves, frowning as her skin blanched then returned to its pinkish tone. "Feels a little warm, do they hurt?"

"Ache, but not really hurt," Carrie answered.

"Have you been taking your medication?" He wrapped the sleeves she had worn in the hospital around her lower legs despite her protest.

"No, but please, I really don't like those things. They're so hot and itchy."

"I've got to get you some Lovenox. You were supposed to be taking those shots daily. What have you been taking for pain?"

"I'm okay. I haven't needed anything. I don't think Caleb even brought in the bag Joyce gave us at discharge. It's probably still in his truck." She shrugged.

"I'll get your medication," Padraic sighed. There was no point in discussing the importance of her care plan.

He could see the exhaustion in her face as she lay against her pillows. "Don't be mad. There was so much going on, I never really thought about it."

"Did Joyce give you a Depo shot before you went home with Caleb?" Padraic turned on the machine and adjusted the settings.

She nodded her answer. He could tell by the way she dropped her stare that she didn't want to talk about it.

"Your honest answers to my questions help me make the decisions necessary to keep you safe and healthy." He lifted her chin.

"I know. It's just weird." She let out her breath, giving a simple grin.

"I agree." He sat down beside her on the bed. "I'm not only concerned about your health, but your safety as well. The investigation of your father's crash revealed the fuel distribution company is corrupt. This means you are a major liability."

"I don't understand what you're saying."

"You're dad's death wasn't an accident. The information you gave with the fuel samples is very damaging. It is possible that this company may try to stop you before the investigation goes any further."

"You mean kill me? I don't understand. Why kill my dad in the first place? Why would they want to do that? It doesn't make any sense."

"I don't have a lot of details, just bits and pieces I've picked up from talking to Caleb. I guess they've already contacted him—because when you disappeared, he just about came out of his skin." He watched her flinch at this information.

"He's so mad at me right now." She pressed her lips together, eyes brimming with fresh tears. "If looks could kill, I'd already be dead."

"Tomorrow is a new day. Let's get some sleep."

"Please, don't leave me alone." Her labored breathing provided the warning of an oncoming panic attack.

"I'm here." He cupped her face in his hands, leading her in a slow breathing exercise that for the moment seemed effective. "We are all scared, but we cannot let our fears control us. You are safe. No one, not even Caleb, knows where you are right now. It's recovery time for you and for him."

"Is Caleb safe?" Her question caught him off guard.

"Do you want to talk to him?" He placed his phone in her hands.

"No." She shook her head, "I texted him on your phone earlier." Her fingers wrapped around the cell phone, gripping it like a security blanket. "He didn't answer."

He waved away her attempt to return it. "Keep it. You may want to talk to him later."

"Will you pray me to sleep?" She settled in the bed, accepting the blankets he tucked around her.

"God wants to hear your voice, not mine." He turned out the overhead lights and pressed the dimmer switch for the nightlights.

"Caleb prays me to sleep." Her voice muffled into the pillow.

"You don't need Caleb to seek God." He offered her a cool washcloth and then settled in a chair beside her bed.

It wasn't long before her breathing became slow and rhythmic. The SCD machine hummed a perfectly timed tune, inflating and deflating the sleeves wrapped around her calves. An analogue clock ticked the seconds as he focused on the light snowfall illuminated by a distant street lamp.

He needed to get her medicine. It would be easy enough to pocket some blood thinners. It was handed out like candy on the ICU. *I don't want to have to steal it. I'd be acquiring it, not stealing.* The rationalizations consumed his thoughts for the longest time until he could no longer sit still. He would get her medication from Caleb.

A copy of Caleb's truck and apartment key remained forever on his keychain, a decision they had made as boys and kept to this day. It would be easy enough to walk in and take whatever he wanted. He wouldn't even have to lay eyes on Caleb if he didn't want to.

Is Caleb safe? Carrie's question gnawed at his mind, leaving little chance of sleep.

Chapter 17

Caleb awoke with a start. He'd fallen asleep on his couch and landed hard on the floor, cracking the side of his head on the corner of the coffee table. His ring tone continued to scream out to him as a warm gush of fluid washed over his left eye and flowed across his lips. Grabbing his work shirt from the floor, he applied pressure to the wound.

Great, wonderful. He found his way to the kitchen, exchanging his shirt for a damp dishtowel. *Better soak it,* he told himself while filling the sink with cold water. *I hope this doesn't need stitches.*

He walked himself to the bathroom and examined the cut in the mirror. It was a small, superficial wound, but the amount of blood it produced gave the appearance of much more. Squeezing the cut together he applied the liquid bandage in hopes that it would stop the bleeding long enough for him to get the sterile strips in place.

This is not what I needed today. Tossing the bloody dish towel in the tub, he washed his face and re-examined his work in the mirror. It would have to do. A quick shower and shave was all he could accomplish before his phone started ringing again.

"Where is Padraic?" The woman's terse voice further confused his already befuddled state.

"Hello?" He asked, trying to head off the caller.

"Padraic said that if I couldn't find him, then you'd be the one to talk to." Her tone remained stern and unwavering.

"With whom am I speaking?" He shoved his foot down hard into his work boot and tightened the laces.

"This is Gail. Do you know where he is?" She spoke with an accusatory tone rather than one of concern.

"I thought he was with you." The picture of the dark-haired woman flirting with Padraic invaded his mind.

"What makes you think he's with me?" Her response made him wince.

"I—" it wasn't his place to say anything. "He's probably at work. Did you try his cell?"

"He only answers when he's so inclined." The fierceness in her voice faded with this revelation.

"Welcome to the club." Caleb finished tying his boots and grabbed his coat. "I'll track him down. If I find him, I'll let him know you're looking for him." He shoved his wallet into his pocket and grabbed his keys from the counter.

Caleb snapped his phone shut and tapped it on his forehead. The girl last night was familiar. He'd seen her before, but it couldn't have been Gail. He'd never met Gail.

How could I just assume that's who it was? The flirting, the obvious nature of her visit to his apartment. Obvious? Maybe not so much.

His phone. Caleb looked at his cell phone. *She had Padraic's phone! She had Carrie. I'm so stupid!* He set down his keys and grabbed Carrie's discharge papers from the kitchen table. *Joyce, that's her name, that's Carrie's nurse. I should have followed him.* He set the papers down, caught his breath and shook his head.

No. He gulped a breath of air and forced himself to set the discharge papers aside. *I didn't go there looking for Carrie. I can't help him if I don't stay focused. How did I get so worked up about Carrie when I intended to talk to him about all the other stuff going on?*

Without warning, he opened his phone and hit Padraic's number. *Why am I calling? He's not going to answer.*

"Talons," Padraic answered half out of breath.

"Where are you?" Caleb's voice jumped in before he could think.

"She's not with me." Padraic sounded drained.

"I'm not looking for her. I need you." Caleb inadvertently rubbed the cut on his head, withdrawing his touch as a trickle of blood slid down his cheek. "We have to talk. Are you working?"

"No, I start orientation for anesthesia tomorrow."

"Granddad came by last night, told me about your results. He also mentioned a medical administrator from the city calling about early admission—"

"I spoke to Granddad this morning," Padraic interrupted before Caleb could complete the sentence.

"Will you come and talk to me? I think we really need to check in."

"I'm not talking about Carrie."

"Me neither," Caleb sighed, not realizing he had been holding his breath.

"Joe wants you to recover the parachute. I'll meet you at Ben's Lair around three." The ominous click told Caleb the conversation was over.

Caleb looked at his watch. There wasn't much time to prep, and he hadn't seen his gear since Padraic borrowed it to bring in Reyn. You could count on Padraic's obsessive nature when it came to cleaning, inspecting and packing the equipment. Caleb suddenly realized how dependent he'd become on Padraic in this regard.

Where is my gear? How am I supposed to meet him at

Ben's Lair with no equipment to get there? Taking a quick walk through his apartment, he saw no sign of his stuff. *Maybe it's in the truck?* He grabbed his keys, trying to think. *I didn't see it there last night.*

Trudging through the snow, he unlocked his truck. Setting on the passenger seat, he found his gear neatly packed and ready to go, along with a steaming cup of coffee. *He could have at least waited for me.*

Caleb started the engine and turned on the heat, then went back to lock up his apartment. He hadn't noticed initially, but as he climbed into his truck and looked at all the other vehicles in the lot, he saw that his was the only one completely cleaned of snow and ice. Even the hedge of snow left behind from the plows was not blocking his tires.

Pulling into the ranger station at Colter Bay, he met Brileigh at the trailhead. Padraic's truck was already parked in Caleb's spot. "The whole parking lot is empty and he parks in my space," Caleb said as he donned his gear and grabbed a radio from Brileigh.

"It was *his* first," Brileigh reminded him.

"True enough." Caleb shook his head and signed the log. "He didn't sign in?"

"He didn't have a pen." Brileigh shrugged, placing the log back in the lock box.

"Never does." Caleb adjusted his pack and looked at the trail. "How much of a head start does he have?"

"Maybe forty-five minutes." Brileigh scratched his ear while chewing on his bottom lip.

"All right, we should be out no later than nine. Radio checks every two. Give Joe a call for me and Reyn. Let them know where we are."

"Roger that, and good luck." Brileigh offered a firm

handshake.

"Thanks." Caleb smiled and headed up the trail toward Columbine.

Caleb kept a steady pace, knowing that it was unlikely he'd see Padraic until he reached Ben's Lair.

I need to put my thoughts in order, figure out exactly what I want to say. Lord, help me. I want both of us to come away from this stronger. Give me the courage and strength to say what needs to be said. Grant him the patience to listen and understand. Use me, God, to speak Your will, Your agenda, and not my own.

Padraic left enough of a trail that it was fairly easy to track him. Caleb popped a piece of gum in his mouth before attempting the final assent into Ben's Lair. The sun was high above the horizon, creating a blinding force with the reflection from the whitewashed slopes. It offered a false sense of hope of warmth, as the mountain air remained so cold it hurt to breathe.

"You're going to damage your lungs." Padraic grabbed his arm and pulled him up to the top of Ben's Lair.

"I think all the crack I inhaled as a kid took care of that already." Caleb gathered his ropes and brushed off his jeans.

"We don't need to add mischief to misery." Padraic gathered the rest of his equipment, inspecting each caliper and rope as he repacked Caleb's gear.

"Where's the parachute?"

"Where you left it," Padraic answered, keeping his attention focused on his work.

"Thought you'd have it down by now." Caleb hefted his pack onto his back and followed Padraic toward the canyon.

"You thought wrong." Padraic kept a fast pace, stopping only when they reached the site.

"All right, what did you see first when you arrived and assessed the scene?" Caleb dropped his pack beside Padraic's and grabbed his shoulder, leading him away from the drop-off.

"I saw nothing. It was night." Padraic stepped away from the scene and pointed to the pine he'd used as a baseline. "We did an air glide from there to here."

It wasn't an ideal slope. The angle was off to such a degree it would have taken a great deal of strength to get anything, especially a person, from the other side.

"You threw her across and made her think she was gliding?" Caleb called him out.

"It worked." Padraic faced him, accepting the challenge.

"Not really—she hit the tree, the harness released, she fell to the ground and woke up with a concussion and a displaced ankle fracture."

"My options were?"

"I don't know. I wasn't there." Caleb stepped around him and assessed the scene. "Why are the harness ropes over here and the nylon over there?"

"She climbed up after she landed." Padraic pointed to the release lines on the chute. "The nylon she was using like a blanket."

"Any ideas on how to bring it in?" Caleb turned and faced him, catching him off guard.

"That's your job." Padraic backed away, grabbing his canteen.

"What are you drinking?" Caleb followed him and opened his own.

"The same thing you are." Padraic offered his canteen forward; Caleb pushed his hand away.

"Reyn said you were drinking on trail." Caleb waited for

a response that was not forthcoming. "His face looks like something you'd do to him after drinking."

"That was done long before any alcohol was consumed." Padraic snapped the lid shut. "He got exactly what he deserved."

"With his mouth, I'm surprised you didn't pummel him."

"I would have had to carry him out." Padraic shrugged his answer.

"True enough." Caleb stood and followed Padraic toward the edge of their quest. "We're getting a bit too grown to be settling things with our fists."

"Best get out your crampons. The Lord sent rain last night, and the temps haven't been cooperative."

"Seems like lots of rain lately." Caleb returned to his pack and grabbed his crampons while Padraic set the ropes.

"The lines are twisted and frozen. I'll work from the top." Padraic leapt to the rock face, dug in, and started climbing.

Caleb finished strapping on the crampons and lowered himself toward the base lines of the parachute. *Lord, I wish I could climb like that.* He watched as Padraic spread his body against the surface and maneuvered up and out of sight. Caleb swallowed hard, looking at the debris at the bottom of the canyon.

Did he not take any notice of that drop just now? What about when he threw Carrie across? He glanced one more time toward the top, but Padraic was well out of view. Tethering in, he lowered himself until a good vein could be determined.

Making the jump, he dug his crampons deep into the icy rock surface.

"You okay?" Padraic must have felt the jerk in the lines.

"I'm okay! There must be like six inches of ice here!"

Caleb adjusted his position, trying to get a steadier stance.

It took the better part of an hour to free the chute from the ice and entanglement, and both men returned to the safety of Ben's Lair, bedraggled from the experience.

"I'm not done talking to you about this thing with Reyn. Were you drinking on trail?" Caleb accepted the hot coffee Padraic offered from a thermos in his pack.

"Do you not carry a flask in your med pack?" Padraic poured himself some coffee and sat back, inhaling the steam.

"That stuff can raise Lazarus!" Caleb couldn't stop the smile that crossed his face or the chuckles rising within him. "You funneled it when he couldn't take it. Oh, I wish I'd been there to see his face!" His laughter was contagious.

"It was pretty funny." A slight grin appeared on Padraic's face.

"That was absolutely the wrong thing to do, but man I wish I'd been there when it happened."

"It felt good though." Padraic stretched out his legs, flexing his feet and ankles.

"Initially, but what about now?" Caleb finished his coffee and rinsed the cup with water from his canteen.

"Nothing was intentional, or regretted, at least not as far as I'm concerned."

"What about last night with Joyce?" Caleb shifted the subject, hoping Padraic would stay with him.

"What about it?"

"If you're sleeping with Gail, what were you doing with Joyce last night?" It was tender ground. They usually did not discuss what happened behind their bedroom doors.

"Joyce was…" Padraic sipped his coffee, obviously in search of the right word, "entertainment."

"So you were using her?" Caleb asked, receiving a shrug

from Padraic. "Like you used Gail to change Carrie's lab records? She works in IT at the hospital, I checked."

"Some people enjoy being used."

"Most of us don't," Caleb answered too quickly.

"Isaiah six." Caleb broke the tension-filled silence between them. "What did you want me to get from that?"

"You're the Jesus freak, not me."

"You referenced it, now back it up and tell me what's going through your head." Caleb jumped to his feet as Padraic grabbed his gear and headed down the trail.

"My head is not someplace you want to be."

"It's exactly where I want to be." Caleb stepped in front of him, stopping their progress. "We need to talk about what happened to Reyn's face. And what's going on with you, Joyce and Gail? You're walking down some pretty shady paths." Caleb grabbed his arm, stopping him from passing.

"You're accusing me of being promiscuous and a bully?"

"Yes." Caleb released Padraic's arm, stepping away from him, "but that's because you are."

Padraic raised his hand quickly, pushing back his fire black hair, and then faced Caleb. "No one got hurt."

"Depends on your perspective, doesn't it?" Caleb stayed at his pace until they reached the face of Ben's Lair. "Reyn, Joyce and Gail aren't Christians."

"So?" Padraic had the lines set, slipping his caliper into place.

"What do you think is going through their heads when you ask them to sleep with you or hack into the hospital's mainframe? How can they see Christ in you?"

"Do you see Christ in me?" Padraic's question cut into Caleb's train of thought, leaving him speechless. "I can't represent something that isn't there." Padraic stepped over the edge as Caleb stood on the ground, dumbfounded.

Caleb finished the rappel, searching for the right words to address the situation. Nothing—no revelations, no inspirations, not even a "tide me over" verse—touched the empty void of his mind.

"Put that stuff down and explain to me what you are saying." Caleb managed to find his voice before Padraic could finish repacking.

"I don't have the same relationship with Christ that you do. That's all I meant."

"You said Christ is not in you." Caleb pulled the pack away from Padraic's grip.

"He's not present; he's just there. Never mind." Padraic stepped away from the conversation.

Caleb swung his pack onto his back, ready to follow him down trail if need be. "By not present, do you mean not involved?"

"Probably." Padraic finished gathering his equipment and readied himself to go.

Caleb felt his heart beat in his throat as he followed Padraic down trail toward Wilderness Falls. "Do you ever feel his presence?"

Padraic set the ropes for the descent, and then looked toward Caleb. "It's been awhile."

Caleb kept silent as they finished the rappel. *How could he not feel God's presence in his life? After all he's been through? How could he not feel You there?*

"What happened to your face?" Padraic's voice ripped through the silence as they walked down trail toward Columbine.

"I fell." The words choked deep in his throat as he continued to lament.

"You'll recover." Padraic stopped their progression, facing him with determination. "I will, too."

In the same moment, Padraic turned and continued down trail.

"I messed you up." Caleb found his voice as they tethered in at Columbine.

"That had been accomplished long before we met." Padraic dropped over the edge for a tandem rappel.

Caleb slid into place, raking his anchor caliper against the ice and just missing the hitch. It was a moment he couldn't see. Filth covered his face as his feet tipped away from the rock surface. The harness cut deeply into his back, suspending him centimeters away from safety.

"Get up." Padraic spit out the words as he braced himself against the rock, locking the belay lines with every ounce of his strength.

"I can't move." The cords ripped through his skin, threatening to sever his arms from their sockets.

"Try harder." Padraic coughed his words, bowing his head against the rock.

"Let go." Caleb spit the debris from his lips as a slight breeze rocked his body. Padraic's grip tightened. "I said let go. Nothing's going to change until you do."

"I need you to trust me." Caleb wiggled his fingers, praying the dexterity would return quickly.

The cords loosened. Caleb thrust himself into a somersault and planted his crampons into the ice-covered vein below him.

"I'm okay." He wiped his face and untangled the ropes. "Hey, come down here."

Padraic didn't respond, and the ropes remained motionless.

"I said, come." Caleb gripped the rope and waited. "Padraic?"

Locking in, Caleb ascended, following the ropes until he reached him. Caleb met his eyes, realizing the dissonance on Padraic's face. "Let's put our feet on the ground, okay?"

Caleb waited for Padraic to process. It was only a moment before they were moving again, but it was long enough for Caleb to feel the abundance of emotion surging through his friend's body. Caleb breathed a sigh of relief as they planted their feet at the basin. Padraic remained silent and inventoried every inch of their gear, repacking it meticulously at record speed.

"You didn't want to trust me." Caleb slowed their pace, knowing the four miles back to the trailhead was not enough distance to cover the ground unveiled by the fall.

Padraic remained silent.

"Things worked out better when you did." Caleb drew in his breath feeling the presence of God inside him. "Feeling God's presence requires the same level of trust and letting go."

The moment dissipated as Padraic turned from him and continued toward the trailhead.

Lord, don't let him walk away from You. Whatever it is that needs to be done, I pray that he feels Your embrace.

"You're praying for me." Padraic crossed the parking lot and tossed his gear into the cab of his truck.

"I am." Caleb stood his ground as Padraic faced him.

"I didn't release the line." Padraic climbed into the driver's side of his truck and slammed the door.

Caleb tossed his gear into his truck and gathered what was left of his strength to walk over to the ranger station. He needed to turn in the radio, as well as the parachute. He'd give Padraic a few hours to regroup, and then maybe they could try again.

Brileigh took the items and offered Caleb a steaming cup of coffee. "Everything all right?"

Caleb signed the log. His back ached from wrenched muscles. His clothing was battered, stained with a mixture of dirt and blood. Tingling in his fingers and toes and a swift burn over his cheeks and face forced him to acknowledge how close he'd been to frostbite. Slumping down into an old easy chair by the stove, he sipped the warm liquid and watched Brileigh sign everything in.

"What do I do with him?" Caleb tilted the cup toward his face, feeling a wash of condensation on his forehead. "Do you like Padraic?"

"I don't dislike him," Brileigh answered, slipping the radio back into the charger. "His skills are like a gift from God around here."

"I never feel like I can reach him." Caleb downed his second cup and tossed it in the garbage.

"Don't stop trying." Brileigh walked him to the door, handing him his truck keys. "You're the only one who is."

Chapter 18

Padraic forced a smile on his face and opened the door to Carrie's room. She sat engrossed in the news program, munching on microwave popcorn and drinking Diet Pepsi.

"The twins are still missing. Come watch this with me." She beckoned him in beside her. "The boy's name is Austin and the sister is Hilary. They're only six years old. There's a whole story; they keep replaying it. Both of them are divers. The little girl is number one in her division for the nation. Watch some of her footage. She's phenomenal."

"Have you eaten anything besides popcorn and Pepsi?"

"Stop parenting me and come watch this." She patted the bed.

He did as she asked, halfheartedly listening to the program. The little girl was indeed a gifted diver. The television replayed her performance at Nationals. She was shy and mousy compared to her brother. It was obvious he was the dominant twin, even though she was more talented.

"There are no leads. It's like they've just vanished off the face of the earth," Carrie sighed as Padraic took her hand, noticing the absence of her ring.

She timidly pulled her hand away from his.

"I don't want him to always think of me as his mistake." She reached inside her bedside stand and pulled out the ring, wrapped carefully in some pink tissues. "Can you return it? Get your money back?"

"I don't want to."

She placed the ring in his hand. "This is your promise, not Caleb's." She closed his fingers around the ring and held his fist. "Your promise doesn't belong to me." She released a deep sigh and lifted her hands away from his. "Apparently, Caleb's doesn't either."

"I'm not sure what I'm supposed to do." He kept his eyes on his closed hand.

"I want you to keep it." She lifted her hand to his cheek. "The girl who wears it will be very special. I hope I get to meet her."

He secured the ring in his wallet, unsure of what to think or feel. He picked up his cell phone from the nightstand. "Any calls?"

"Gail. I talked to her. I hope you don't mind."

"You did? What'd you talk about?" He smiled at her sheepish grin.

"You," Carrie laughed. "She really cares about you. We talked a long time. She told me she spoke with Caleb, too."

"He mentioned it." He brought her a sandwich and a carton of milk from the small refrigerator.

"I want to meet her." She opened the carton of milk and lifted it to her lips.

"You're supposed to be hiding. Remember what I told you about the people who may be responsible for your father's death?"

"That has nothing to do with me meeting Gail. Anapaytoo, I remember. You told me in the cabin." Her eyes sparkled with delight, bringing a smile of acknowledgment that this was a battle he would not win.

"Anapaytoo." He rubbed his eyes, wishing the word had never passed his lips. "I saw Gail this morning." He busied himself clearing the trash she'd left at her bedside. "She doesn't want to see me anymore."

"Padraic, she's lying! It's not true!" Carrie pushed her tray aside, nearly coming off the bed.

"Gail and I want different things." He drew up the Lovenox in the syringe and pinched her skin, preparing her for the injection. "She wants to marry a doctor, live happily ever after. She won't marry me unless I go to medical school."

"She said that? You asked her to marry you, and she said no?"

Padraic nodded his answer. He had accepted the answer and been relieved at the outcome at the time, but standing before Carrie now and facing it head on, he felt lost.

"Tell me what happened." She winced at the needle stick, and then opened her eyes as he tossed the needle in the plastic container on the wall.

"There really isn't much to tell." Padraic brought her a glass of water and her medications. "I'm not what she wants."

"What happened with your medical school application? Did it not come through?" Her voice struck with defiance.

"Early acceptance. I could start as soon as January if I wanted to." He sat beside her.

"Oh." Carrie let out a low sigh, reaching for his hand. "Is that it? You don't want to go? And Gail, she wants you to?"

"Something like that." His fingers interlocked with hers for a moment.

Carrie was quiet for a long time.

"I watched you the whole time when you took care of my mom." She turned off the television and faced him. "The medications, the shots, the machines. Balancing them all, my mom said you had the hands of God."

"I'm well-trained," Padraic countered.

"You're gifted, Padraic. Medicine is your calling."

"Those who are gifted, or have callings, are passionate about what they're doing. I'm nonchalant about medicine. That fact alone tells me I shouldn't be a doctor." He breathed in a deep sigh, shifting in his chair.

"Tells me you haven't found what you're looking for." Carrie reached for him, giving him a playful push. "How many different types of doctors are there? Maybe you just haven't found the kind of doctor you're supposed to be."

He faced her, offering a coy grin. She wasn't going to let him off the hook so easily this time. There were some things he could easily lead her away from; this was not going to be one of them.

"I want to see the medical school you applied to." She broke his train of thought.

"What for?"

"It's the closest I'll ever get to going to college."

"Is that what you think?" He powered up his laptop and uploaded a site from the hospital education center. "All you've got to do is log in, there's your account number and password."

"Caleb said I didn't have to go back to school." Her shocked expression brought a smile to his face.

"I am not Caleb." He hit the button, opening up her account.

All of her information had been uploaded from her school, showing everything up to her current classes and grades.

"This is a satellite site. It connects with the education center here at the hospital. They work together so that students don't miss out academically while hospitalized or recovering. It looks like you've got plenty of homework."

"I don't like school." She pushed the tray table away.

"Name someone who does." He stopped her efforts, returning the table to its position. "You finish, and you keep the laptop."

"Really?" She lifted her hand from the second attempt to push it away. "Like a graduation present?"

"No, more like a bribe."

"You're terrible!" Her laugh eased the tension in his mind.

Grabbing her book bag, he placed everything within easy reach around her. "I went through everything. You should have all the resources you need, either on the laptop itself or here in the bag. Next time I see Caleb, I'll get your phone. Until then, you can keep mine."

"I'm never going to go to college, so why do…" She tapped the table, looking first at the computer then at him.

"We're not talking about college. Let's just get through high school." He lifted her chin, drawn to her pouty smile.

"I still want to go see that school, and I want to meet Gail." She grabbed his hand away from her chin but did not release him.

"You're not going to let it be until I relent."

"Probably not." She offered a pretty smile.

"I have Friday off. I'll take you to the city." He kissed her forehead.

"Can Gail come?" she asked, lifting her voice in a hopeful tone.

"Sure." He snapped off the lights and adjusted the dimmers. "You invite Caleb; I'll invite Gail."

"I knew you were going to say that." She cast her eyes upon the computer, then back toward him. "Do you have to work tomorrow?"

"Yes, but you'll be able to page me if you need anything." He took his phone and showed her how to work the paging system. "Let's call it a night, okay?"

"Are you sleeping here?"

"I can stay in the sleep chair here in the room, or take the adjoining room. Which would you prefer?" He waited for her answer.

"Will you leave the door open between us?" She chewed her bottom lip.

"Always." He crossed the room, opened the door and turned on the dimmers in the next room.

"Wake me up before you leave?" She turned the television on and pulled the blankets to her chin.

"I will."

Settling in the adjoining room, he felt exhaustion claim its rights against his body. Fatigue would force his systems to comply with the demand for rest, but his mind would not adhere to the order. There would be no peace.

I don't want you. I don't need you. I don't trust you. I don't love you. The faceless voices accosted his solace. Hollowness engulfed his very being. The loudest of them all echoed deeper, carving his name upon the confines of his soul. Just as the prominent hand sketched upon the walls in the book of Daniel, the message etched tonight was clear. *You are forsaken.*

Chapter 19

Caleb studied the file Joe had given him. In the past five years, there had been seventeen fatalities in the northwest region, all involving small-engine planes. Three could be ruled out to weather, although all of them stated pilot error as the primary cause of the crashes. The families stood to receive little to no insurance benefits due to the unsubstantiated claims. Fourteen years, twenty-six years, a veteran Navy pilot with thirty-four years. Caleb sorted the data in his mind.

These were men and women with vast knowledge and experience in aviation. Was it possible they all made mistakes? *It's possible.* He rubbed his forehead. *It's just not probable.*

Gregg had been flying planes since Caleb could remember. Before Carrie was born, Gregg and Helen would fly out to remote Indian reservations to share their faith. There were no landing pads, no safety measures.

Did Gregg not fly all over Africa, in and out of areas under extreme duress from poverty and war? With the result being his life and that of his daughter, would he now make the wrong call? What's the commonality? Lord, give me direction.

Pushing away from the table, he refilled his coffee cup. *This apartment looks like a war zone.* Bloodstains from the living room peppered his path to the kitchen, where his shirt still lay soaking in the sink. Carrie's blood-christened sheets still covered his bed. *How did it get this bad?* Grabbing the bleach, he headed for the bathroom—maybe cleaning up would help clear his mind.

"You can't mix bleach and ammonia." Padraic's voice sounded so far away.

The windows and door of his apartment lay wide open, and the frigid November air poured in. A blur of colors passed before his eyes as the room continued to move in an unsteady top-like fashion, raising a wave of nausea within him.

"I'm going to puke," he heard himself utter.

In a movement too quick for him to process, he found himself outside face-down in a snow bank. "What the—"

"Fresh air." Padraic stood at the window, looking down at him.

"Did you just throw me out a second story window?" Caleb sat up, wiping his bloody lip.

"Cured you, didn't it?"

"You could have killed me." Caleb staggered to his feet, brushing the snow from his clothes. "That was just evil."

"Leaving you be would have been evil." Padraic climbed out the window and leapt into the snow bank, knocking Caleb down again.

"Would you knock it off? What's wrong with you?" Caleb pushed him away, trying unsuccessfully not to smile.

"Looked like fun." Padraic stood and offered a hand to Caleb.

"There is something seriously wrong with your brain." Caleb accepted the help to his feet.

"True enough." Padraic followed him back inside.

"What are you doing here anyway? Aren't you supposed to be orienting this morning?"

"I'm oriented enough." Padraic went straight to the refrigerator and helped himself. "I think this orange juice is fermented."

"Stop drinking it." Caleb grabbed the jug out of his hand and tossed it in the sink.

"Why? It's better that way." Padraic shrugged and finished his glass.

"What do you want?"

"Cell phone, clothes." Padraic grabbed an apple.

Caleb tried to reorient himself to his apartment. "What in the world just happened? Why did you throw me out the window?"

"It seemed like a good idea at the time." Padraic shrugged, taking a big bite from the apple. "Basic chemistry: mixing bleach and ammonia equals toxic fumes."

"Is that why I feel like I'm two days hung over?" Caleb touched his lip then grabbed a dish towel to address the bleeding.

"Depends, might be too much of that orange juice." Padraic's jovial tone seemed out of place, but Caleb dared not question it at the moment.

"Hey, where's the file that was on this table?" Caleb scanned the room, suddenly aware of his loss.

Padraic ignored him, went to the bedroom and grabbed Carrie's bag. Caleb followed him, standing on the threshold.

"Where was I when you came in?" Caleb threw the dish towel on the bed.

"Bathroom. Looks like you were trying to bleach the sheets." Padraic stepped aside as Caleb crossed in front of him and opened the bathroom door.

"I was." Caleb looked around and cast his eyes back toward Padraic. "I wasn't using ammonia. I don't think I even own any."

"Apparently you do, because there was an open bottle

of it right under the sink." Padraic set the suitcase down and located Carrie's phone on the floor.

"Where is it now?"

"Capped and in the kitchen."

Caleb pushed passed him and went to the kitchen to retrieve the bottle. "You found this in my bathroom?"

Padraic nodded his answer.

"It's McConnlie's brand. I never shop there." He pointed at the label, and then returned to the table. "There was a file on the table. Did you see it when you came in?"

"I really wasn't looking." Padraic scratched his head. "What are you thinking?"

"When did you get here?" Caleb left the table and grabbed his coffee mug, feeling slight warmth from its contents.

"Twenty, thirty minutes ago."

"Was my door locked?"

"Door wasn't locked. You didn't answer, so I let myself in. I went to get Carrie's things, and smelled the fumes. Opened the bathroom door and there you were."

"The bathroom door was closed?" Caleb put his coffee down.

"Yes." Padraic followed him back toward the bedroom.

"Someone else was here." The pounding of Caleb's heart grew so loud it echoed in his ears and vibrated in his throat.

Caleb scanned the apartment; nothing else seemed out of place.

"Do you have a copy of whatever it was you were looking at?"

"That was a copy. I left the original at work."

"Do you want to tell me about it?"

"Yeah I do. Give me a ride to the office and I'll tell you what I know." Caleb grabbed his coat and keys, still feeling a bit nauseated from the fumes.

Talking helped. Padraic seldom offered any input, just an occasional nod of acknowledgment that he was listening. Caleb briefed him on the timeline of events. The crash fires had incinerated almost all the evidence; in most cases the victims were not identifiable except by dental records, and in two separate crashes, only the flight plan filed could identify the ashes.

Seventeen different fueling stations were involved, with Dixon's having the most reported incidents. Verchante Distributors serviced thirteen of the seventeen sites. Narrowing his focus to the one distributor disregarded an entire set of information as a distraction.

"I think you should stay in my apartment," Padraic interrupted Caleb's train of thought.

"I'll be okay."

"Gregg is dead, Carrie is in hiding, and you've just experienced a very suspicious accident. I don't see how that's okay." Padraic pulled into the parking lot next the ranger station.

"Is Carrie at your apartment?" Caleb opened his door.

Padraic shook his head.

"Eventually, you will return her." Caleb leaned over his seat and removed the keys out of the ignition.

"She will return to you," Padraic corrected.

"I'm taking your keys. That way, I'm pretty sure you won't drive off and leave me." Caleb slammed the truck door and hurried into the office.

Joe stood at the coffeepot as Caleb went to his work station.

"What happened to your face?" Joe offered him a cup of coffee, watching as Caleb dug through his files.

"Padraic threw me out the window this morning."

"He's not playing well with others again?" Joe leaned against the desk, sitting against the edge.

"You could say that." Caleb grabbed the file he was looking for and opened it. "What else do you know about the twins' father?"

"Walter Ross drives the fuel truck for the northwest route. At least, he did until last month. He filed a safety complaint and was fired a month later."

"Do you think the kidnapping is related to this incident?"

"He's a whistle blower." Joe opened his phone, scrolling through his list of contacts. "I'll send you his number. Walter is a good guy; just involved with the wrong people." Joe pushed some buttons on his phone then looked up at Caleb. "Like you."

"Will he talk to me?"

"He's expecting your call." Joe closed his phone and tapped his chin. "Caleb, I want you to call him, and then I want you to drop this case. Go home, take care of Carrie. You've got a month before you take off to the ranger program. Leave this case here. Take Carrie and go."

"This is Carrie's father we are talking about."

"No, son, it's a whole lot more than that. Talk to Walter, and then you take that pretty little girl of yours and ride off into the sunset."

"I can't do that." Caleb stepped aside as Joe pulled out a picture of Walter Ross' children.

"He's lost his pretty little girl. Are you willing to lose yours?" Joe forced the picture into Caleb's hand.

"Are we sure this is not just a coincidence?"

"There's no such thing as coincidence." Joe walked away from the conversation.

Caleb bit hard into his sore lip, re-cracking the skin, tasting the salty warmth of his own blood as it trickled over his tongue. Placing the photograph inside the file, he checked his phone to ensure Walter Ross's number had come through. *What am I supposed to say to this man? Lord, what am I supposed to do?*

"I need to get back to the hospital." Padraic opened the door and walked over to Caleb's area.

"Yeah, okay. I'm ready." Caleb pushed away from his desk and walked toward the door.

"You want this file or not?" Padraic lifted the green folder containing the Verchante information.

"Leave it." Caleb zipped his coat and tossed his coffee cup in the trash.

"Yeah, right." Padraic tucked the file under his arm and followed him out the door.

Caleb sat lost in thought. Padraic turned the key, awaiting direction.

"Where do you want to go?" Padraic released the steering wheel.

"I don't know." Caleb fastened his seatbelt. "I've got to make a call, but I need some time to figure out what to say. There's so much chaos going on. I just can't think."

"I'd take the machine eleven miles out." Padraic started the engine and pulled out of the parking lot.

"That hut is still standing?"

Padraic shifted into second as the truck slid on some black ice. "I bought the land as soon as I got my Indian money."

"I thought you partied that money away." The words fell out of his mouth, and he instantly regretted them.

"You thought wrong," Padraic answered after a slight hesitation.

"I'm sorry. I didn't mean it to sound that way. It's just, buying land is like settling, and I didn't think you were ready for that."

"God found me there once." Padraic turned his truck, heading toward the outskirts of town. "Maybe someday he'll go looking for me there again."

Caleb swallowed hard digesting the information Padraic had laid before him. *Lord, give me the right words.* "Are you lost, Padraic?"

"I don't get lost," he answered as quickly as Caleb had asked.

"Can you tell me what you mean? I'm a bit confused and a whole lot concerned, especially after the other day." Caleb grabbed the dashboard as the truck rocked through the uneven terrain.

"I wanted it, so I bought it." Padraic shifted into four-wheel drive as he turned up his grandparents' driveway. "The hut is stocked. You could stay there all winter if you wanted to. There's wireless and cell phone service. You'll need the machine to get in and out. I haven't had time to build a road."

"Wow, really? How come you never told me?" Caleb waited for Padraic to take the keys out of the ignition.

Padraic opened his glove compartment and pulled out another set of keys.

"Are you coming with me?" Caleb followed him to Granddad's shed.

"I can't."

"You need to."

"It's not about me." Padraic led him to the back of the shed and uncovered the snow mobile. "Here, take this with you; no one's going to get it where you're going." Padraic slid the green file folder into the storage compartment of the snow mobile. "There's an extra gas can already there. Greater Lake should be pretty well frozen. You may be able to cut some distance and go over rather than around it."

"I know you don't feel it, but God's fingerprints are all over you." Caleb helped Padraic move the machine toward the back door.

"You're right." Padraic started the engine and handed Caleb the helmet. "I don't feel it."

Caleb donned his helmet and climbed aboard, unable to respond.

Lord, please give him some sort of guidance. He needs more than I can afford him right now. Lord, I'm going to have to trust You with him. I'm running out of strength.

Chapter 20

"Son, what's going on? Is that Caleb?" Joseph Talons came around the shed with an armload of wood.

"Yeah, he needs space," Padraic answered, casting his eyes toward the ground.

"Ah, yes, I suppose he does. How's Carrie?" Joseph motioned for him to grab an armload of wood and follow.

"She'll be all right." Padraic entered the familiar kitchen that radiated warmth and welcome.

"Were you two raised in a barn? Look at the mess you traipsed into my kitchen." Sarah turned from a sink full of dishes. "At least you brought in the wood to atone for your sins."

"If it were that simple, I'd have brought in the tree line," Padraic stated under his breath, feeling his granddad's hand heavy on his shoulder.

"Where are you supposed to be?" Joseph led him back out the kitchen door.

"It's my orientation for anesthesia. But it's just paperwork and computer stuff today. I don't need to be there." Padraic braced himself, feeling a lecture approaching.

"Doesn't the hospital have rules about skipping the orientation?" Joseph scratched his silvery-orange beard and followed Padraic toward the trucks.

"They don't apply to me. I mean, not all the rules apply to me." Padraic raised his head to face his granddad, but a fierce assertion from within forced his gaze toward the wood line.

"You're wrong, son." Joseph grabbed the door handle of Padraic's truck, stopping him in his tracks. "All rules that are assigned over you by an authority are applicable.

"Once you've identified the authorities in your life, you need to submit. Through submission, you will learn to commit. Commitment brings peace. I'm talking about a commitment to yourself, for your career, your character, your relationship with Christ. Until you've mastered those three "C's," the last one—the covenant of marriage—should not be entertained." Joseph opened the truck door. "Carrie called your grandmother this morning and told her about Gail."

Padraic remained in place, digesting the information Granddad was offering.

"Each authority in your life has its own rule book. It would behoove you to look at them." Joseph ushered him into the truck.

Padraic placed his key in the ignition, and then noticed the deerskin Bible on his dash.

"What's this?"

"I want to say it was your mother's," Joseph sighed, "but I don't know. I found it in the driveway the day you first arrived."

"It's got a name in it." The soft brittle pages crinkled against the brisk winter breeze. "It's a Bible. I can't read Sioux," Padraic reminded him.

"Learn. Develop your character and your relationship with Christ at the same time."

"You didn't mention anything about my career." Padraic smiled, placing the Bible on the seat beside him.

"I'm sending you back to work, aren't I?" Joseph shoved the door closed and offered a slight wave.

"I'll learn to read it." Padraic rolled down his window.

"Anyone can learn to read it. The challenge is learning to follow it, submitting to the authority over you, over us all. You're a good man, Padraic. Your friends are blessed to have you, and they know it."

"I feel more like a nuisance than a blessing." He leaned against the back of the seat, letting out a deep sigh.

"You're not often on belay. It takes a great deal of physical strength and mental agility to manage two belays at the same time." Joseph rested his arm on the window ledge.

"I'm not following."

"On belay, isn't that the term you boys use when one of you is climbing, and the other is watching, holding the safety ropes?" Joseph smiled as Padraic turned off the engine.

"Yeah, it is. But I'm usually the one climbing."

"Hmm," Joseph tapped the window and stepped away from the vehicle. "Sometimes the good Lord does some cross-training of His own."

Padraic pulled onto the highway. The forty minute trip back to the hospital was over before he could piece together the entire conversation.

Gathering the battered Bible, he headed for the front door. *I can do this. If it means I'll find this piece of me that's missing, Lord, help me do this. I'll follow the rules, just lead me.*

He slid into an empty seat in the back row as a HIPPA video projected onto the screen. Sinking low in his seat, the weight of the transgressions against the hospital, his coworkers and the patients fell upon him.

I knew it was wrong when I did it. Knowing it was wrong and doing it anyway is deliberate disobedience. A chill crept up his spine, causing his legs to move in quick and constant motion. *I don't need to be here. Yes, I do. I can't do this, I need to move, do something, go somewhere.*

"Are you all right?" A man who looked to be in his early thirties, wearing a white lab coat, offered him a cup of coffee while taking the seat beside him. "That's for you. You looked like you could use it. Actually you could probably do with a little less caffeine in your life, but we won't go there right now. My name is Aaron."

"Padraic." Padraic accepted Aaron's extended hand in a firm but gentle grip.

"Padraic Talons? You're the one who was managing my patient a few weeks ago." Aaron adjusted his position to one that locked Padraic into a confrontational conversation. "I was impressed. I did a little digging later. You managed her care well."

"Not well enough." Padraic shifted his stare to the floor casing.

"She lost the baby?"

Padraic forbid himself to react.

"Altering medical records is a serious ethical and criminal offense. I can't prove you did it, so it's not going any further than right here, right now. I just thought you needed to know that somebody noticed." Aaron kept his voice low, in an unreadable tone.

The video ended, and the lights were turned on as people began filtering out of the room for the ten-minute break.

"Padraic." Aaron stood, stretching his arms, and then placed a firm hand upon his shoulder. "Don't waste the gift the good Lord gave you by making haughty decisions." Aaron walked away and joined a group of doctors across the room.

Beads of sweat peppered Padraic's forehead at the realization of the encounter. *God's calling my bluff.* Fingers intertwined in a tight fist tapped his chin as his silky black hair fell forward, hiding his face. *It's about time.*

He kept silent through the presentations, grateful when the last speaker released them for the afternoon. The day's antics had taken their toll. *This must be what exhaustion feels like.* Every muscle in his body ached, and even his eyes burned, blurring his vision. He pushed himself through the corridors, fashioning a quick smile and greeting for his co-workers. He scanned the area, unnerved by an eerie sense that someone was watching him.

"Are you scrubbing in?" The unit clerk grabbed his sleeve and pushed him through the OR doors. "If Cathy's back there, you don't need to go in. Go check."

The OR doors closed and latched behind him, providing safety. Whoever caused the tickle in his spine dare not enter the operating suites. Cathy was already scrubbed in and elbow deep in someone's abdomen. *Better you than me.* He passed through a set of antique doors leading to the old hospital.

Carrie sat with her knees propped and a sea of pillows around her. The television played low but easily audible. The twin story replayed; her attention never waned from the television until the newscaster led into the next story.

"How was your day?" He tossed his jacket on the bed, brought her medications, and then prepared her for her shot.

"Uneventful. How about yours?" She grabbed his jacket as it slid toward the floor.

Should I start with finding Caleb on the floor overcome by toxic fumes? Maybe the come-to-Jesus lecture in Granddad's lair? Or, how about the confrontation with Aaron?

"What's this?" Carrie took out the tattered Bible and opened it.

"Granddad gave it to me this morning. He says it might have belonged to my mother." Padraic prepped her skin and injected the medication.

"Do you mind if I look at it for a while?" She ran her hand across the old leather, awaiting his response.

"It's written in Sioux." He tossed the needle in the sharps container.

"Oh, that reminds me." She grabbed the bedside table and pulled it over and tapped wildly on the keyboard. "Clarkson, that's where you were accepted, right? Look at this."

The screen flashed, and the steady rhythm of Indian drumming cascaded through the speakers. Twelve different tribal leaders stood in stoic fashion, all in traditional attire, each representing their own nation. The bureau of Indian Affairs, along with collations of Universities nationwide had joined forces to re-immerse tribal children and adults through language. Clarkson would be offering free Sioux language classes to any enrolled member of the Sioux Nation.

"That's you, Padraic. You have to go. You want this." Her enthusiasm made him smile, but left his decision unaltered.

"I'll admit it's tempting, but I'm pretty schooled out right now. I think I need to work a year or two." He scratched his forehead, feeling even more drained then he'd ever felt before.

"Are you okay?" She reached for his hand.

"It's just been a long day. I'm going to take a shower and lie down. Do you need anything?" He rubbed the back of his neck and met her eyes.

"I'm okay. Get some rest." Carrie released her hold on him and settled under the covers.

He placed a gentle kiss on her forehead and turned off the lights, retiring to his adjacent room. A scalding shower left him exhausted. His body crumpled onto the crisp white sheets, his strength depleted as he surrendered. His head sank into his pillow.

His body's necessity for rest conquered his mind's quest for solace. Tormented by the demons that possessed his soul, he gripped the side of the bed, wishing he had the strength to open his eyes. Voices crowded his thoughts, and the hands of love and hate reached out toward him, some grabbing at him, some pushing, others retracting—none actually contacting his body. *A touch riddled with repulsion would be enough, God. I'll take disgust over nothing at all.*

Chapter 21

Caleb's watch read noon when he removed his helmet and secured the snowmobile in the lean-to. The area remained as he remembered it: the mountains swallowed the tiny alcove from all directions. It stood a beautiful, but impenetrable, fortress of rock, trees and sky.

It shouldn't surprise me that he bought it. Caleb wandered toward the east slope and looked down the only possible vehicle route. It was five miles to the old Shaw barn going that way. The Shaw family owned the barn and all the surrounding land at the base, or at least that's what he'd always been told. He'd never seen or heard from the Shaws, and from the look of things, no one else had either.

Did Padraic know who the Shaws were? Did he buy this land from them? How did he know who it belonged to in order to purchase it in the first place?

Caleb kicked the snow off his boots and entered the hut. From the work that had been done, it could be considered a cabin more than the shanty they built so many years ago. Insulation had been stapled in and covered with sheetrock panels. A small wood stove and an army cot lay in the corner adjacent to the only window. Crafted shelves lined the anterior wall.

Joseph prided himself a master carpenter in the Colter Bay area and had taught Padraic well. The wood was smooth, but lacked the distinct design or personality that Joseph would have applied. The wood box was full. A pile of books lay neglected in a basket beside the cot. The blankets, he knew, would be pulled so tightly that even a drill master would have difficulty finding fault with Padraic's precision. A few pots and utensils hung from the rungs, and canned goods lined the shelves, all with the labels dutifully facing out. He grabbed the water pump handle, lifted it and pushed it down hard. Running water? He left the pump and opened the door to what he thought would be a closet but revealed a small bathroom with a camp shower, water heater and generator. *He's serious about staying here.* Caleb used the facilities then returned to the wood stove and lit a fire. Within an hour, he had a cozy cabin.

He found a pair of shorts and a T-shirt and clean socks in a duffel bag at the foot of the bed. A change of clothes was a welcome accommodation—almost as much as the indoor plumbing. He found himself all too relaxed with a cup of coffee and a steaming bowl of beef stew.

I've made such a mess of things, yet You place me here, in the midst of all this beauty. I look outside and feel like I must be in Your throne room. I've been rescued without reprieve. All that I've done against You, against Carrie, against Padraic...I don't understand how You still love me, how they still love me. I am in awe of Your mercy. Lord, I need more than Your mercy right now. I need Your guidance. The decisions I'm facing concerning this case, Carrie and my career, I lay them at Your feet. I've tried things my way. Please don't allow me to do it again. I am surrendering—whatever is Your will, whatever it is that You would have me do, lead me, make my voice Yours. Enforce my compliance and acceptance of Your complete authority over me.

He waited. Evening settled and with it came a fresh foot of heavy snow. All signs of his coming were erased. The

Ross twins, Gregg, all the other pilots and families that had been affected by the atrocities of this company…walking away seemed so wrong. Endangering Carrie any further in this mess was not the right answer either.

Lord, I don't know what the right answer is. I need Your guidance to make the decision You want me to make. Silence overwhelmed him. His head sank deep into the goose down pillow. The coolness of the evening filtered between his toes. *Lord, this case is bigger than me, but You are greater than it. You are in control.*

"Take your girl and go." Joe's command invaded his mind.

I'm scheduled to leave anyway. I'll need a month to get all our personal affairs set straight. Leaving just makes sense. Caleb rubbed his temples.

That's the problem. It does make sense, too much sense. But is it what I'm supposed to do? Is it what You want me to do? Silence deafened his soul. He lifted his eyes toward the window. Pure white flakes christened the foreboding darkness. *What do I say to this man who has lost his children? Maybe he has something to say to me.* The thought caught him off guard. Caleb opened his phone and glanced at his watch before pushing the buttons. In a last effort he pushed the record button—if Walter Ross did have something to say, he didn't want to miss it.

The phone rang more than twelve times before a muffled, tired voice spoke incoherently into the phone.

"My name is Caleb Cohen. I was told I could reach Walter Ross at this number."

"Just a minute." The man sounded as if he was just waking up. "Caleb? Joe's trail kid?" The voice returned a few seconds later. "I'm who you're looking for. Son, it's one o'clock in the morning."

"It's only ten in Wyoming," Caleb heard himself answer before he could think.

"You're young, aren't you boy?" A forced sigh emptied into the receiver.

"I'm twenty-two." Caleb drew in a deep breath letting it out slowly. *Lord, help me know what to say.*

"Are you married?"

The question took him aback. He looked down at the platinum band that encased his left ring finger. Already it had blanched his skin—a farmer's tan that would mark its place if he removed it.

"I am," he sighed, *but I'm not much of a husband.*

"Any kids?"

His mind immediately shot to their lost baby. So much had happened, and he hadn't had time to feel the reality. He did have a child, and if Carrie had never been in that plane crash, she'd still be pregnant. The thought crushed him upon impact. He tried to gather his thoughts to speak.

"Carrie lost the baby in the same crash that killed her father."

"You make a child together, and when you lose one, you lose it together as well." Walter Ross's voice touched a hidden nerve within him.

This baby was real. She was a part of us, a part that I never even acknowledged. A part that Carrie had to turn to Padraic for, for physical and emotional healing. An aching in his chest spread throughout his body. *I've abandoned this child. Child.* He wiped his eyes with his free hand. *I never even perceived it as a child. Lord, I only saw it as a condition.* Bile rose up in his throat. He fought the urge to vomit. *God, forgive me. Can Carrie forgive me? When did I turn so calloused?*

"I've lost my children, too," Walter spoke as Caleb tried to recover.

"They've found the twins?" Caleb cleared his throat, dreading the answer.

"No," Walter's voice countered. "My penance is never to know. It's far worse than anything else imaginable."

"Did my report trigger the abduction of your children?"

Walter's voice softened. "Verchante had a standard practice and hefty incentives for drivers who could accomplish more with less. From day one, I was shown how to alter the driving logs so that I could actually drive more hours than the regulations allowed. I should have walked out. Nothing good comes of something like that. But I really needed the job."

Caleb closed his eyes and nodded. He understood the necessity of work, especially in today's depressed economy.

"Within a month I was driving. I hadn't even completed the CDL licensure program. No one seemed to care about that though. Then there were all the safety measures. Driving HAZMAT is some serious stuff. I was getting nervous at my lack of training and the things they were having me do."

Skirting around the rules was something Caleb was familiar with as well. How many times had he filled out documentation for something Padraic did?

"Some guys were more interested in those bonuses than anything else," said Walter. "They'd carry one fuel and not allot the proper time and maintenance necessary to carry another type of fuel. I reported it, and it got me fired. I didn't know that the report would bring me where I am today."

"The fuel itself is contaminated," Caleb restated putting all the pieces together in his mind. "And it's all related to the distribution process. Sir if you hadn't reported those the unsafe work practices, it would have been next to impossible for the investigating team to put this all together."

"That's where your report came in, Caleb. You provided the investigating team here a fresh path to pursue.

"Transporting fuel is not simple. Different techniques are utilized depending on what kind of fuel it is. With automobile gasoline, for example, it's not a big deal if you have an extra high test to unload it into the lower test," explained Walter. "It's a shortcut we take so we can get ready faster for the next run—but it's not the same for aircraft.

"Given what was going on with the carriers and the company, it was a tragedy waiting to happen," sighed Walter. "Your report was just enough evidence to continue the investigation here."

"If I hadn't sent that report when I did, it's possible your children would be safe at home with you tonight." Caleb swallowed hard.

"There's no proof of that either. All I can tell you, son, is that if God has offered you a way out, you'd be wise to take him up on it."

"Joe told you?" Caleb grabbed his canteen and finished what was left of his water.

"No, not much has been said to me about your situation, but I know my own. I do believe that the good Lord has a plan. He's tapped all the players He needs for his purpose. You and I both have been identified—there's good in that. In His time, we will move according to His will."

"What about in the meantime?" Asked Caleb.

"Sit the bench. Stay ready. He'll let you know when it's your turn."

"I just feel so helpless."

"If you were helpless, you wouldn't have been put on the

team. You just don't understand your role yet."

"Sitting the bench?" Caleb scratched the side of his face as he processed the analogy. "It just seems so wrong. I know too much to let everything go."

"You're not letting it go. You're waiting your turn." Walter's words struck Caleb with such force he had to sit down.

"He wants me to wait?"

"We're all receiving a lesson in waiting." Walter's tone became a whisper as a woman's voice sounded in the background. "I need to go."

Caleb sent the recorded conversation to his e-mail then closed the phone and tossed it on the wooden stand beside the cot. *How do I let this go? How do I wait? Why can't You just use me now? I'm ready.* He massaged his temples and attempted to process all that Walter Ross had told him. *If this is what You want me to do, Lord, I will abide.* He stretched out on the cot and hoped a few hours of sleep would help him unwind.

At three in the morning, his eyes were open. Padraic had invaded his dreams. Always the same, the terrain radiated warnings of certain death. There was Padraic, hand raised ready to cut his belay line.

He's just as much a part of this as I am. He's on the team, is that what you're trying to tell me? I can't let him cut me off. Caleb grabbed his phone, hitting the speed dial.

Chapter 22

Carrie glanced through the entryway leading to Padraic's adjoining room. He had been sound asleep for over an hour. True exhaustion must have corralled him because he rarely slept this hard.

All this stuff with Caleb and me—his relationship with Gail, starting a new job, medical school— Lord, I'd be exhausted, too. I'm tired just thinking about it. She lifted his Bible from her bedside table. She checked one last time to ensure he was sound asleep, then slid her fingers under the tattered leather cover.

The page was well hidden. Her mother had told her about the Bibles they had distributed on the reservations. The page that credited the translator and publisher could not be omitted. It would be there, and as she feared, have her father's name on it.

God forgive me, but he will never get past that page if he sees it. The bold black lettering stood and bore witness to what she already knew. It was one of her father's Bibles. She lifted her eyes one last time in Padraic's direction, then carefully removed the page and replaced the cover. *Story Running Brook*, was the penciled-in name on the backside of the page. She hadn't noticed it until now.

Padraic's ringtone interrupted her thoughts. She grabbed the phone and stuffed the page in with her school notes.

"Hello," her voice shook and hands trembled.

"Carrie?" The sound of Caleb's voice nearly tore her in

two.

"Yes, it's me. I didn't want you to wake up Padraic." She swallowed her initial fear.

"He's usually up and going by now. Is he sick?"

"No, not sick, exhausted." She sighed and admitted to herself his voice felt like a warm blanket wrapped around her. "He's been through a lot these last few weeks."

"He said something about orientation for the anesthesia position."

"Did he tell you about early acceptance to medical school?" She felt her body relax as she listened to his gentleness.

"He didn't mention it."

"He turned it down. Said he's all schooled out. When he told Gail, she left him."

"I can't believe he didn't say a word to me. I just talked to him this morning."

"He didn't go see you for his own benefit." She felt her lips tighten with the sudden remembrance of their situation.

"I know." He deflected her anger. "Carrie, I'm really sorry for everything I've put you through. All the things I kept saying that you weren't ready for. It was actually me. I wasn't ready to be a husband, much less a father. Please forgive me."

"I can't." She squeezed her eyes shut tight, refusing to fall prey to his apology. "You don't love me, Caleb."

"Yes, I do." His answer came before she could finish speaking.

"No, you don't. You should love me like Christ loves the church." Tears escaped down her cheeks as she wiped her nose with her hand.

"I do."

217

"Christ never asked for an annulment." Her voice shook as she cried into the phone.

"Kimimela." Padraic took the phone. "You two aren't ready to talk yet." He pressed the off button and wiped her tears with his thumbs. "You'll just hurt each other."

"He wanted to talk to you." She surrendered to him as he lifted her onto his lap and wrapped her in his arms.

"It can wait." He withdrew his touch as a sharp pain shot up her right leg and radiated in her hip. "Pain?"

"It's okay." But it wasn't. She buried her face in his chest.

"You are going through enough without having to deal with physical pain, too." He withdrew his hand and brought her medicine and a glass of water.

"You have a physical therapy appointment today." He sat down beside her, taking her glass as she swallowed the medication.

"I don't care. I wish I was dead."

"Wait until after you experience PT, then you'll really wish you were dead." He grinned as she started to smile.

"You're making me laugh." She sighed, grabbing his hand as he tried to leave her bedside. "I don't want to go to PT today."

"What would you like to do?" He cupped her chin with his fingers.

"Let's run away. We can get married and hide somewhere in the mountains and never have to deal with other people again."

"You're already married." He offered a cheeky grin.

"Details." She let out her breath as they both laughed. She settled after a few minutes and looked up at him. "You'd do that wouldn't you, Padraic? Just take me away and leave everything behind?"

"Would it make you happy?"

She hesitated, dropping her gaze from his. "No."

"So, if we're choosing to stay miserable then maybe physical therapy isn't such a bad option." He turned off her overhead light and tucked her into bed. "It's still early. Why don't you try to get a little more sleep? I'll check on you before I leave."

Padraic finished his shower and grabbed a set of hospital scrubs. One last check on Carrie revealed that she'd fallen back to sleep. Leaving the remote on her table, he gently kissed her forehead.

"Kiss me again." Carrie opened her eyes as he started to back away.

He caved at her insistence and placed a simple kiss. She moved her head quickly, bringing his lips over hers.

"Please, I just need to feel loved." She held his forearms, drawing him closer to her.

"So do I." He tapped her lips lightly with his finger and released her hold. "My touch will never satisfy you."

"I love you, Padraic." He allowed her to capture his glance and accepted her hand.

"No one will ever be more in love with you than I am. For that reason alone, you shouldn't tempt me." He lifted her chin, brushing her lips ever so gently with his.

"Please," her whisper caught him.

She lay back against her pillows as his lips teased hers. He was slow parting her mouth, probing ever so slightly with his tongue. As his passion increased his touch lessened, then the kiss was over, leaving her breathless and confused.

"Gail said no to you?" She caught her breath as he sat down on the edge of her bed.

"I'm not the kind of guy girls want to take home to their mothers." He brushed her curls aside, catching her lopsided grin.

"My mom thought you were awesome."

"That's because I did all the chores while your dad gallivanted all over China."

"Africa," she corrected with a slight cough.

"Whatever." He scratched his head, knowing he was leading toward a discussion he didn't want to have.

"He said that he was led by God." Carrie's voice wavered as she gave her answer.

"Attaching God's name to it doesn't make it any less of a transgression." The words came out too fast and harsh to restrain. "I'm sorry. You know what, let's not talk about this. I've got to get to orientation. I'll come get you for PT around ten." He gathered his things and headed toward the door.

"You'll never forgive him." Her voice rose as he opened the door.

"Would you?" He didn't face her.

"No."

He turned, hearing her start to cry. He returned to her side, sorry the conversation had taken place. "This is not about you, Carrie. Your father used God as his tool to dehumanize me when I was too young and too weak to defend myself. I'm not going have a sudden epiphany just because he's dead."

She hid her face. "I hated him for what he put you through. I wish he'd never come back from Africa. He never cared about me or my mother." Her words came out choppy as her breathing started to spasm.

"Take some good deep breaths for me." He grabbed a towel and wiped her face. "You're right, he didn't care about you or Helen. If he had, then he would have stayed home. God's first call is to take care of your household. It's in the book." He pointed at the Bible on her bedside table. "What he did to me was nothing compared to the hell he put your mother through. The only reason I didn't kill him was because your mother loved him."

"She supported his decision to go to Africa."

"He has another family in Africa. She couldn't ignore that fact, and they needed him over there more than she did."

"Mama never told me that." Her body shook as she screamed, "I hate him!"

"He cannot hurt you anymore. Find solace in that." Padraic wrapped his arms around her. "Death was too good for him. He didn't have to suffer like your mother did. Your mother hurt, but nothing so deeply as when Gregg didn't come home when she was sick."

"I didn't know. Why didn't she tell me?" Carrie rocked in his arms, following his breathing patterns.

"She wanted you to make your own decision. He was still your father; she wasn't going to take that away from you."

"It's my fault. I slept with Caleb because I knew my father couldn't stop me." Her words broke between sobs. "Twice he had me go through those exams. He said if I didn't, Caleb would go to jail." She sucked in her breath. "After the second time, everyone stopped listening to him." She pushed away Padraic's hand. "I slept with Caleb because I knew he couldn't stop me."

"You get accused often enough, you may as well be guilty of it." He released his hold on her and resettled her in the bed. "I've been there."

"But I didn't mean to hurt Caleb."

"Maybe you need to talk about this with Caleb." He adjusted her leg sleeves and turned on the machine.

"I can't. He'll hate me if he finds out." She grabbed a tissue, accepting his comfort.

"Maybe he won't." Padraic released his hold as she pushed out of his embrace.

"I'll burn in hell for this."

"If we were all condemned for the sins of our youth," he cupped her chin, giving her a sly grin, "there would be no Heaven."

"Is this the part where you tell me that I'm not condemned because of the blood of Christ?" She pushed his hand away.

"No, because we both know Christ won't condemn you. It's Caleb we're not so sure about."

"Don't ever tell him." She shivered wrapping her arms around herself.

"Caleb probably has a few confessions of his own before any condemnation gets handed out."

"It's what happens next that scares me the most." She dropped her stare and chewed her bottom lip.

"If he sends you to the city, I'll go too." He lifted her chin.

"What would you do in the city?"

"I could go to med school, maybe even relearn some Sioux." He sat down on the edge of her bed.

"What if he sends me to the city and never brings me home again?" She drew in a deep breath and let out a long sigh.

"I will bring you home."

"What about Gail?"

"Gail doesn't want to be with me." He shrugged at the mention of her name.

"You just haven't really committed yet. When you do,

she'll say yes." She reached for his hand.

"Are you going to be all right?" He pointed at the clock.

"Go to work, I'll be okay. Can I have your cell phone?" She dropped his hand, and it lay against the bed.

"Page me if you need me." He placed the phone on her table. "I'll try to remember to bring your cell phone in from my truck later."

He closed the door behind him taking a deep breath before starting toward the main hospital building.

Morning was in the earliest part of dawn—when the birds were still chirping and the new day's snow dampened everything it touched. He'd understood Carrie's confession more than he'd professed. She had used Caleb.

"Some people like being used," he heard himself say nonchalantly.

"Most of us don't." The solid response of Caleb's tone lay heavy on his shoulders.

Chapter 23

One day turned into a week, then bordered on two. It was the first time in a while that when Caleb placed his feet on the ground, he had no other place to be. Joe had all but told him not to come back to work. Carrie didn't want him. Padraic had his hands full. He cleared his mind and let God take over, spending his days hiking the nearby trails or taking the snowmobile out toward the lake.

He accepted the truths that Padraic had laid out. *I'd become too comfortable in my faith. I thought I was strong. I thought I knew how to thwart off temptation. I'm no better than anyone else. I was worshiping myself. I gave in to lust, pointed my finger at everyone else, and sent up complaints and reports of blame. Lord, thank God You've provided the way for me to come back. Enforce Your message upon my memory, so I don't repeat my mistakes.*

Caleb reset the cabin, ensuring there was more wood and kindling than what he started with. To him it looked tight, but with Padraic's insatiable desire for order, he was sure something would be out of place.

He needed to see Carrie. Two weeks without the chaos, without the mystery, without the constant nagging on his soul, and now he finally felt the peace that God allotted him.

He pulled the green folder from the cargo bin and added a hard copy of the conversation with Walter Ross. One final glance at the Ross children reinforced his decision to take Carrie and leave everything else behind. He reopened the cargo bin and tucked the folder in the weatherproof side pocket.

He locked the lean-to and looked at the two trails. The one to the east was an easy five-mile trek; the western trail led back toward the Talons' home, with an eleven mile span between the two. *I've got nothing but time.* The morning air covered him like a shroud—not cold, but enough to entice him to shiver.

The night had provided a fresh foot of wet snow, and without his gear his feet were soaked, as were his jeans. Thankfully, the temperature stayed above freezing. He determined that as long as he kept moving, he could ward off the chill.

I should have taken Padraic's gloves. He blew on his hands and rubbed them together as he passed the trail break that indicated there were four miles to go. The sun was high in the sky as he breached the wood line of the Talons' property and slid down the back side of the hill that led to their shed. An old metal rung sled hung on the outside wall. A closer look at it revealed a coat of rust forming on the rudders. *One sled, two boys. Work it out*, Joseph Talons would say when they requested he make another.

"Thought you rode the machine out?" Joseph walked around the far side of the shed.

"I felt like walking back." Caleb shrugged, pulling his jacket around him.

"Go on inside and shower up; there are clothes in your room. Sarah probably saw you coming. She'll have something hot on the table before you're through." Joseph swept him into a bear hug and led him through the kitchen door.

"The audacity of all of you! There isn't a one of you boys who are house trained! Get them boots off! Look at my kitchen! Look at you, boy! Stopped eating a week ago, no doubt! Get upstairs with yourself!" Sarah stopped them as they entered the kitchen and claimed their boots and jackets.

Caleb climbed the stairs. This was the only home he really knew. It was the place that cared if he was cold, hungry, sad or elated. His own home had been shattered by drug use. Both his parents were users—nothing mattered more to them then getting their next fix.

When there's one, there are two. Sarah's voice tickled his ears as he turned on the shower. It was true. He and Padraic were considered a matched set after the incident with Brileigh and Brody.

Gregg lobbied to send Padraic to detention; Carrie countered with a request of her own—go back to Africa and mind your own business. Caleb heard himself laugh out loud in the shower. The father and daughter wore the same expression on their faces—neither would be moved. Padraic went to detention. Gregg won the battle of wills, but it cost him the love and respect of his daughter.

Caleb dried his hair with a fresh towel he found hanging in the bathroom. No doubt Sarah had anticipated his homecoming today. On the king-sized mahogany bed that he and Padraic had shared many nights were an old set of blue jeans and a hunting shirt that he hadn't seen in quite a while. He lifted the shirt off the bed, and beneath it were socks, underwear, a razor and a toothbrush. *Padraic got a good deal coming to the Talons'.* Caleb dressed quickly and brought his things back to the bathroom to shave and brush his teeth.

Sarah was a natural mother, but never blessed with children of her own. Caleb threw his dirty clothes in the hamper and looked at the picture of himself and Padraic that stood alone on the vanity. They were fourteen. He could make out the markers of the summer camp behind them. It was taken just before they left. He tapped the picture absentmindedly.

He never hated his parents the way Carrie despised her father. Maybe it was better never to have something than to be in constant yearning for it.

Caleb met Joseph at the foot of the stairs.

"Just coming to get you. Food's on the table. Come eat, and then I'll give you a ride to your truck." Joseph's strong hand landed firmly in the center of Caleb's back, drawing him toward the kitchen.

Sarah Talons' talent in the kitchen never ceased to amaze him. Buttered, homemade yeast rolls lay in a wicker basket in the middle of the table. If that wasn't enough to tempt his senses, steaming corn chowder stood at the ready in an old clay pot with a matching ladle. Caleb inhaled the aroma of garlic and warm cream. He didn't need to taste it to know how good it was. Toasted corned beef sandwiches with dripping provolone were placed in front of him as he took his seat at the table.

Joseph said the blessing, and then Sarah immediately stood and filled their plates.

"Do you have a plan?" Sarah grabbed Caleb's roll off his plate and split and buttered it before he could respond.

"I think I'll start with the soup." He grinned as she slammed the roll back in his hand.

"Me, too," Joseph chided.

"That's not what I meant. You keep quiet." She pointed the butter knife at Joseph. "Look at the ring on your hand. What does that mean?" She laid the knife down and grabbed Caleb's hand, forcing him to look at the ring.

"We're trying to figure that out."

"You should have done that before the rings were exchanged." Sarah buttered a roll for her husband.

"I know." Caleb savored the sweetness of the yeast roll as it melted in his mouth. "I really just want to get Carrie and leave."

"You're supposed to start that job next month." Joseph wiped his mouth, then lowered his napkin to the table. "You taking her along?"

"I want to. I'm just not so sure she'll want to." Caleb lifted his glass of milk.

"She'll be alone more than not. You'll be in the field all the time," Sarah interrupted.

"We knew that before vows were exchanged." Caleb had finished half his sandwich before he answered.

"True enough," Joseph stated before Sarah could respond. "I have a buddy who owns a year-round camp in Jackson Hole. Would you be interested in staying there at least until you can find something?"

"That might work." Caleb finished his soup and started in on the other half of his sandwich.

"I'll give him a call. It's off season so it shouldn't be a problem. Maybe you and Carrie should take a drive over the weekend. See what you think of the area."

"Acclimate?" He set his sandwich down and finished his milk.

"It's a three-year commitment, isn't it?" Joseph finished his bread and soup, wiped his mouth and placed his napkin on the table.

"It is," Caleb confirmed.

"Renting or buying?" Joseph pushed away from the table and returned with two mugs of coffee.

"I can't afford to buy anything right now," he answered.

"What are you going to do with Carrie's estate?" It was a

question he hadn't even considered until this point.

The house had been Carrie's grandparents, then inherited by Helen. Her parents' vehicles remained untouched in the driveway. He really did need to take care of a lot of business before they could restart in Jackson Hole. He hadn't filed the insurance claims, or even paid for Gregg's funeral. There was no shortage of things that needed to be done.

"Caleb?" He jumped, feeling Joseph's strong grip on his arm.

"I'm sorry. I guess I hadn't thought about the estate." Caleb glanced at his watch and then cleared his dishes.

"Padraic bought tickets to the hockey game tonight. Told us not to hold dinner; he'd be eating in the city." Joseph cleared his plate and grabbed his keys and jacket.

"He told you that?" Caleb chewed the inside of his lip and pondered the invitation.

"He did. He also said Carrie's cast came off today, the one on the right side." Joseph Talons passed the information along just as he knew his son intended him to.

"Has it been six weeks already?" Caleb followed him out to the truck.

"Give or take." Joseph started the engine then buckled his seat belt. "You haven't seen him on trail anywhere?"

"No." Caleb shook his head. "I wasn't looking though."

"I thought maybe he'd stopped in and checked on you."

"He probably did, but you know him—if he didn't want me to know he was there..." Caleb rubbed his eyes as the truck plowed through the slushy roads.

"That'd be my boy." The truck became quiet for a moment, and then Joseph asked, "Have you talked to either of them?"

"Earlier last week Carrie answered Padraic's cell phone.

From the sound of her voice, I honestly don't know what's going to happen."

"She must be missing you." Joseph stopped as a herd of does passed in front of them. "He wouldn't have told you how to find her otherwise."

"True enough." Caleb scratched his head, seeing his truck cleaned off and ready to roll outside his apartment.

"Have you spoken with Padraic?" Grandad's voice acquired a sullen tone.

"No, not since I left for the cabin." Caleb chewed the inside of his cheek uncertain at the somberness of Grandad's voice.

"Something about him, is laying heavy on my heart these days and I can't quite grasp it."

"He's been through a lot as well these last few weeks." Caleb sighed as they pulled into the parking lot of his apartment building.

"It feels like more than that. Do me a favor and make sure you listen to him. He needs to know we care about him." Grandad shifted his truck to a stop.

"I will." Caleb opened the door and slid from his seat."Caleb." Joseph opened the glove box and handed him his wallet and keys. "Charge your cell phone."

"Thanks, Granddad."

"Game starts at seven," Joseph stated as Caleb slammed the door.

Caleb looked at his watch as Joseph Talons drove away. Unlocking his truck, he plugged in his cell phone and noticed the pile of mail covering his passenger's seat. *I need to pay my bills. Lord, I need to pay Carrie's bills. I don't even have a job right now.* He sifted through the pile, and then tossed it into the back seat, unable to process it all. *Give me strength.*

Do I even have enough gas to get to the city tonight? He turned on the engine and watched his gas gauge stop on the full line. Padraic had gassed up his truck, *probably changed the oil and…yes, he did.* Caleb tapped the sticker in the corner of his windshield, indicating the last date of service.

Why had he not noticed all the little things? Why hadn't he appreciated Padraic for the great person he was, rather than always looking for the wrongs in him? No one had a good word to say about Padraic, but that's because he was surreptitious with his kindness. *I just have never chosen to see it, Lord. I want to see it. Lord, I want to love him the way he loves me. I don't want to be envious or jealous. Make me a better friend to him.*

Caleb pulled into the parking lot at his workplace. He closed his eyes, whispering a prayer of thanks and requesting strength as he went to his work station. Brileigh was alone going over some files.

"You're leaving, too?" Brileigh stood and offered him a firm handshake.

"This place looks deserted." Caleb noticed that all of Reyn's things were gone.

"Reyn enlisted in the Coast Guard, left this morning. I've been trying to reach you. He wanted to see you before he left for basic." Brileigh tapped the back of Reyn's empty chair.

"It's the right move for him." Caleb emptied his desk.

"When do you start at the other place?" Brileigh grabbed the inventory sheets and signed off on Caleb's equipment.

"Second week of January." He took his ID card from his wallet and handed it to Brileigh, then signed the paperwork. "I hate leaving here."

"You'll be back," Brileigh clapped his shoulder and crossed the room to file the paperwork. "Once you two start having kids, you'll come home, settle down, and become the *Leave it to Beaver* couple."

"True enough." Caleb relished the thought.

It probably was more true than not. Colter Bay was his home and Carrie's, too. He didn't really want to leave, but it was time for them to go.

"Are you going to rent out Carrie's house?" Brileigh came back to the work station and watched as Caleb tossed a slew of papers in the trash.

"I don't know—that's probably not a bad idea. Why? Are you looking for a place?"

"I am." Brileigh folded his arms across his chest. "Jerica's due in less than two months. Matty will be three this fall. Putting him in with the new baby's not really ideal."

"Jerica was one of Carrie's nurses. She looks like she's going to have that baby any time now."

"There's no doubt in my mind that girl is definitely thirty-two weeks."

"And it's definitely yours." Caleb stated conclusively.

"Matty is my son. The state did a paternity test before they placed him in my custody." Brileigh stiffened.

Caleb bit his tongue too late.

There weren't many people who knew Brileigh's secret, and even fewer who would care. Marissa, his ex-wife, signed their son over to him the day Matty was born. She was taken to prison, and supposedly no one had heard from her since. Matty was a little replica of his father, who just happened to be Brileigh's identical twin brother, Brody.

"About the house." Brileigh stepped away from the confrontation.

"I think Carrie would be okay with it. I'll talk to her and give you a call tomorrow."

"Thanks." Brileigh walked him to the door.

Caleb surveyed his vacated work space, shook Brileigh's hand and then grabbed his stuff, heading for his truck.

It would take him at least an hour to get to the city. He knew exactly where they would be. He knew what parking garage, even what space Padraic would be in. Sure enough, as he entered the second floor of the garage, there was Padraic's truck facing out of space 218. Caleb pulled in beside him. He slid out from behind the wheel and walked to the elevator. Two blocks from the garage was the stadium, but a block in the opposite direction was the Spaghetti Factory. Going to the city without stopping at the Spaghetti Factory was like going to church without your Bible. *I know where they're sitting, even what they've ordered.* He trudged downtown, realizing that a tender snow had started falling.

"She's very happy tonight. Don't ruin it." Padraic met him as he tried to open the door.

"Does she know I'm here?"

"I ordered bruschetta." Padraic tucked two tickets into Caleb's jacket pocket and walked away.

The warmth and aroma of tomato and oregano accosted his senses as he entered the restaurant. Carrie sat in her usual seat. She lifted her eyes in his direction, a slight grin welcomed him closer. For a moment, he couldn't breathe. *She's too beautiful, too perfect to be mine.* She wore her Cowboys jersey too well, and he realized he was staring as he sat down beside her.

"I knew you were coming. Padraic hates bruschetta, says it tastes like dirt." She averted her eyes as he took her hand in his.

"He just doesn't know what's good for him." He released her hand as the waitress brought their food. "I've missed you."

She tried to meet his eyes but lowered her glance toward her meal. "Smells delicious, I'm starving. Aren't you?"

"Not so much. I hiked out today, and Mrs. Talons greeted me with a feast fit for a king." He picked up his fork and looked over his entree. "It does smell great though."

"Is Padraic coming back?" She pushed her food around her plate with her fork, indulging in a few bites here and there.

"I don't think so. He gave me his tickets and walked out the door."

"Did he say where he was going? What he was doing?" She grabbed her cell phone and started texting.

"Carrie, stop." He placed his hand over her phone. "Please leave him alone. It was hard enough for him to walk away. He doesn't need you texting him right now."

"He shouldn't be alone. You don't understand. We need to find him." She pulled her hand out from under his and sent the text. "Call him."

"Carrie?"

"If you love him, call him now." Tears brimmed in her fluorescent eyes as she pushed her plate aside.

"You're serious?" He sat back, reluctantly took his phone out and hit speed dial; no answer. "It just went to voicemail."

"Did he say he'd see you at the game? Or tomorrow, anything like that at all?" She summoned the waitress for the check.

"What's wrong?" He helped her with her jacket as she prepared to leave.

"Your tab has already been paid. Would you like me to box this up for you?" The waitress cleared their plates and met them at the door with their to-go boxes.

"Carrie, please. You're acting like this is a matter of life and death." He stopped her wheelchair in front of the parking garage elevator.

"It is." Her breath escaped her lungs as she reached for the button.

Caleb followed her into the elevator, trying to piece together her concern. "Is someone trying to hurt him? Does this have to do with your father's case? I don't understand what's going on right now."

"He's cut himself off. Don't you see it?" She tried his phone again, biting her lip at the sound of his voicemail. "He broke up with Gail, cut his ties with the school, made sure you were ready to take care of me. Why won't he answer? He always answers me." She texted again as he buckled her into her seat.

"Do you think he's suicidal?" The thought struck him hard as he got behind the wheel.

"I didn't ask." She was texting again. "I don't know. I just don't know!"

"Calm down, don't panic." He pulled the truck out onto the highway and headed for Colter Bay. "I'll find him."

Chapter 24

Caleb dropped Carrie with the Talons. In earnest prayer, he drove to the old Shaw barn. Padraic's truck was parked on the far side, barely visible from the driveway. He laid his hand on the hood. The engine ticked and still held a hint of warmth. Caleb grabbed his gear and followed the moonlit path.

The slope was slick with ice forming by the moment. The day's melt crystallized as the night settled with a new layer of precipitation. He pressed further, focusing on the journey rather than the sentiment.

The cabin was dark and vacant, as far as he could tell. He pushed open the door and was met with nothing but a rush of air.

"Padraic!" He turned toward the door and stood on the threshold. His voice rebounded from the rocky slopes, "Answer me!" He dropped his gear, grabbed his flashlight and searched the lean-to. "Padraic!"

"What are you doing here?" Padraic gripped his forearm as he started to slide down the North Slope.

Caleb caught his breath and secured his footing. "You're not answering your phone."

"And that surprises you?" Padraic led him back to the cabin.

"You didn't answer Carrie." Caleb closed the door behind him and watched Padraic light the lanterns and focus on the stove.

"I really thought the two of you would have other things to do tonight, rather than follow me around." He lit the stove and opened the flue.

"Carrie seems to think you need to be followed." Caleb sat at the table and watched as Padraic kept himself busy. "Is she right?"

"I can take care of myself." Padraic set a kettle on to boil and poured instant coffee into two mugs.

Caleb watched him as he unrolled his sleeping bag and tossed it on the floor beside the stove. "Carrie's afraid you may be having suicidal thoughts, and quite honestly, so am I."

"I'm not suicidal." Padraic tested the water and poured coffee for both of them before settling on the floor.

"Would you tell me if you were?" Caleb accepted his coffee and moved to the floor beside the stove.

"I'm not saying the thoughts never cross my mind. I recognize them for what they are and dismiss them," Padraic answered after a long hesitation.

"You're impulsive Padraic, so even the thought crossing your mind is concerning." Caleb set his mug on the floor and watched Padraic retreat inside himself. *Lord, help me draw him out.* "Do you have a plan?"

"A plan for what?" Padraic stirred the fire and added another log.

"For when the thoughts overcome your reason. The enemy is stronger than you are. And I sense you are going into this battle alone." Caleb extended his legs, stretching his calves.

"I thought I was never alone." He closed the stove and met Caleb's stare.

"We're provided with the resources to overcome all

temptations that we face. Using those resources is a choice." Caleb drew in his legs and looked down at the floor. "Several opportunities were afforded to me to remain chaste with Carrie. I chose to ignore them. Every step I took away from what I've been taught was a deliberate decision on my part. The further away I got, the harder it was to find my way back. The wrong answer became the right answer, and look where it got me. I don't want this to happen to you."

Padraic sighed into his cup, and then finished off the lukewarm liquid. Caleb took both mugs and placed them on the table. Silence overtook them, the lantern flickering in the darkness. The stove warded off the definite chill as the wind howled against the cabin.

"What are your plans for Carrie now?" Padraic settled back on his sleeping bag placing his hands behind his head.

"We really didn't have a chance to talk about anything. She nearly had a panic attack when you didn't come back to the table."

"Is she with Grandmother now?" Padraic closed his eyes.

"Yes."

For the longest moment, there was nothing but silence. Caleb wrestled his way to his feet and realized Padraic was asleep. He breathed a sigh of relief and decided to step outside. *Maybe the chill will revive my senses and give me some sort of direction.* He wandered toward the north face, following Padraic's footprints to the ledge. The moonlight reflected off what he thought was an ice formation at first glance. He placed his hand upon the smooth surface, retracting his touch at the sharp sting of jagged glass. The mass stood almost as high as his waist; from what he could tell it was shattered clear glass, maybe a windshield? His foot kicked against a bottle that tipped over, spilling some of its contents into the snow. He lifted it and brushed the snow off the label.

Whiskey? That can't be what all this is. He sniffed the top of the bottle and lifted a finger to his lips, verifying what he'd discovered. There is no way he drank all of this himself. Caleb brushed the snow from the broken glass structure. Only the bottle in his hand remained intact; everything else lay frozen in its fragmented state. This was over time, but this... he lifted the bottle and saw that two thirds of its contents had been consumed...maybe. Caleb inhaled the frigid air.

Can he really consume that much alcohol and still do the things he was doing? He lit the stove, made coffee, held a conversation. Wouldn't I have noticed? He didn't stumble, he didn't slur his words...He's normal, beyond normal. He's calm, approachable...oh my word, he's asleep.

Caleb turned his eyes back to the cabin. Never before had Padraic fallen asleep in front of him. He brought the bottle to the cabin and set it down on the table.

A deerskin-covered Bible lay open to the book of Isaiah. A quick scan of the page showed him it was not in English, nor were the notes in the margins. *What's going on with him?*

Caleb sat on the army cot, folded his hands and bowed his head. *Lord, I am at Your feet.*

"Let's go." Padraic laid a heavy hand on his shoulder, shaking him awake. "Sun's almost up."

Caleb placed his feet on the floor. *When did I take off my boots?* He looked around the room. The wood box was filled, the shelves restocked, the stove emptied and clean. Every utensil, cup, and plate were washed and stacked with exact precision and neatness. *How did I not hear him?*

Caleb pulled on his socks and grabbed his boots. He lifted his eyes to the table. The Bible and the bottle were gone.

He tied his boots, grabbed his coat and gear, and slammed the door behind him.

"Did you make the bed?" Caleb nearly jumped out of his skin as Padraic came up behind him.

"I forgot." He caught his breath as his feet sank in a fresh six inches of snow.

"I got it." Padraic dropped his gear and re-entered the cabin.

Caleb waited, adjusting to the dawn and the sudden chill. His breath crystallized upon expiration. It wasn't more than a few minutes before Padraic secured the door and grabbed his gear.

"Are you drinking?" Caleb remained still as Padraic started toward the trail.

"Not at the moment." Padraic faced him, startling Caleb with direct eye contact.

"You know what I mean."

"Caleb, I refilled the flask in my aide pack as well as the one in the cabin. Would you like to verify?" Padraic stepped toward him, tearing the flask from the corner pocket.

"I'm sorry." Caleb averted his eyes, pushing the offer away.

"It's okay. I do drink, but I'm not irresponsible about it." Padraic put the flask away. "I wouldn't have even cracked that bottle if I had known you were coming. I was planning to finish it until you showed up."

"On the North Slope at night, as slick as it was, you would have drunk a fifth of whiskey?" Caleb followed him through the snow.

"I would have slept better and longer if I had." Padraic waited at the bottom of the culvert, monitoring Caleb's progress.

"That's called self-medicating." Caleb steadied his footing and continued to follow.

"Call it what you want. I don't care."

"I care." Caleb grabbed his arm, forcing him to turn around. "I'm on belay here, and I need to know when you're in trouble."

"I'm okay." Padraic freed himself and stepped away from Caleb. "I promise, if I thought I needed help, you'd be the first person I'd call."

"In all things Padraic, I'm holding you to that promise."

"I'm sure you will." Padraic glanced up at the rising sun, then headed down the trail again.

They loaded their gear and cleaned off their trucks. *Do I just let him leave*? Caleb approached his window.

"Carrie wants to see you."

"I'll text her. I'm on call for the weekend. I'll stop by your apartment on Tuesday."

"I'll tell Carrie you'll see her on Tuesday after work. If anything changes you'll call us and let us know?" Caleb placed his hand on Padraic's shoulder.

"I will."

Caleb stepped away from the vehicle as Padraic shifted into gear, rolled up the window and pulled out onto the road. Caleb walked toward his truck, uncertain of all that had transpired. *Am I doing the right thing by him? Can I trust him? I have to trust him. He needs me to trust him.*

Chapter 25

Carrie lay in a restless sleep, tucked safely into the mahogany bed in the upstairs room of the Talons' home. Caleb sat on the edge watching. Her golden hair contributed to a paleness he hadn't recognized earlier. He placed his hand gingerly against her exposed calf, surprised at the heat it exuded. Her face grimaced. She opened her eyes and moved her leg away from his touch.

"Does it hurt?" He laid his hand on the bed, allowing her to establish the boundaries.

"Did you find him?" She sat up and tucked her curls behind her ears.

"He's having a tough time right now. But he's okay. He said he'll text you later. He's on his way to work."

"Thank you for checking on him." She lowered her chin.

"Thank you for noticing. He's my best friend, and I never saw it coming." He lifted her chin and looked at her hand. "You took off your ring."

"I did." She withdrew her hand from his and looked at her fingers.

"I'm sorry for everything I put you through. Will you ever forgive me?" He slumped under the weight of his shoulders.

"I'm in love with you, Caleb. I have been for as long as I can remember. But I'm willing to wait until you love me, the way God intended you to."

"Thank you." He could not resist taking her into his arms.

Burying his face in her hair, he hid his tears.

She slid the ring off his finger and placed it in the palm of his hand. "This belongs to Padraic. Please return it to him."

"I will." He closed his fist around the band. "Carrie, I didn't do it. I didn't annul our vows." His voice trembled as she met his stare.

"I'm annulling them." She placed her hands over his closed fist. "Just between us, no one else needs to be involved. When you're ready, I'll wear your ring."

"There's a lot going on."

"I know." She winced and started coughing. "Padraic told me."

"Are you catching a cold?" He grabbed some tissues from the vanity and handed them to her.

"Probably pneumonia with my luck." She accepted the tissues and wiped her eyes.

"Do you want me to pick up some cough medicine later?"

"That probably wouldn't be a bad idea." She settled against him.

Caleb closed his eyes, trying to turn off his desire to touch her. "I can't be this close to you." He broke his embrace and separated himself from her. "Carrie, I have to leave. I want you to come with me. Move to Jackson Hole with me."

"You'll be the best ranger in Wyoming." She looked up at him with a shy smile.

"You'll come?" He knelt in front of her.

"No." She shook her head placing a warm hand against his face. "You need to go first. Prepare a place for me, both out there and in here." She tapped his chest.

"Carrie." He bowed his head as she drew him into her arms.

"By giving me your name, you've provided me with a

shield of safety. There isn't anyone else who knows I have it. These people, this company—they'll watch you walk away and fulfill your dream to be a ranger. They'll think you've forgotten all about them, and they'll do the same about you.

"I'm going to stay right here with Mr. and Mrs. Talons, graduate, and wait."

"You're going back to school?" He sat up beside her on the bed.

"I never left. I was signed up for a satellite program in the hospital. I'm all signed in as Carrie Cohen. I should graduate right on schedule." Her cough returned.

He slumped back against the headboard and toyed with the ring in his hand.

"I want you to do this. I would be in your way right now. I don't want you to resent me or our relationship."

"I don't resent..." Caleb interrupted.

"Please, don't make this harder than it already is for me." She grabbed the bars around her left leg and moved the entire contraption to the side of the bed.

"I thought you'd come with me." He dropped his legs over the side of the bed. "I'm at a loss right now. I don't know what to say or what to do."

"You could help me downstairs and join us for breakfast."

He scooped her up in his arms and carried her to the wheelchair waiting in the foyer.

"You found my son, I trust?" Joseph slapped him on the shoulder as he settled Carrie in her chair.

"He's at work, on call for the next few days. He says he'll check in as soon as he can get a minute." Caleb pushed Carrie toward the kitchen, where Sarah Talons had already prepared pancakes and bacon.

"There's nothing like the aroma of maple bacon in the morning." Joseph grabbed his wife's waist and nuzzled her neck.

She slapped his hand as he stole a piece of bacon and popped it in his mouth. "To the table with you already. Is Padraic coming?"

"He's working," Caleb answered, sitting beside Carrie.

"All that boy ever does is work. I wish he'd find a greater purpose," Sarah huffed as she set a platter of pancakes on the table.

"So does he." Joseph filled his plate then reached for Caleb's hand to say grace.

After the dishes were cleared and washed, Caleb brought Carrie to the front room and settled her on the couch beside the fireplace. He covered her with the afghan that was draped over the back of the couch. Her cough concerned him.

"Maybe you should see a doctor. The cough doesn't seem to be getting better."

"I'm fine. I don't feel sick. My legs ache, but that's not unusual."

"Do you want your pain medication? Or some aspirin or something? I'm supposed to give you a shot, right?"

"I'll take the aspirin. All that other medication just makes me sleepy. I don't need anything else." He handed her the remote and went to the kitchen to get her a glass of water.

When he returned, the story of the Ross twins was replaying on the screen. He handed her the glass of water and pills, then folded the wheelchair and stashed it behind the couch.

"Do you think they'll find them?" Carrie's eyes met his.

"I pray they do." He leaned in, leaving a kiss on her cheek. "I'm going to go get you some cold medicine. Do you want anything else while I'm out?"

She shook her head and turned her attention toward the television. Caleb grabbed his coat and checked his pocket for his keys. Sarah followed him to the door, handing him his phone.

"Bring back some milk," she instructed as he kissed her cheek and headed for his truck.

"Anything else?" He opened his truck door and hesitated before climbing in.

"That's all." She waved, then crossed her arms in front of her chest, shivering in the crisp morning air.

It would be mid-afternoon before he could return. He had phone calls to make and his apartment to clean, and he had to pack his things. Christmas music bombarded him from all directions, every radio station, every store. Christmas? He had pretty much forgotten they had entered mid-December. Carrie would turn seventeen on the twenty-first.

"What did she name the baby?" He regretted having to call and ask Padraic the information. He had chosen to buy her a mother's ring with the baby's name engraved on the inside and her tiny birthstone embedded in white gold.

"Rebecca," Padraic's voice revealed his fatigue. "Is everything all right?"

"I called Verchante Distributors back this morning and accepted a settlement. Hopefully, that will end everything for everyone."

"What about the twins?" Padraic asked.

"I'm trusting God. I've prayed about this, and I really believe this is what He wants me to do." Caleb turned off his radio. "Have you contacted Carrie?" He stopped at the jewelry counter and placed his order.

"Yes, she says she's developed a cold."

"And a nasty cough. I'm bringing her some cough medicine now," replied Caleb.

"Don't forget to give her the other medicines as well. Stay ahead of her pain, because if it gets out of control, it's going to be hard to catch it."

"You really should rethink this doctor thing. You'd make a good one." Caleb breathed in a deep sigh as he headed back toward the Talons' home.

"Not you, too," Padraic chuckled. "I gotta go."

Carrie was asleep on the couch when he came through the door. Sarah shushed him and motioned him to the kitchen. The savory smell of beef and herbs reminded him that he had skipped lunch. He breathed in the unmistakable scent of homemade biscuits and felt his stomach growl.

"Move her things into the den. There's no point in her having to manage those stairs just now."

Sarah had turned the den into a bedroom. Joseph was busy in the downstairs bathroom installing a bench in the shower.

"Thank you for taking care of her."

"Caleb," Sarah patted his cheek as he kissed her. "I harassed God for years to give me children, and I nearly missed the three he placed in my quiver."

"I love you, Grandmother."

"I love you, too. Now run upstairs and get the down quilt off the bed in the second bedroom. It can get cool in here at night, and our girl is already coughing."

Caleb decided to stay close to home, rather than go check out the cabin in Jackson Hole. The cough medicine seemed to have little effect on Carrie's cold, and Sarah called a friend from church that was able to get her an appointment at the local clinic on Monday. Caleb called Brileigh and had him come over to sort through Carrie's house.

"We're going to have to put all this stuff in storage if you don't use it." Caleb finished tossing Carrie's things into the back of his truck.

"I can't guarantee we won't mess something up. I have kids." Brileigh chewed his lip.

"I'm not worried about it, nor should you be. It's yours if you want it. If you want something moved, you'll have to call Padraic."

"I'll do it myself." Brileigh smiled, accepting the keys. "Thanks, I really do appreciate this."

"It helps us out, too. Funny how God works sometimes, isn't it?" Caleb slammed a heavy hand down on Brileigh's bad shoulder.

"Yeah, I guess it is." Brileigh removed Caleb's hand with a playful shove and straightened his shoulders. "Tell Carrie thank you for us."

"I will." Caleb checked his watch and headed for his truck.

In the darkest hours of Monday morning, the mournful sound of sleet and wind peppered the Talons' house to no avail. Caleb sat up, placing his feet on the hardwood floor. Sweat poured from his body as he tried to regain his breath. It was the dream again. Every time he had it, it seemed that he'd have to run further in order to grab the belay line. This time, he barely had time to snatch it and pull it taut before Padraic withdrew his knife.

I need Your help, Lord. Help me keep him engaged in my life. Bar me from isolating him. Grant him direction and purpose so that he feels, believes, and realizes his true worth in Your eyes, as well as ours.

Headlights drew him toward the window. Padraic's truck pulled into the driveway. Caleb grabbed his clothes off the floor, dressed and met him in the foyer.

"You don't want to be out there if you don't have to be." Padraic kept his voice barely above a whisper.

"Carrie has a doctor's appointment at nine." Caleb stood at the base of the stairs as Padraic placed his boots meticulously by the door and hung his coat on the drying rack.

"She still has that cold?" Padraic grabbed a towel from the hall closet and dried his hands and face.

"Regardless of how much medicine she takes, her cough doesn't seem to be improving."

Padraic stopped and met Caleb's stare with a look that pierced his being.

"Is it a cold or a cough?"

"Same difference." Caleb received the damp towel from Padraic.

"No, it's not. Does she have a fever?"

"Not really. It's been between ninety-eight and a hundred and one. She's been in bed most of the weekend, says she feels achy and it hurts to move. She doesn't want to take her pain medication because it makes her sleepy, so I've been giving her…"

Padraic turned from their conversation, "Where is she?"

"In the den."

Padraic crossed the living room and made a beeline for Carrie's bedside. Blood-tinged tissues lay on the nightstand as she reached a cyanotic hand in his direction.

"Call 911." He placed his fingers on a throbbing vein in her neck. "Granddad! I need one of your heparin shots now. Call 911! This is a pulmonary embolism, not a cough."

Joseph and Sarah Talons came in, Sarah carrying the

necessary syringe. Padraic grabbed the needle. "Granddad, I need your CPAP machine."

Joseph pushed past Caleb as Sarah turned on the lights. Caleb tried to answer the 911 operator's questions as quickly as possible.

"I need a heparin drip and a vent. Send me the closest EMT they have. I can do the rest if I have the equipment."

"The interstate is closed. No medevacs right now. The weather…"

"Get the medical rack at the ranger station. I need an IV. I want the red box. Granddad, bring me all your heparin. I need to make a drip. We'll need to sustain here her until the weather breaks. Grandmother, get Mercy ER on the phone. I need someone to talk me through this."

"The lines are down," were the last words Caleb heard as he tossed his cell phone to her and headed out the door.

Chapter 26

Twenty minutes may as well have been two years. It was taking Caleb forever to return with the supplies he needed. Padraic adjusted the settings for the CPAP and secured a face mask in place of the nasal cannula his granddad wore. The combined effect of oxygen and blood thinners seemed to be working, restoring color to her face and torso.

"I've got to do something about her pain." He grabbed the bottle of aspirin from the bedside. "Caleb has been giving her aspirin?"

"She says the other medications make her too sleepy." Sarah accepted the bottle as he thrust it toward her.

"Thank God he did. It's probably what's kept her alive all weekend." He lifted his head as Caleb and Brileigh burst through the door with the supplies.

"Check the box for Altepase." Padraic started the IV and handed the bag to his grandfather. "Hold it up. Caleb put a nail in that wall to sustain the IV. Brileigh set up the EKG." Padraic seized the Altepase and realized suddenly that he had no orders to follow, and nothing look at to tell him this was the right decision, the right dose.

"Were you able to get the ER?"

"It's the doctor on call. He says he'll help us."

Padraic accepted the phone and rattled off Carrie's condition, vital signs and medications administered, giving a full report before he stopped to breathe.

"I have Altepase, but I'm not sure if I should use it."

"Is it indicated?" The man's voice plagued him with familiarity.

"I don't know. I'm not skilled or trained well enough to be making life and death decisions."

"You are not trained, but you do possess the skills to keep her alive. Look at your patient. Are the treatments rendered effective, or are more needed?"

Padraic drew in a deep breath, stood back and looked at Carrie. Her IV fluids were infusing; the heart monitor chirped in a perfect sinus rhythm. She lay quietly awake, awaiting his next move.

"I trust you, Padraic," the voice over the phone and Carrie stated simultaneously.

"We'll wait." Padraic set the vial aside. "I just gave her heparin, and she's been taking aspirin. We don't want to instigate instability."

"That's a fair assessment." Padraic set the phone on the table, letting everyone know the line was dead.

"I'll get breakfast." Sarah interrupted the sudden hush.

"I'll help." Brileigh followed her out of the room.

"I better go tend the woodstove." Joseph made his way out as well.

Caleb placed a gentle hand on Padraic's shoulder and took the phone from the bedside table. "Are you okay?"

Padraic caught his breath and reviewed the situation in his mind. Nothing more could be done. They would have to wait and see if the therapies they'd initiated would be effective. Fatigue engulfed his whole being. He bowed his head, defeated.

"We have to wait." Padraic sighed.

"You did a great job."

"Shut up." He'd had enough. "I should have foreseen this

and prevented it from occurring."

"You're not a doctor." Carrie reached her hands out to both of them.

Padraic knelt beside her. "All the risk factors were there. How could I let this happen to you?"

"Padraic, you are no more responsible for my blood clots than you were for my mother's cancer. These hands," she focused on him, taking both his hands in hers. "These hands are special. Look at you two." She drew Caleb down beside her. "Just like Caleb will make the finest ranger in Wyoming, you would be the most gifted surgeon in the northwest."

"Surgeon?" Padraic shook his head.

"Surgeon, doctor, whatever it is you medical people do in the ER." Carrie smiled as he moved away from her bedside.

Caleb tucked her in and dimmed the lights. "I'll stay with her." He turned to Padraic. "You probably need to get some rest."

"I'm okay," he answered after a slight hesitation.

"I didn't know." Caleb chewed his bottom lip, dropping his stare to the floor. "I didn't know that you felt a responsibility toward Helen's death."

Padraic backed away, not wanting to face the history behind his pain. "I need a shower and a nap. Wake me if anything changes."

Caleb nodded and returned to Carrie.

Upstairs, Padraic turned on the shower, thankful for the momentary solace that it offered. He closed his eyes, seeking much-needed rest.

When Padraic awoke, the house was dark. The storm hadn't let up. If anything, it had worsened. He wiped his face with his hands and ran downstairs.

A game of Monopoly was unfolding in the living room by the fire. The door to the den lay open, and it looked like Carrie was sleeping. An oil lamp dimly lit the corner of the room.

"Power's out." Caleb lifted his eyes from the game momentarily.

"Brileigh go home?" Padraic crossed the room and gathered the monitor strip.

"All the commotion here got him worrying about Jerica and Matty." Caleb moved his piece around the board and drew a card.

"Carrie has been okay?" He stood on the threshold between the rooms.

"I would have awakened you if she wasn't." Caleb counted out some Monopoly money and handed it to Granddad.

"I guess it wasn't as bad as I thought." He accepted the coffee that his grandmother brought him and allowed himself to be led toward the couch.

"You recognized it for what it was, treated it, and prevented it from escalating into a fatal situation. No one else could see what you saw or do what you did. You've got a glimpse of God in your eyes, and His grace in your fingers. It's up to you what you do with it." Caleb put down his cards and offered Padraic his full attention.

"It's not a blessing." Padraic settled back on the couch, breathing in the aroma of strong Colombian coffee.

"Not yet, but maybe once you develop it—figure out what you're supposed to do with it."

Joseph interrupted as he finished his turn. "The gifts you're given aren't usually meant to bless you. You'll be a blessing to someone else or to God, usually both."

Padraic sat forward, resting his elbows on his lap. "Carrie and I visited the medical school last week. She wouldn't let us leave until we completed all the interviews and filled out all the forms." He kept his stare at the edge of his coffee mug. "I'll be starting in January." He waited for someone to break the silence. "She even enrolled me in the Sioux language class."

"You're really going to do it?" Caleb pushed himself away from the game.

Padraic shrugged his answer.

"What about Gail?"

Padraic lifted his eyes toward Caleb and shrugged again, "She told me not to call her until I've completed my first year."

"That's a good plan," Grandmother spoke, keeping her attention on the beading in her lap. "You'll need to stay focused on what you're doing."

"Maybe." Padraic stood and stretched.

Dawn struck hard. Caleb paced at Carrie's bedside as Padraic talked to the ER doctors on the cell phone. The roads were impassible, all flights were grounded, and Carrie's condition had begun to deteriorate. Padraic had started the Altepase drip, calculating and concentrating the exact drip rate.

Carrie's color had waned to a gray paleness. Even with the oxygen, her saturation rates remained in the eighties.

"What can I do?" Caleb knew that short of praying there was little else he could offer.

"We don't have the equipment to treat her effectively. We don't even have an IV pump. I'm titrating the rate, but God only knows if it's right."

"It's right. Show some faith."

"I have very little." Padraic checked for color and blood

refill in Carrie's feet.

"Very little is all that is required," Caleb stated under his breath and rested his hand on Padraic's shoulder. "God doesn't need you, Padraic. He chose you."

"Would you please stop? I don't want to hear this."

"That's because you're still beguiling the truth and embracing the lies of your youth. Regardless, God is going to use you. Your choice is either to act as a vessel or an obstacle." Caleb sat down, taking a long, hard look at Padraic. He had neglected him and, in doing so, placed much more than their friendship at stake.

"I don't think I want to be either right now."

"Doing nothing is a choice." Caleb sat up as Padraic let out a hearty laugh.

"I said those very same words to Reyn not too long ago. They must have come from you."

"Reyn left last week, enlisted in the Coast Guard." Caleb tried to contain his smirk as he read the surprised look on Padraic's face.

"Good. Maybe you'll finally get a decent partner." Padraic turned back toward the monitors.

"My paperwork came through. I've accepted the Ranger position in the National Park System. I'll be moving to Jackson Hole first of the year."

"Carrie?"

"She's asked me to go without her for now."

"How do you feel about that?"

"Honestly?" Caleb caught his eye. "I'm more concerned about your relationship with Christ than I am about mine with Carrie."

"My relationship with Christ is going through a lot of changes right now, but I think we'll be all right." Padraic pushed away from the bedside, pointing toward the obvious improvement in Carrie's color.

"Good changes? Bad changes?"

"I'll let you know." Padraic sighed and backed out of the room.

Carrie opened her eyes and squeezed his fingers lightly. He didn't deserve to be loved the way she loved him, he knew that. He moved closer to her bedside and brushed her cheek with his lips.

In the early afternoon, the television announced the lift on the roadway ban. Caleb looked out at the trees drooping heavily, some cracked from the weight of the oppressing ice. Everything glistened, radiating a false sense of harmony.

He and Padraic took the better part of the morning placing the studded chains on his tires. The road warden had deemed those chains illegal, but there wasn't a native of Colter Bay that didn't own at least one set.

Lord, I am going to miss him. Caleb turned away from the window and looked at Carrie.

"He loves you." She beckoned him to her bedside and insisted he help her sit up. "He has no trouble loving others, but he won't accept it. He believes he's unlovable."

He lifted her fingers to his lips and breathed a kiss upon them. "The enemy's lies are difficult to overcome."

"I think we're ready to move." Padraic opened the door as Caleb lowered her hand. "Do you want me to drive?"

"I'll drive. That way if she needs something, you'll be available." Padraic tossed his keys at Caleb, then slid three leather belts under Carrie's legs.

"We don't want your legs to move if we can help it." He wrapped a blanket around her legs and fastened the belts. "We don't know how many clots there are. Moving around may dislodge some, and we'll end up in a bad situation." He locked her IV and set the bag on her lap. "Take the red box just in case." He shot a glance in Caleb's direction, then lifted Carrie and headed out the door.

It was a long and tedious trip to the hospital. Caleb was glad he had opted to drive. Padraic's patience would have been tested to its limits. When they arrived, the radiologist was on standby with the phlebotomist in the emergency room.

"Scrub up, Talons. Now that you're back, you're not leaving." The charge nurse caught Padraic's attention as they released Carrie to the ER personnel.

"You want anesthesia or a nurse?" He whipped his ID badge from his pocket and grabbed his keys from Caleb.

"All of the above. Dawn is upstairs doing an epidural right now, and we have three pending OR cases. Everyone you see has been mandated since Monday. So if you take the OR cases now, Dawn can take a break. When you're finished, follow up in the ICU and see what needs to be done."

Padraic disappeared without so much as a goodbye. Caleb sat alone in the waiting room until the nurse led him to a room on the fourth floor. Carrie looked more alert and awake, although she had a plethora of monitors and tubing crossing all over her body.

"I'm okay," she stated as he put their stuff down in a chair and went to her bedside. "You guys did a great job of taking care of me."

He kissed her and pulled a chair up beside the bed, not letting go of her hand. "Padraic had to go back to work; otherwise, he would be here."

"I figured they'd snag him as soon as we walked in the door. That's okay; it just reinforces everything we've been telling him," said Carrie. "Now if we could just patch things between him and Gail."

"That relationship doesn't need encouragement." Caleb rubbed his eyes, caving toward the exhaustion that consumed him.

"How can you say that? He really cares about Gail. Anapaytoo. He doesn't speak Sioux for just anyone. Sometimes I don't think you really know him at all."

"He's not walking firmly in his faith right now as it is. Gail not being a Christian doesn't help." He dropped his guard, trapped by her beautiful smile.

"Well," she took his hand, "I guess that means we pray for them both."

Caleb placed a gentle kiss on her fingers, thanking God one more time for the blessings bestowed upon him.

DELIBERATE DISTANCE

Book Two

Colter Bay Series

Chapter One

Padraic ignored the incessant blinking light of his answering machine. Most likely it was Caleb reminding him of the rehearsal dinner tomorrow night. Caleb and Carrie had said their vows over a year ago opting to go to the court house, sign the papers and call themselves married. Why they would want to go back through all this pomp and circumstance, was beyond him.

He plugged in his cell phone and turned it off. *Let it charge, but leave me in peace.* He checked the refrigerator realizing that the long stretch of on-call nights had depleted his grocery supplies. He didn't feel like takeout. That would require interaction with people, not something he thought he could tolerate right now.

His first year of medical school had proved little more than annoying. He was able to at least test out of several of the classes and pre-req's based on his prior experience as an ICU nurse and his anesthetists training.

Mercy Hospital was more than willing to let him clock extra hours in their OR and emergency room especially since they were familiar and comfortable with his level of expertise.

He'd scrub in, circulate, or even provide them with anesthesia. He would serve in whatever role they wanted him to do, as long as he could count it as clinical time for school. In a year, he'd been able to count more clinical hours than most first year residents.

Work was good, at least it gave him purpose and a place to be. With Caleb serving as a forest ranger for the National Park System in Jackson Hole, and Carrie focused on preparing for the wedding, his role in their lives had become minuscule. *As it should. If I were marrying Carrie, I certainly wouldn't want Caleb underfoot.* Padraic sighed, that wasn't the total truth, but it was true enough.

He grabbed his Bible off the coffee table and thumbed through some references he'd heard on the radio. Nothing about this book came alive to him without Caleb's drive behind it.

He knew there was power in there; he'd experienced the cataclysmic events that could only be explained as the breath of God soaring through his body purifying the indignation of his soul.

He entered medical school and started the integration into the Sioux language and culture courses that his friends and family pushed for him to do. He could now read and interpret most of the Bible his Grandfather had given him last year.

The language came back to him like a warm fluid saturating his brain. Little memories tickled his mind whenever Sioux words crossed his tongue. It was likely he was immersed in his native tongue as a small child, though he had no recollection of his parents or life before moving in with the Talons when he was six.

"Akicito je miye." He felt her words caress the back of his neck as he obediently waited on the door step of an old farm house outside of a town more than a car days drive from his home on the reservation.

"Ina," the word slipped off his tongue.

Padraic sat up. He didn't need or want that memory. *Forgive you?* He grabbed a bottle of whiskey that he kept tucked away for just such occasions.

A tall glass would surrender his mind toward sleep and save him from the memories of his *ayusta*.

He debated the action only for a moment. There was a lot of homework to catch up on; people to call back, his apartment needed cleaning, laundry to be done. There was no shortage of things that needed his attention. *Half a glass would chase the demons away long enough for me to clean up and throw in a load of washing.*

He set the bottle on the counter and turned his attention toward the chores that needed tending. His friends had always teased him about his obsessive nature, but now in the midst of medical school it was a trait worth having.

Within twenty minutes, everything was in its proper place, and the washing machine clicked into spin cycle. He spared a few minutes to glace at his e-mail, but regretted it when he saw hundreds of queries awaiting his response.

His stomach rumbled redirecting his attention to the kitchen. A last look in the refrigerator, he settled on some left over spaghetti. He only wished he knew how long it had been leftover. He shrugged at the thought, poured himself a full glass of whiskey, and then settled on the couch with the remote.

"Wake up sleepyhead." The room swayed in an array of color as he forced his eyes open.

"That's better."

"Gail?" He sat up and pushed his hair from his face. "What are you doing here?"

"I wanted to see you." She straddled his lap and placed his hands on her slender hips, then lifted his chin forcing him to drink in her dark blue eyes. "I've missed you." Her kiss ignited the passion within him. "I think you've missed me too."

The year apart didn't matter nor the fact that she had turned down his proposal. It was all insignificant. He became physically and painfully aware of how much he wanted and needed her at that moment.

A still small voice echoed in the hollow of his mind, yield.

Not tonight Lord, not tonight.

About The Author

H. Amore was born and raised in New England. She currently resides in Oklahoma with her husband and four children. She is a registered nurse specializing in labor and delivery. *The Colter Bay* Series is her debut series.

Publisher

Stonebridge
Publications

For more great titles, visit Stonebridgepublications.com